FROST CLAIM

DEMONS OF FROSTERIA
BOOK ONE

ELLE BEAUMONT
CANDACE ROBINSON

Midnight Tide
PUBLISHING

Frost Claim

Copyright © 2022 by Elle Beaumont & Candace Robinson

Midnight Tide
PUBLISHING

Published by Midnight Tide Publishing
www.midnighttidepublishing.com

Cover design by Covers by Aura

For the beauties who love the beast, this one is for you.

CHAPTER 1

NOEL

WHAT THE FUCK IS THIS PRICE?

Noel arched a brow at the price tag of a skimpy Belle costume. It was literally a piece of yellow fabric that barely covered one's ass and the top didn't seem like it could hold her assets in for the entire night.

There weren't many options left at the party store, though, or good ones anyway. They were all overpriced for cheap material that she'd wear once. She could've come up with something back at the sorority house using the clothing she already had, but nothing she owned would look like a costume —unless she wanted to wear all black and dress up as her former self from high school.

Screw that.

But… there was something she could do. The old Noel was creeping in, telling her to just take the costume into the dressing room and stuff it into her purse. There wasn't a security tag on the fabric. It would be *easy*. So damn easy.

Noel closed her eyes, slowly inhaling, then exhaling. *No, I've changed.* She'd put that life behind her.

"I mean, the costume will do," Ivy said, interrupting Noel's dark thoughts.

She flicked open her eyelids and cocked her head, her gaze meeting Ivy's bright hazel irises. "You're only saying that because you've had your Crow costume made for two months." A fucking glorious costume at that.

Ivy bumped Noel's shoulder with hers. "Hey, I offered to make you something."

"I know." Ivy had listed several movies from the nineties, but Noel didn't want to make her friend waste her study time working on a second costume that would only be worn once. Besides, Noel just didn't want anyone doing extra things for her. Her dad was already using her mom's money on Noel's college. He hadn't wanted to, but it was in her mom's will before she passed away from cancer. After her mom's death, her dad had turned into a real prick. She'd only been ten then and she'd really needed her father, but he hadn't been there. Each year she'd waited for him to change, to realize she was there, that he still had a daughter. He hadn't though, and she was glad she was gone from that depressing house.

Hell, Noel was surprised she hadn't ended up in jail. During her senior year in high school she focused as much as she could on classes, aced the SATs, and ended up at the University of Vermont. Even though she'd focused more, she still hadn't been able to control her pickpocketing urges until last year, when she'd joined a sorority to meet new people and better herself. Hoping she'd possibly get those sisters that all the happy-go-lucky movies with sorority girls had shown. She'd thought it was a lie, but meeting Ivy showed her it wasn't. And if she'd had someone like Ivy during high school, Noel might have had her fucking act together back in those days.

"If you don't want to buy it, I can get it for you." Ivy pushed her auburn hair over her shoulder and took the Belle costume from Noel's hands. "My mom sent extra money this month."

"No." Noel snatched the costume back from Ivy. "I'm not letting you do that. Anyway, I need to try this… rather fine attire on," she drawled, gazing at the costume rack one more time, wishing there was something else. It was nothing against Belle—she loved the damn princess, but if she was going to dress like her, she wanted the *actual* yellow gown. However, there wasn't another costume she was even remotely interested in. Harley Quinn? No thanks. Not unless it was the classic tight and sexy jester style, which, no luck here.

Skimpy Belle it is.

Noel left Ivy, who was looking at feathered masquerade masks, and headed toward one of the dressing rooms. The party store was small, cluttered, and smelled like moth balls. It wasn't one of the big party supply chains that she'd had closer to her old home, but it did have more choices of fun party items that she couldn't find at other stores. Except for the Halloween season, apparently.

Out of the three dressing rooms: one was without a door, the other was occupied, and the third stood wide open with several pieces of plastic trash sprawled across the floor. She kicked the mess aside and shut the door.

After hanging her purse on the hook, Noel looked at herself in the rectangular mirror for a few moments. Purple bags no longer hung beneath her green eyes, her face wasn't gaunt like it used to be, and her acne was gone. She'd been eating better, no more drinking except for at parties, and she hadn't touched drugs since early high school. For the past year she'd been coloring her long hair dark blue with streaks of green throughout. The small changes, for the better, made her smile. She was finally getting used to seeing that expression on her face instead of a strained version staring back at her.

Noel unbuttoned the front of her shirt and removed it, followed by her Converse and jeans. She took the Belle costume from the hanger and shimmied into it, gritting her teeth as she pulled on it. "Come on." She hopped a few times just to get the fabric up. It was so tight across her ass that she thought it would tear the seams, but it showed off her curves well enough.

"Dear Beast, will I find you and break your curse tonight?" Noel joked to herself in the mirror and bowed slightly before giving a flashy spin. She still ached to retrieve her old hoodies, but she was more comfortable in her body now. With a little makeup, she'd look halfway decent tonight, and she believed she was ready to have fun with someone. It had been too long since she'd dated—much less fucked a guy. This was her third year at the university and she'd been too focused on her school work.

"So, Belle," Ivy cooed as she tapped on the dressing room door. "How does it look?"

Noel opened the door and leaned on the frame while arching her back, giving the most seductive pose she could.

"Ooh la la," Ivy purred, stepping forward and adjusting one of Noel's sleeves. "Now, we'll just have to find you a prince tonight."

Noel grinned, remembering how she used to watch *Beauty and the Beast* over and over as a child. She would even wear the princess costume and perform the dance scenes by herself when the couple would come on, or she'd rearrange her books on her shelf, pretending she owned Belle's library. "I'd much rather have the beast. The prince at the end looked like shit."

Ivy tossed her head back and laughed. "He *so* did not!"

Noel arched a brow, thinking about the close-up of the prince's face in the film. She'd been disappointed then, and she still was.

"Okay, maybe he did." Ivy held up a finger. "At least in the cartoon version."

"That's what I thought. This is why we're friends." Noel's smile grew wider as she closed the door behind her with her foot. While peeling off the tight costume, she clenched her jaw as if that would prevent the material from ripping, but she managed. She hoped she could get it on one more time without tearing the cheap piece of shit. It was the only size the store had, but it fit well... once it was on anyway.

As she hung the costume back on its hanger, the urge to steal it rose to the surface again.

You're worthy. You don't need to do this. She repeated the mantra her counselor—Mrs. Hilliard—had told her a year ago to fight the urges, when she'd finally decided to make herself stop. It was the same counselor who'd been there for her since her 9th grade year. The one who'd gotten her through everything and helped her develop study habits so she could get better grades and ace the SATs.

As quick as blowing out a candle, the urge vanished, and Noel released a calming breath. If the temptation got any stronger, she might need to call Mrs. Hilliard.

Once dressed, she gathered her things and spotted Ivy back at the masquerade masks, trying them on. A bird mask rested on her friend's heart-shaped face and Ivy slowly stroked the long beak. Noel chuckled to herself, then smiled at how cute her friend was and headed toward the counter. An older lady with tight gray curls was stitching part of a ripped Santa costume's pant leg. The store rented out costumes, too, but the price was about the same as just buying them. So what the hell would be the point of that? Besides, she didn't know how good they were cleaned afterward, or if people went and had sex in them, which she was pretty sure a decent number had been fucked in.

"You're going to be the prettiest little thing," the woman said, taking the costume from Noel. "I wish we had costumes like this back in my day to get the fellas' attention."

Noel grinned wide—the old lady was thinking about *sex*. "It's never too late." Still smiling, she took her card from her purse and handed it to the lady. Noel's dad didn't send her money like Ivy's parents. She worked full time during the summers at an ice cream shop and saved almost all her money by eating ramen noodles and shopping at thrift stores. During the school year, she mostly stuck to selling her crochet items on Etsy. That was another thing she missed—when her mom would sit beside her and teach her how to crochet, her berry scent enveloping Noel.

The lady handed her the bag, pulling Noel from her thoughts. She turned and found Ivy putting up a mask before walking toward her.

"Ready?" Ivy asked.

Noel checked her phone—it was still hours until the party started. "I suppose killing time at home it is."

They hopped into Ivy's car and drove back toward the sorority house. A few sprinkles of rain dotted the windshield while Noel leaned her head back in the leather seat. When she'd started college, she hadn't brought her car with her since she could pretty much walk everywhere and save money on gas.

Noel stayed zoning out toward the trees, their red, yellow, and orange leaves drawing her attention. She hadn't realized how much time had passed until Ivy pulled into her assigned parking spot.

They walked past several students *trying* to break dance, then circled around a building and crossed through the freshly-cut grass to their orange brick sorority house with the words *Tri Sigma* above the door. The *faithful to death* motto was a bit extreme when she'd first joined, but she'd thought *what the hell?* after seeing the skull and crossbones symbol.

A garden of evergreen shrubs rested in the front, and a couple of empty beer cans lay at their bases. *Fuckers*.

Ivy sighed and scooped up the cans before they headed inside the house.

As soon as Noel stepped into the bright green hallway, her gaze fell to Winter and Holly, who were dancing around the room in hot pink bikinis while recording themselves on their phones to the loud music. The black leather couches were covered in white sheets, most likely for some weird reason.

Laughing, Noel palmed her forehead and shook her head.

"You two want to join in?" Winter whirled around, swinging her dark ponytail up and down like a whip. "We're trying to get double the views this time. Holly and I were so close to hitting a million when our last video went viral."

"No thanks." Ivy cringed. "Unless you get better music and I don't have to dance around in a bikini."

"What's wrong with this?" Holly placed a hand on her hip and batted her thick eyelashes.

"Nothing, per se…" Noel trailed off. Everything was wrong with their taste in music. "Maybe if I'm drunk enough tonight, I'll join in." She knew she could dance, but hopping around in a bikini just so people could watch her boobs bounce didn't sound entertaining while sober.

"Party poopers." Winter gave an exaggerated huff. "But hey, we won't deny a drunk Noel later!" she called after her as Noel followed Ivy up the stairs to their shared room.

Noel was the opposite of Winter and Holly in every way, but they were still her sorority sisters and she genuinely liked them since they could lighten her moods.

Ivy opened the door to their room—which was clean courtesy of her. There wasn't much in the small space besides their two twin beds, two nightstands with Noel's crochet stuff on one, a shared desk, and posters covering the walls. Ivy's side consisted mainly of old movie posters, while Noel's held art of mythical creatures.

A ding came from Ivy's phone as soon as Noel tossed her things on the mattress.

"Can't he just leave me alone?" Ivy whispered, sinking down on her bed and staring at her phone.

Noel furrowed her brow, wondering what the dickhead wanted now. "Why don't you block his ass?"

"I don't know."

Ivy's ex-boyfriend, Jace, cheated on her a few weeks ago, even though they'd been together since the eighth grade. After Ivy found out, the jerk still wanted her as a girlfriend while getting to go and have his dick sucked by someone else. Ivy only knew about the one time, but Noel believed he'd cheated on her more than that.

Noel plopped down beside her roommate, grabbed Ivy's phone and typed: *Fuck off and leave me alone, asshole. Emphasis on the ASSHOLE.*

"I should have done that myself," Ivy said softly. "But thank you."

"If he bothers you again, just block him."

Ivy rested her head on Noel's shoulder and wrapped her arms around her. Noel froze for a second, her eyes widening, before hugging her friend back. She was still getting used to being touchier with people and needed to remember that this was her new life, that she had actual friends who cared about her, friends who didn't just use her for things.

"All right." Ivy straightened. "Let's get ready for the party and find our princes for the night." She paused and smirked. "I mean, *beasts*."

Noel chuckled. "Damn right."

CHAPTER 2

AERYX

"DON'T DO IT," AERYX GRUNTED AS HE STARED AT HIS younger brother, who currently sat on top of Dral—their father's familiar, and often, Ryken's guardian. He was a reindeer, but nothing like the ones of the mortal realm. His massive ivory rack jutted from his skull, looking more like barbed wire. Each point was a gnarled bony structure that surely would've killed an attacker. Dral's legs were thick, and they needed to be to support his heavily muscled form. And his eyes glowed a brilliant red hue.

The reindeer groaned and pawed at the freshly fallen snow as if he wanted to be anywhere but here. Part of Aeryx wished Dral would dump his fourteen-year-old brother into the nearest snowdrift, but he was determined to prove himself, and that was something he could respect. How many times had he done the same thing with his father? Pleaded with him for a chance to show him how capable he was?

Tall balsam trees reached for the sky as if they were in search of more sun—not that Aeryx could blame them, since

Frosteria was a land of snow and ice. Days full of the sun were few and far between, and even when they graced the land, it did little to warm the realm.

Winds rustled through the branches, shaking the heavier laden boughs and depositing more snow onto the ground. Winter wasn't quite upon Frosteria, but it would arrive in a few weeks' time, and with it, the constant storms.

Fortunately for his brother, all he had to do was saunter off into the comfort of their parents' home. It was right there, a warm cottage brightly lit inside with a fire. Evergreen trees nearly hid the structure from view, and that was likely because of their father not wanting intruders.

Ryken scowled and brushed his sandy blond hair from his face. A few pieces tangled in his black horns, which had yet to begin curling. "Quit telling me what to do," he ground out between clenched teeth. The next moment, he shoved his hand beside the saddle and drew up his sword. "If you're too afraid to come at me, I'll find someone else."

Idiot. Was I ever as foolish as him? Probably. Especially at fourteen. And, he *had* requested a sibling sixteen years ago. Time had flown, and to think, he was now twenty-two, in Morozko's Immortal Army, and fighting the changelings just as his father was.

Chuckling, Aeryx lifted a gloved hand and dipped his head down. Tika, his mare created from ice, shook her head. Her mane chimed against her thick neck, creating a lovely melody.

"I've warned you once. This is your second warning, and I won't do it again, Ryken." His tone was gentle but held a cautioning in it. Like their father, Aeryx could use snow and turn it into a weapon. He'd been a year younger than Ryken when his abilities appeared, chaotic and unrestrained. Idly, Aeryx wondered, would his brother take after their parents? Or pull from distant relations, like their cousin Efraun, who could track and hunt like no other?

Particles of ice halted in the air, then—as he swiped through—a jagged sword formed. All he had to do was picture the object in his mind, and the weapon would take shape.

From several yards away, Aeryx could see a flicker of doubt in Ryken's sky-blue eyes. Frosteria was a harsh land, and the younglings were raised to survive from the time they were infants.

But, it had been Aeryx's wish to join the Frost Demon King, Morozko's, Immortal Army. He'd created the krampi from a drop of his blood by letting it drip into fresh snow. From that, he formed a male and a female—his superior demons, as he'd called them. Brought to life to snuff out the threat of the changelings. His last touch had been to grant each krampi an ability, whatever it may have been. Morozko went on to create other demons, including the tomte.

Aeryx would not go easy on his little brother.

A slow grin tugged at Aeryx's lips. "All right." With his other hand, he ran it along Tika's flank. The subtle pulse of their familial bond hummed in his mind, and for a moment, he saw through her eyes. Saw as she homed in on Dral, then Ryken. Aeryx felt her body tense, preparing to bolt forward. "Now!" All he did was lean forward, and Tika launched across the snow, her hooves kicking up dust in their wake.

Ryken urged Dral forward, much too slowly. Aeryx was already bearing down on them, and before they met halfway,

Aeryx took up the sword in his right hand. Tika changed her path, shifting to the left as he leaned in the saddle.

"No!" Ryken's eyes widened. He was too slow gathering Dral's reins, and in repositioning his mount, the flat side of Aeryx's ice blade crashed into his shoulder, sending Ryken toppling onto the powdery ground. "You fucking cheated!" he roared, pounding his fists on the snow before launching forward toward Tika.

The ice horse reared, its black hooves cutting through the air, then crashing down. "I did not and would not. I outmaneuvered you. Let that be a lesson to always be prepared, little brother." Aeryx relinquished his grip on the sword, and it turned back into snow. "For now, don't brood too much. I must return to the barracks." His gaze flicked to the bright gray sky. More snow was on the way. If he had to guess, it'd be flurrying by the time he arrived at the fortress.

"Be sure to eat something." Aeryx smiled warmly, which wasn't reciprocated. All he could feel was the heated glare from his brother. Envy oozed from Ryken, but there was nothing to be envious about. Aeryx had been in the same position as his little brother. Training hard, wanting eyes on him, needing the recognition from anyone—everyone. Ryken's time would come, too, if that was what he wanted.

Aeryx whistled. "Dral, it's time to head back." The reindeer swung his head up and plodded forward. "Come here," he murmured to the beast and bent over to tie the reins, so they didn't tangle in his antlers.

Tika nickered to him and pressed her muzzle into his furry neck.

"One of these days, I'm going to best you, Aeryx." Ryken spat at the ground.

He would, and when that day came, Aeryx would welcome it because it'd mean his brother had grown mentally and physically. Blinking, Aeryx looked up from beneath his eyelashes. "I don't doubt that, Ryken. Keep training, and you will." He clucked to his mare, and she launched forward. Dral galloped behind them, occasionally making a low grunting call to Tika.

The cluster of trees grew sparser, giving way to tiny, twig-like bushes with soft pink flowers. Aeryx had always enjoyed how stubborn of a bush it was to defy the bitter cold and bloom amidst the snow and ice.

After traveling for a half-hour, the fortress' impressive structures came into view. Smoke billowed from the furnace, and the acrid scent of burning changelings filled the air. They'd been in full force as of late, more so than they had over the past years—testing Aeryx's abilities, as well as his comrades.

Aeryx had grown up knowing the harsh truth of the changelings. They'd invaded his home while he and his father were out, but that wasn't the worst of it. When he'd returned, Aeryx had been the one to find his mother's bloodied body— if one could call it that. Her chest cavity had been ripped open, half-eaten lungs pulled from her. If he closed his eyes, he could still see it clearly, could still smell her blood.

He pressed Tika on toward the training yard, and a familiar voice barked orders. Warriors grunted as they dropped to the icy ground into a push-up, then leaped to their feet, crouching as if they were ready to pounce the krampi closest to them.

In the middle of the throng, a tall, lean male walked around, his hands behind his back as he barked a new order.

"Down again!" His father jerked his head toward the stables, his black horns gleaming in the dim lighting. Knowing better than to interrupt one of his drills, Aeryx prodded Tika forward.

"Not now, Dral," Aeryx murmured.

Once he was in front of the stable, he hopped down from Tika. She nudged him with her muzzle, covered in black leather. Glowing blue eyes peered at him, full of intelligence and affection. She'd been a gift from Zira not long after she moved into the command building. It seemed like just yesterday that he'd snuck into the sleigh to join his father and the trainee on a mission. He hadn't known then that Zira would become a mother to him, or his father's mate.

Life hadn't been predictable or kind, but Aeryx wouldn't have changed a thing. He chuckled as he stepped into the stable, thinking of how Zira challenged his father, and how much Ryken was like her.

He shook his head and continued down the aisle until he reached Tika's stall. The scent of shavings permeated the air, as did the musk from the other reindeer and horses. First, he tended to Tika, removing her tack, then placed her in the stall. Tika wasn't fed a normal diet of oats and hay, she lived off water. For a reward, Tika often munched on chunks of ice and, if she had been particularly good, they were peppermint flavored.

When he was done, he moved on to Dral next, which took a little longer since Aeryx needed to brush out his fur. The reindeer grunted low, jabbing Aeryx with one of his barbed antlers. Yelping, Aeryx narrowed his eyes. "You'll get a treat after." Dral made a noise that sounded suspiciously like a laugh.

Aeryx scratched at the reindeer's rump and grinned as Dral snorted in approval. After, he pulled out an oat cluster from his pocket and arched a brow. "Looks like I have one more left for you." He offered it to Dral before leaving his stall.

Just as Aeryx was rounding the barn door, Lyra, a comrade and—at times in the past—a lover, came into view. Thick, black curls framed her sandalwood face and twined around her ebony horns. But it was her cherry-colored lips that teased Aeryx's senses. However, he could see in her dark eyes that she wasn't here to play. She wore her red and black leather uniform, which accentuated her lithe figure.

"Major Enox is asking for our band to gather." Lyra's lips pulled back into a smile, revealing her pearly white teeth. She wasn't his mate, and he certainly wasn't hers, but oh did that mouth know how to bring him to his knees.

Aeryx had always been clear, he never wanted a mate, because he believed in choosing for himself. The idea of anyone taking the choice away from him sparked his anger.

"Any word as to why?" Aeryx pushed away the images of her lips circling his throbbing member and focused instead on the news.

"What do you think? Of course not." Lyra pivoted on her heel, leaving him to watch as she walked away, purposely swaying her hips. The leather pants clung to each curve in a way that left little to the imagination. Not that he needed it.

With a sigh, he blew a strand of brown hair from his eyes and followed her inside the command building. One step through the door and his gaze widened as he took in the crowd of similarly ranked krampi.

Sidling up to Lyra, he turned his attention to Major Enox.

Long tresses of black licked at the major's shoulders, and from his head, large, rounded horns jutted. Much to Aeryx's dismay, his piercing green eyes homed in on him.

"Aeryx, I didn't think you'd be joining us." The major's tone implied that he wasn't thrilled he was the last one to file in.

Pounding a fist against his chest, Aeryx bowed. "Had I known an assembly would be called, I'd never have ventured off to see my brother."

Major Enox huffed. "As I was saying, the changelings have grown active once again. It seems as if the lull is over. Several nests have hatched lately—they're more aggressive, and not living peacefully amongst the humans, either. Chaos is erupting in their realm."

Chaos? Aeryx's eyebrows furrowed in question, but the major continued on.

"It has been reported that the changelings are growing more violent and acting out." Enox flexed his fingers. "Other children have suffered from it. No deaths yet, but do we want to wait for that?"

No. Aeryx's lip curled as he thought of all the mortal children he'd helped over the years, and to his first. She'd been so curious and unafraid. The way she'd rested against his chest as he'd taken her home on Dral, and her green eyes, like emeralds, had twinkled while observing him. He didn't want to imagine what a changeling could've done to her.

The changelings were desperate, and likely felt cornered by the krampi. A year after Ryken was born, the changelings had nearly ceased all of their attacks. They still occurred, but were few and far between—over a decade of relative quiet.

Now, they were surfacing with a vengeance that made Aeryx's blood boil.

The changelings were demons, but unlike the krampi, they hadn't been created by Morozko. They were wicked creatures, born from a place of hatred. Aeryx had once asked where they came from, and Efraun, always one to spin wild stories, said they were born from a curse. Before Morozko ruled, his mother sat on the ice throne, but she was wretched, and her people plotted against her. In the end, she was slain, but not before laying a curse on Frosteria.

Changelings were born to terrorize, to slaughter, just as the queen had intended.

Eventually, the lesser demons discovered they could open portals to the mortal world, and thrive within the bodies of children. Their parents were none the wiser.

In the scheme of things, that was minor, but it was how they tore into the krampi villages—slaughtering the younglings, and ripping infants from expecting mothers' bellies that was the true horror of the wretched changelings.

"A nest hatched and broke through a defense line. Several krampi were victims of their attack, and now those bastards are in the mortal realm. So, all of you will be leaving today. Understood?"

Aeryx bowed his head. "Yes, sir," he called out, pounding his fist to his chest again.

When the krampi began filing out of the building, Aeryx approached Enox. "Major, can you—"

"Relay that you'll be heading off?" Enox's lips pulled back into a slow smile. "Of course. I know your father is busy training the recruits. May Morozko be with you." The major turned on his heel and walked away.

Someone's hand clapped against Aeryx's back, and when he turned to see who it was, Lyra's dark eyes met his. "How about we make a little game out of this, Aeryx? Whoever returns first has to feed the other's tomte for an entire month."

Tomte were short beings, no taller than three feet. Their hair, whether female or male, was the color of snow, and a tomte's nose always reminded Aeryx of a skinny slope on the mountainside. They were robust creatures who often took it upon themselves to live amongst the livestock, which was fine because they groomed and fed the animals. All they required was a bowl of food. A task never to be forgotten unless one wished for ill to fall on their animals.

"Fine. We have a deal." He chuckled and strode out the door into the blinding snow. He'd been off in his assessment of the sky, but now, the flakes fell at a dizzying speed. They caught in his thick lashes, melting and leaving trails of moisture, which quickly froze against his cheeks.

"And so it begins," Lyra sang as she dashed away to the barracks.

Aeryx narrowed his eyes and ran after her. He would not lose to her. He would gather his supplies and tack Tika up, then beat Lyra to the mortal realm.

He had to.

He didn't want to play servant to his friend.

More importantly, he wanted to be the one to haul the changelings back to the whipping post. Aeryx enjoyed having fun, but when it came to a mission, he wouldn't stop until it was complete, and time was of the essence.

CHAPTER 3

NOEL

"Holy hell," Noel gasped. "You look so badass." She may have even been a smidge jealous of Ivy's sleek black costume.

"I offered to make you something," Ivy sang and patted the feathered crow attached to her shoulder. The black wig hanging to her waist looked real, not like that cheap shit at most stores during the Halloween season.

Her friend did one more twirl, her leather pants hugging her thighs, the black corset drawn tight around her waist, and her long sleeve shirt pulled taut to show off Ivy's normally-hidden breasts. The makeup was a darkish kind of sensual, a soft white powder across her face, black lipstick elongating her mouth, and mime-like dark eyeshadow around her eyes—very much the Crow. Frankly, it was hot as hell, and Noel wasn't even into girls.

"You look so adorable!" Ivy said, scanning her over while adjusting Noel's yellow sleeve.

Noel peered at her Belle costume in the oval mirror

hanging on the wall and still didn't find it that bad. She should turn the costume into a dead Belle though, add some blood and rips to the dress, but she wasn't going to waste time while making Ivy wait for her.

Winter and Holly had already left for the party about an hour ago—most likely close to being wasted as they filmed themselves. The rest of the girls in the house had other plans or different parties to go to, while a few lingered in their rooms, studying for upcoming exams.

Noel tucked her phone into her small leopard-print backpack purse, slipped on her black flats, and followed Ivy out of the house into the darkened night. Lights flooded the area of the campus and sprinklers made clicking sounds as they rotated, watering the bright green grass.

The party was being held at a house just down the street, so they wouldn't need Ivy's car.

Three tall guys with broad shoulders stumbled across the campus lawn through the sprinklers. One, with a buzzcut, let out a shrill whistle toward them while another dry-humped the air like an idiot.

"Ladies!" the jackass still humping the air called. "We'll show you a good time if you want to come to our place!"

"Fuck off!" Noel yelled and flipped them the bird.

"Ah, don't be like that!" the whistling guy whined, puckering his bottom lip.

"Forget those losers," Ivy said, rolling her eyes as the guys laughed. She tugged Noel away before she said something about how their small penises wouldn't be able to get her off.

A cool breeze drifted through the air, chillier than earlier, and Noel shivered. She should've brought a damn jacket.

They walked past a group of students drinking out of Starbucks cups. A few wore costumes, either going to the same Halloween party or a different one.

After several minutes passed, they approached the massive two-story house. Or, in other words, a mansion. Cream brick covered the front with two iron balconies circling the tall windows of the second floor. Green ivy wove between the bars or dangled down from the top. The lawn was freshly-cut with pristine bushes planted in the small garden.

Ivy stepped onto the bare porch, then pushed open the door. Rap music greeted them, thrumming through the house, but not loud enough to drown out someone's voice. Wooden stairs were at the entrance, and a couple was getting a bit frisky on the bottom step. It practically looked like the guy was eating the girl's face—Noel held back a snicker as she shut the door.

Portraits of cats wearing different objects—hats, sunglasses, and neon clothing—covered the walls of the narrow hallway.

The hall opened to a room filled with people drinking, dancing, and talking. Almost everyone wore some kind of costume. One guy dressed as a taco was already passed out in the corner of the room with an open bag of chips in his lap. She and Ivy stepped into the kitchen area littered with various alcoholic drinks across the wide granite island and counters.

"Didn't Belle have brown hair?" Winter asked playfully from behind Noel, nudging her shoulder. She was wearing a Harley Quinn costume with the short shorts and jacket but missing the wooden bat. Her eyes were glazed as they focused on Ivy. "And what in the ever-loving fuck kind of evil clown are you? I thought you were going to be Little Red Riding Hood?"

"Surprise!" Ivy waved jazz hands in the air and smiled. "I always dress up as her, so I figured I'd do something different and go as the Crow tonight."

Winter wrinkled her nose. "Who?"

"Never mind." Ivy sighed. "We'll make you watch it tomorrow." She and Noel were always forcing Winter and Holly to see movies they hadn't heard of. Which was a lot of the time.

Reaching forward, Winter tugged on a lock of Noel's blue and green hair. "Again, not brown."

"The wigs at the store were too tacky." She wasn't going to bother with sweating like a pig while wearing one all night, either.

"O-kay," Winter said the word slowly, then perked up and waggled her brows. "Holly and I are about to play strip poker with a few *hot* guys if you want to join in?"

Ivy petted the crow at her shoulder and tilted her head toward its beak as if waiting for something. "His answer is not right now."

Winter palmed her face and shook her head.

"Same here," Noel said. She wasn't drunk enough to take off her clothes, and she knew the type of guys Winter and Holly went for, so a big pass on that ball of joy.

"Fine," Winter huffed. "But remember, we're recording a video together later."

"I said if I got drunk enough," Noel pointed out.

Winter turned to the keg next to her, then filled a red cup and shoved it into Noel's hands, the liquid sloshing over the sides. "Start now." Noel dried her hand with a napkin as Winter poured shots and tried to pass Ivy one.

"I'm not drinking tonight." Ivy shrugged.

"You never do." She grinned and handed it to Noel. "More for Noel, then. This will get you closer to tipsy."

Noel rolled her eyes but tossed back the shot, the liquid burning as it slid down her throat. "Damn, that was strong," she rasped, but took another one, just to get the edge off.

"I'll see you sexy girls later." Winter turned on her booted heel and sashayed out of the room.

Noel sipped from her beer as Ivy grabbed a soda from an ice chest. They stood in the kitchen for a while, watching people come in to grab drinks before deciding to venture into the living room. The space was practically the size of a small one-story house.

"This party is lame," Ivy said after a while.

"No hot beasts tonight." Noel grinned.

"Let's just go dance with ourselves then."

Noel followed Ivy past a few comic book characters to an area near a couch that wasn't occupied. The rap music changed to a techno dance song, and they swayed their hips to the music while Noel drank down her beer.

A slim body brushed past Noel and stopped in front of them. Jace wore a superman costume, his hair parted to the side. He looked like a dickwad, as per usual.

"Ivy, can I talk to you?" Jace asked. His expression was a bit melancholic, which was most likely because Ivy wasn't running back into his arms like he'd probably expected.

"She doesn't want to talk to you anymore," Noel answered. It wasn't her place, but Ivy was her best friend and she didn't want to see her hurt again.

Jace's jaw clenched as his hard stare latched onto hers. "No one asked *you*."

"Jace," Ivy said in a firm voice, placing her palm on his chest.

His gaze softened as he focused back on Ivy. "I just need to talk to you. Please."

Ivy blinked a few times, her expression remaining neutral. "Give me a minute, and I'll meet you out front."

"Anything for you, Ivy. I'll be out on the porch." Jace slowly turned around, wading through the crowd. Ignoring the people bumping into him, he glanced one more time over his shoulder, seeming to expect that Ivy would already be there, following him.

"You're not going to give in to him again, are you?" Noel bit her lip. She really didn't think Ivy should, but it was her friend's choice, and she would have to support her no matter what she decided to do.

"No, I'm not." Ivy's shoulders relaxed. "I am going to talk to him back at the house, though. I've known Jace for a long time. He was my best friend since elementary, and it's like I lost him. We change throughout our lives, and that old Jace didn't come to college with me. It's like that part of him was left back at home. But he needs to understand, I can't be his friend, either. I can't be his anything."

Noel understood that better than anyone, except she'd left a darker part of herself back at home. "I get it, Ivy. Do you want me to come with you to the house?"

"Thanks. But no. You stay and have fun."

"If you need me, call." Noel raised her cup. "I'll keep an eye out for any beasts."

Ivy gave her a quick hug before leaving Noel to herself. The space where Ivy previously stood still hadn't filled, so it was just Noel and her empty cup. She went back into the kitchen, brushing past a few bodies before taking a few more shots. A frat guy then filled her cup with more beer from the keg.

Noel started to feel good as she swiveled through the crowd to the spot in front of the couch. She would listen to a few more songs, then she'd be tipsy enough to find her sorority sisters and join in on their naked game of fun.

An older rock song poured out of the speakers, and the heavy riffs coursed through her. She set her cup on the side table, figuring she'd dance with herself for a bit. The room dipped while she spun in circles, threw her hands in the air, and jived to the music. She probably looked like a fool, but she was having a fucking blast as she danced facing a *Dracula* movie poster hanging on the wall.

Noel attempted to do some sort of backward shimmy with her feet and stumbled over the rug. "Shit." Her ass didn't land on the floor, or the couch, but in someone's lap. Two hands grasped her hips, preventing her from falling to the side. She slowly turned around, catching the sight of a fancy button-up crimson leather shirt and part of an even deeper red jacket lined with fur. Her gaze drifted up, finding darker fur and a very hairy neck.

"Why, hello, Chewbacca," she drawled, not getting up from her comfortable seat on the stranger's legs. Her eyes focused as they lifted to his face, then widened. "No, not Chewbacca. You're a… beast." *A beast*! Dammit. Ivy had missed him. If she found a second one, she would haul him back home to her friend.

The guy didn't say a word as he smirked down at her with sharp, protruding teeth. She adjusted herself in his lap, becoming more forward while she straddled his hips to get a better view. The alcohol roaring through her was making her brazen.

She cradled his face and brought it closer to hers for inspection. His costume was so lifelike. Long curving black horns rested atop his head, his hair falling in short waves across his cheeks. Soft fur covered most of his face and the warmest brown eyes she'd ever seen studied her in return. There was something familiar about him, like a dream she'd had long ago, one that had felt real. She pushed the past away and focused on the guy in front of her.

"Why are you sitting all by yourself on this couch?" Noel asked.

The stranger's smirk turned into a devious wide grin. "I was entertained by your dancing."

"At least one person was." She smiled. "What's your name? I don't suppose it's truly Beast."

"Aeryx." His voice was deep, and that one word sent a rush of heat through her as his fingers pressed into her hips.

She arched a brow. "Eric?"

"No, Aeryx." He chuckled, the sound even more euphoric with what could possibly be an Eastern European accent. Damn alcohol.

"Aeryx. I like it." She brushed a finger across the fur of his neck. "Your special effects makeup looks real."

"Does it now?" he purred. "I preen quite a bit—perhaps that's why."

Well, then. She cleared her throat but needed to fan herself. "You want a drink?"

"I would drink a cup of ale, but I have a job to take care of soon."

"A dance then?"

He leaned forward, whispering in her ear. "I can spare a dance, but only if you tell me your name." His breath on her neck sent a heavenly shiver through her.

"Noel," she cooed. She wasn't as flirty without alcohol. But she might've been this time even without it. Because, hell, it had been three years since she'd had sex. That was almost a lifetime, really.

Aeryx easily lifted her from the couch, her breasts sliding down his chest, her feet touching the rug that had made this all possible. *Thank you, ugly rug, for making this magic happen.* She already missed sitting in his lap.

Noel now got a clear view of his costume: tight leather pants, knee-high boots, the red leather jacket falling to mid-thigh, and a high popped collar along the neckline of his shirt. "Do you go to school here? I like your accent." Noel drew him closer as they moved their hips to the beat of the new dance song.

"No, I just saw people coming into the house wearing costumes and thought it looked like fun."

"You know"—she leaned in—"if you keep dancing with me, you may get a kiss."

"Is that so?" He leaned in even closer. "What kind of kiss? And is this a challenge? I'll have you know... I don't back down from challenges."

Her hands trailed down his sides, gripping his firm ass as she pulled him even closer. "How about a game of strip poker first? Just you and me, then I'll show you what kind of kiss."

CHAPTER 4

AERYX

NOEL. THAT WAS HER NAME. IT SUITED HER CHERUBIC features, but her gem-like green eyes told a different story. Within them, he saw mischief—he saw a fraction of himself. The daring side, the one always willing to accept a challenge.

It shouldn't have shocked him that this mortal wanted to play a game he'd never heard of. Aeryx was willing to partake in the test—he enjoyed puzzles, and while he wasn't certain how the cards had anything to do with stripping, he was willing to learn. "Strip poker? What is that?" His reply must've surprised her because her eyebrows furrowed in question.

"What? You don't *know*? Well, you're in luck. I'll show you how to play. Follow me," Noel purred, then glanced around before scooping cards off the table next to the couch. She pocketed the cards, then curled her fingers around the fur of his jacket, and tugged him through the house. How she managed to navigate the room without falling again was beyond him, but she led him down a small hallway with bare walls.

He tried, at first, to ignore how short the skirt of her dress was, yet it was impossible. Her bare legs taunted him, inspiring thoughts of her straddling him.

Noel opened a door, flicked on the light, and motioned for him to enter. "A room all to ourselves."

Whose room is it? He looked around, not finding any picture frames with Noel's face in them. Not to mention, the drab blue and gray blanket didn't seem to reflect her taste, either. Not when her hair was so bright.

"So, Aeryx," she said his name a little breathier than most, likely due to the alcohol he smelled on her breath. Striding forward, she splayed her fingers against his chest and boldly stared up at him. Why didn't she look away from his face? He knew without a doubt he wasn't attractive in this state. In fact, he appeared wretched, *beastly*. But, in the age-old tale of Krampus, he would be considered even more hideous. Aeryx looked nothing like the more humanized monsters bustling around outside in costume, and everything like what nightmares were inspired by. Not that he could *see* himself as she did, but over the centuries, many had drawn true portraits of a krampi, which eventually had been exaggerated.

Noel continued to walk forward until her chest was brushing against his body and forced him to stumble back onto the bed. Aeryx caught her by the shoulders, steadying her, so she didn't headbutt him.

With a chuckle, he grinned up at her. "I thought we were playing a *game*?"

"You're so soft," Noel murmured, stroking her hand down his neck and along his shoulder. "The fur is so nice."

Aeryx could feel her touch, even beneath the layers he wore. His jacket, his uniform. What would her fingers feel like, he wondered, as they trailed down his bare skin and stroked his throbbing cock?

Still, she wasn't of the right mindset. *Fuck.*

Noel danced her fingers up to his cheek and leaned forward as if readying to kiss him. Aeryx quickly flipped her onto her back, so he loomed over her. Her eyes hadn't widened—in fact, they'd shut as she laughed.

"I just wanted a kiss, beasty boy."

Aeryx yearned for that kiss, even though they'd just met. Yet he hadn't earned it, and he wasn't going to take advantage of the moment. "Only after I win, as I recall." He watched the mortal—her breathing grew slower, and the smile on her face relaxed. "Noel," he whispered, but when there was no response, he pulled away and stood.

She'd fallen *asleep.* He groaned, yet it was perhaps for the best since he still had a mission to complete, and who knew if Lyra had already returned to Frosteria with her prize. One challenge was good enough for him.

Striding to the side of the bed, he gently tugged the blankets down, then proceeded to cover the mortal girl up. "Sleep well, princess," he said quietly, as not to disturb her. Aeryx turned away, then locked the bedroom door. The last thing he wanted was for someone to storm into the room, see her sleeping figure, and decide to have their way with her.

Aeryx ran a hand through his hair, ruffling the feathery locks. Still, not enough time had passed for him to step outside. Not while the humans were milling around.

With a sigh, he walked to the window and peered into the side yard. It was fenced in with chain-link, but it looked to only come up to his hips. With ease, he'd be able to hop it and dash away to the changeling.

Reaching into his jacket, he produced the stone—it blinked a vibrant ice blue at him. The pulses were quick, which meant the changeling was only a few houses away from where he stood.

Aeryx grumbled as he pocketed the stone again and turned toward the sleeping girl. She'd tugged the blankets up even higher, all the way to her chin.

Now that she wasn't stumbling or swaying his way, he noticed more of her features. Her rosebud lips, upturned nose, and thick, blonde eyelashes.

In this state, she looked more youthful. *How old is she?* Perhaps around his age of twenty-two, but it was hard to tell with her more rounded features, unlike his harsh angles, not that she could see them.

"I suppose I could watch over you a little longer, princess. But not much more. I have a mission to complete, and the longer I'm here, the more likely it is I'll be caught," Aeryx murmured as he knelt beside the bed, lightly pushing away the strands of her blue and green hair. It wasn't enough to disturb the mortal, but she did shift closer to him as if searching out his warmth.

What a peculiar human you are.

He fought against the temptation to brush his lips against her forehead. Although it would've been a chaste kiss, he hadn't won the right, which had been the prior agreement. It was a shame she'd scarcely remember him when she woke. No more than a faded dream—it had nothing to do with his magic, and everything to do with how much she'd had to drink.

It wasn't uncommon for Aeryx to use his influence on mortals when he was on a mission. A human couldn't remember seeing a krampi, couldn't retain the memories of him hauling a child away in the night. Their minds were far too fragile. But, since they were clad in costumes, it made traipsing around like a beast easier. Aeryx didn't have to hide.

Judging by the clock on the nightstand beside the bed, Aeryx waited a solid two hours. Noel hadn't roused—she'd scarcely moved from where he'd tucked her in, and part of him wished she had woken. That they'd been allowed a moment so he could learn how to play strip poker before his night shifted from play to mission.

He cast a lingering glance at Noel's sleeping figure before he walked to the window and opened it. Slipping through the space, he didn't have far to jump since they were on the first floor. Dried leaves crunched beneath his boots as he landed. All he could do was hope the humans had grown too drunk to mill around, or that they'd left.

Aeryx rounded the corner of the house and searched the area. He couldn't see any mortals wandering too closely, but he could hear someone near, slurring and laughing. Rather than strolling out into the street, Aeryx remained in as many shadows as he could cling to.

He walked through the neighbor's backyard, grimacing as a canine—enclosed on the back porch—snarled and barked at him. Not wanting to alert the dog further into perhaps leaping over the rail, Aeryx slowly made his way into the next yard and nearly tripped on a stone figurine.

A strangled noise escaped him as he noted the creature. Oddly enough, the creature looked much like a tomte, except instead of a long, sloping nose, it was bulbous.

Deciding it was clear enough, Aeryx pulled the stone from his pocket and opened his hand. The stone sat in his palm, radiating a vibrant blue. Relief flooded him—the demon was still in the area. It hadn't run off, which meant it'd found a child to inhabit.

To his delight, as he walked down the row of houses and drew closer to the woodline, the pulsing grew stronger.

Aeryx glanced over his shoulder. A few bare trees with skeletal branches obscured his view, but if he ducked his head, he could still make out the bedroom window he'd leaped out of.

His lips twitched as the image of Noel sleeping flickered in his mind, but now wasn't the time to grow distracted. Pocketing the stone, Aeryx eyed the back porch and opted to use that as his entry point. He hopped up on the railing and climbed the rest of the way to the porch's roofline.

Luckily, the backside of the house had a window taller than Aeryx that he could see inside. A dimly lit hallway with a stairway straight ahead, and on the left side were two doors, one open and another closed. On the right side, there was only one door.

He bent, dipping his fingers along the seam of the window. If he were truly lucky, it'd be unlocked. Shimmying the window, it slid up with ease, then he climbed through and inched toward the open door.

Several pictures hung on the gray walls. Smiling photographs of a boy with his parents. A portrait, Aeryx assumed, of the boy as an infant. The fact that the changeling was disrupting the family's lives boiled his blood. It was bad enough they slaughtered krampi in Frosteria, thought nothing of destroying countless homes, but to journey to a realm that didn't belong to them and do the same?

Memories of his dead mother rushed back to him, and he wished the faded images of what she *had* once looked like would replace the ones of her torn-open body.

The changelings needed to be eradicated.

As he walked down the hall, his fingers pulled a leather gag free. It was something Aeryx had come up with. Since the changeling's screams were piercing, silencing them would reduce the need to wipe *everyone's* memory in the area. *Gag first, then bind the flailing limbs.*

Aeryx growled as he stood in the doorway to the room. The child should've been asleep, and had the changeling not sensed his arrival, likely would've been. But the boy perched on the edge of his bed, knees to his chest.

The changeling's eyes glimmered yellow as it watched Aeryx.

He would not wait for the lesser demon to move first. Launching forward, Aeryx dove for the changeling, but it leaped from the bed, chittering as it crouched low on the floor. The changeling's eyes were focused on the doorway, its escape, and more than likely a way to rouse the parents.

They always defaulted on the parents for protection. The little deviants.

The changeling ducked lower, then bolted forward, attempting to run through Aeryx's legs, but the lesser demon didn't make it far. Aeryx pressed his weight down on the creature and reached behind to hold the flailing bastard down by the neck.

Quickly, he spun around, hissing as the creature's sharpened nails clawed at the carpet. *At least it wasn't hardwood.*

This way, there was hardly any sound. Aeryx grabbed the changeling's arms, then inched up to use his weight to pin them down. The gag was of far more importance, especially since he could feel the demon suck in a deep breath.

Slipping the gag into place, he buckled it. When the scream came, it was muted and thankfully not loud enough to alert the parents, who slept behind a closed door.

With the hardest part out of the way, Aeryx tugged free leather rope that was hidden away in a small satchel at his waist and used it to tie up the changeling's hands, then its feet.

Not every mission was as easy as this one. Sometimes the changelings bolted out of the house—other times, they roused the parents, and the adult mortals grew violent, not that Aeryx blamed them.

"Time to get you dealt with, filth," he growled. Standing, Aeryx jerked the changeling to its feet before scooping it up in his arms. He took a quick glance into the hallway. No one was there. In a few strides, he was at the window, hauling the creature out onto the roof. It bucked but was unable to break free—the movements were futile.

That was, until it threw its head back hard enough to crack Aeryx in the face. He stumbled, nearly losing his footing on the roof. "You little fucker," he seethed as he picked up the changeling and descended the roof.

The squirming demon tried loosening Aeryx's grip to no avail. Bucking, twisting, wiggling. Gritting his teeth, he slammed his fist into the side of the changeling's head, and it fell limply.

He was readying to curse at it again when someone's feet scuffed on the pavement nearby.

CHAPTER 5

NOEL

SHITTY MUSIC BLARED FROM... SOMEWHERE. NOEL RELEASED a groggy sound as she blindly reached for her phone from her nightstand. Her fingers brushed air. *Not there.* She cracked open her eyes, and a lamp on top of a dresser cast a warm glow around the area.

She wasn't in her room.

Noel quickly sat up, shoving the covers from her body, and peered at her surroundings. *Pokémon* posters in black frames hung across the walls, a set of signed baseballs and cards on stands rested inside a glass display. A bookshelf cluttered with comic books and graphic novels hugged a corner. It was a room fit for a collector junkie, except the bedspread wasn't decorated in memorabilia.

A wintry smell caressed Noel's nose, and she lifted the pillow beside her, catching a stronger scent of it. Then the night started to come back to her in ridiculous waves, the party resurfacing. That was where she was. The smell was from the guy dressed as the beast... the one she'd acted like a complete idiot with.

Did she have sex with him? If she did, it sure as fuck wasn't anything to write home about. She took a whiff of the bed—it didn't reek of sex. And it appeared she was still fully dressed in her Belle costume, except for her shoes. She was pretty sure she would have remembered him hiking up her dress and having a little fun. Damn, she wished that would've happened, but her dumbass self must've passed out at some point.

A sharp pain pulsed above her eyebrow, and she pressed a hand to her forehead. Even though she couldn't remember, she knew she had made a fool of herself. He'd probably dumped her here, then peaced out on her. Hell, she would've done the same.

Swinging her feet to the side of the bed, Noel looked down and found her black flats neatly next to her backpack purse on the floor. She slipped on her shoes, then flipped through the wallet inside her purse, finding what little she had still there. Well, at least the hottie wasn't a thief. Aeryx. That was his name. And a damn sexy one at that. After dumping her here, he probably found someone less drunk to fuck. At least he wasn't an ass. Or, from what she could remember of him. Too bad she didn't get a glimpse of his face behind the badass makeup or discover each hard muscle with her hands and tongue.

Cool it, Noel. He's gone.

She fished out her phone to check the time. Hours had passed since Ivy had gone back to the house to talk with Jace.

Shoving her arms into the straps of her purse, she padded

to the door, finding it locked. "Why thank you, hot beast, such a gentleman." Noel smirked.

The bright light of the hallway made her squint, and she stumbled out of the room. She was still tipsy but no longer completely shitfaced.

As she walked closer to the speaker, the music became louder, making her headache pulse harder. However, a better song choice drifted through the air.

A couple dressed as peanut butter and jelly lay passed out near the kitchen, and a few people were still drunkenly dancing. Most of the packed crowd from earlier seemed to have already left or maybe were scattered throughout the house.

Noel caught a glimpse of Winter and Holly hopping like fucking bunnies into the room, wearing only their panties and bras. Holly held up her phone inside a selfie stick, recording themselves as a scrawny guy in checkered boxers came jumping in after them.

Fuck, Noel had to get the hell out of there before her friends spotted her and she had to live up to her promise and record a video with them. She sure as shit didn't want to bounce around like a damn Playboy Bunny. But in her current state, Noel knew she would give in. A promise was a promise.

Noel hurried to the door, stepping over a mystery liquid that she hoped to God wasn't cum, but it wasn't her problem. She dashed out into the night's chilly air and shivered as she crossed the lawn. Beside one of the trees rested a stocky guy with short dark hair, passed out on his stomach, a red solo cup still in his hand. Squinting, she peered down at the cup as she approached him. The red plastic was practically full of beer. *Damn*, he was a miracle worker if he could manage to not have spilled his drink while falling… or crawling before passing out. Performing her humane duty, she kicked him lightly in his muscular thigh. "Hey, buddy, you alive?"

"Hmph." He lifted his head and studied her with glazed eyes and his mouth hanging open. "Cinderella?"

Not dead. Good enough for her. "Wrong Disney movie. I didn't lose a glass slipper." She grinned before heading to the sidewalk.

A few of the stars twinkled in the night sky as she folded her arms to keep herself from shivering even more. It didn't work. Her teeth chattered, the wind ruffling the short skirt of her dress, and goosebumps coated her skin. As soon as she hit the sidewalk, a muffling sound stirred from somewhere farther down the street.

Noel glanced over her shoulder, spotting nothing but cars and houses. She was about to turn and head back home when the sound came again, louder than before, resembling a… zombie? Over the years, she'd seen enough horror movies to know she should just get her ass to the sorority house and pretend as though she hadn't heard anything. But she was too tipsy to think about her safety and too nosy at the moment for her own good.

With light, tiptoeing movements, she hobbled to the neighbor's pine tree and stood behind it. She cast her gaze up and down the narrow trunk, seeing she wasn't hidden in the slightest behind its thin frame.

Cursing to herself, she rushed a few houses down and dropped to all fours behind the wheel of an SUV.

The muffling noise came again, but it was more like growling. She crouched, then slowly stood, peering over the hood of the SUV. In the distance, she spotted something big and its head was… furry? Bigfoot?

No, not Bigfoot. Long horns sprouted from his head, and he wasn't a naked furred beast. He wore a red leather coat hanging to his knees. Aeryx! He wasn't alone, though—over his shoulder rested what looked to be a body. But the gangly form was limp and small, like a child, short blond curls dangling from the person's head.

Holy fuck!

Noel lingered there like a moron, then realized she needed to move. It was too dark to see clearly, and she wanted to get a closer look. She took off in a sprint to meet up with him, to see what the hell he was doing. Her foot caught on the space between cement and grass—she tripped and fell, smacking her elbows into the ground. Pushing up to her feet, her eyes fell on the area where Aeryx had been, but he was already gone.

She hadn't imagined it, had she? No, she definitely didn't.

"Hey!" she called, her voice coming out weak. "Hey!" Pumping her legs, she jogged to the end of the street, not seeing or hearing anything out of the normal. Her head throbbed again from the headache. A memory swam to the surface, and she thought back to when she was younger, of a dream she once had. In her old room, there'd been a small beast with nubs for horns, and he'd worn a strange red shirt and fancy boots. He'd turned around while she removed her torn nightgown so she could put on a new one from her dresser. She didn't know why it was torn, but once she was dressed, he asked her for the nightgown so her parents wouldn't be afraid, and she'd given it to him. He then spoke words to her before slipping through her window and leaving. What were the words? Something about sleeping…

Over the years, the dream had grown less vivid as all dreams do. But it had been the best dream of her life, one that had involved snow and wind rumpling her hair as they rode a... horse? No, not a horse, something else... She'd felt protected pressed up against the small beast's chest.

The dream didn't matter now because this was real. She was drunk, but not *that* drunk. Whirling around, she hurried home. She needed to talk to Ivy. What if he'd been carrying a dead body? What if he'd almost murdered her, then changed his mind? Her heart beat rapidly, and she needed to ignore her overdramatic thoughts.

The sprinklers on campus were no longer on, but moisture glistened like morning dew across the blades of grass. She rushed to the front of the sorority house, where the porch light shone.

As soon as she opened the door, she found the living room empty, but the TV was still on, playing some awful reality show of two women arguing about makeup.

Noel raced up the stairs, managing not to stumble in her state. Her heart pounded so damn hard, and she hoped Jace had already gone home. Even though she knew Ivy was going to tell him she couldn't be his friend, that didn't mean the jackass wasn't going to try to still have sex with her—or act like a victim.

When she opened the door, she found Ivy lying on top of her made bed with her eyes shut, her fingers lightly tapping against her stomach. Her Crow makeup and costume were gone, replaced with a long *Labyrinth* T-shirt and headphones over her ears, blasting rock music.

"Ivy!" Noel shouted, maybe a bit too loudly as she approached her bed.

Ivy jerked up, ripping the headphones from her head. Her wild gaze met Noel's. "What is it? Are you hurt?"

"No." Noel's chest heaved, her palm pressed to her rapid heartbeat. "I'm not. But I think I saw something."

"What?" Ivy furrowed her brow, scanning her up and down, seeming to look for a sign of injury anyway.

Noel ran her hand through her hair and drew it over her shoulder. "I met this beast at the party, then I passed out, and he was gone—"

"Who the hell is he?" Ivy scowled, balling her fists at her sides. "He's going to be missing a penis if he did anything to you."

Noel held up her hands, having never seen her friend so angry. "No, he didn't take advantage of me or slip anything in my drink." Although she'd found him sexy before, she sure as hell didn't want him to touch her *now*. "But when I left the party, I saw him farther down the street, carrying a passed-out person over his shoulder. I think it could have been a kid, but I didn't see the face. He was there, then he was gone."

"O—kay, Noel," Ivy drawled, grasping her by the shoulders and pulling her to sit beside her on the bed. "I think you may have had too much to drink. You reek of alcohol."

Had she been too out of it? Aeryx couldn't have run or disappeared that fast. Something still didn't feel right, though. "But what if I didn't imagine it? Should we call the cops just in case?"

Ivy pursed her lips, seeming to mull it over. "I don't know. I'm not sure it would be a good idea unless you're a hundred percent sure you saw it. Are you?"

Noel couldn't be sure it was even a child, but she would recognize the gangly build and blond curls if she saw them again. What if he was bringing the person home? It was too fucking weird, and she wasn't sure anymore. "I'm not..."

"If you want, we can check out the street in the morning? See if we hear about any disappearances?" Ivy bit her lip.

Maybe Ivy was right and that was for the best. Noel nodded. "First thing in the morning."

CHAPTER 6

AERYX

SHIT. SHIT. SHIT. SHIT.

No one was supposed to see him. Hopefully, if Noel was drunk enough to pass out, then she'd assume she was seeing things, and with numerous humans milling around dressed up, *surely* she'd think she'd seen something else?

One could hope.

The changeling lay limp in his arms, giving Aeryx a temporary reprieve from the struggles, but *Morozko's fucking teeth*, he had a new problem.

As tempted as he may have been to glance over his shoulder, he didn't *want* to see a colorful head bobbing along after him. Wiping her memory or using his influence on her was at the bottom of his list of things to accomplish. There was something about the small moment they'd shared that he wanted her to keep. However minute it was.

Leaves crunched beneath his boots as he rounded a cluster of pine trees. Soon, snow would powder the needles, and ice would hang from the boughs. There was a subtle crispness to the air, hinting that winter, in this part of the mortal realm, wasn't far off.

Tika's head popped up, her glowing blue eyes training on him as she pawed at the ground. A whinny wasn't acceptable. She knew that during missions being quiet was necessary.

"Yes, you're a good girl for waiting." With his arms full of the demon's slack body, Aeryx couldn't run his hand along Tika's neck to reassure her that she was, in fact, the good girl he proclaimed her to be.

Idly, Aeryx wondered if Lyra had returned yet. He truly didn't want to tend to the cranky tomte that lived in her barn.

He mounted Tika, pinning the tied-up demon against his chest. If he had needed to capture another changeling, he would've brought a sleigh. However, since it was only him, and the one creature, all Aeryx needed was his horse.

His unconscious captive seemed quiet for now, allowing him to lift his hand. Concentrating, Aeryx focused on opening the portal to Frosteria. Magic pricked at his well of power, sapping away a fraction of it. With the aid of the stone in his pocket, a blue spark formed at first, then wound around in a circle that grew larger with every completion it made.

When it was big enough for him to pass through, a snow-filled world glimmered behind the opening: Frosteria. Tall evergreens jutted toward the star-flecked sky, and a white owl flew into the nearest tree, hooting in alarm.

Tika tossed her head—the melodic sound of her mane striking her neck filled the quiet, but Aeryx didn't allow them to linger there for long. He urged her forward through the portal and at once was greeted by the dizzying motion.

The ice mare's hooves struck the ground, churning up the snow beneath her.

It took a moment for Aeryx to clear his head, but as soon as they entered Frosteria, the changeling bucked wildly. Growling, Aeryx secured his arms around it more tightly. "Don't make me hop down and bind you behind us. I'll drag your sorry hide all the way to the furnace." He glared down at the changeling. Although he couldn't see the creature beyond the child's face, Aeryx had seen so many wretched changelings that he could nearly *see* past the shell.

The waxy skin, the tufts of hair, the scrawny bodies with long sharp-nailed fingers and mouths that harbored razor fangs.

If he could kill them all, he would. And Aeryx wouldn't lose sleep over it.

Tika followed their well-worn path on a hill. It overlooked a frozen river down in the valley. In all of his years, Aeryx hadn't ever seen the water move freely.

It didn't take long to return to the fortress, and when he did, krampi warriors milled around. Some were hauling their captives toward the whipping posts, where the changelings would be strapped and beaten until they released their holds on the mortal children. Others were dragging the screeching and wailing changelings to the furnace stairs. They would meet a fiery death—it was the only way to truly kill one of them.

Much to his surprise, Aeryx didn't see Lyra. His brows lifted as he surveyed the area.

"Aeryx!" a male's familiar voice called out.

Aeryx dismounted, narrowing his eyes as the other male hurriedly approached. Xavi. One of the krampi he'd trained with when he first enlisted in Morozko's army. His dark hair was kept short, allowing his ebony horns to steal all the attention.

"What is it?" Aeryx didn't mind Xavi, in fact, they'd been as close as friends, but life and missions always drew them apart. However, it was the way the male almost snapped his name that grated on him.

"Lyra is back," Xavi rushed out.

Aeryx nearly hissed—Lyra was back, which meant he'd lost their bet—but the edge in the warrior's tone made him take pause. "Is she all right?"

"No—or yes—she's hurt, but alive. She's in the infirmary, but Aeryx—"

"Do *not* whip this changeling, understand? I'm doing it, but I need to check on Lyra." Despite the cold air swirling around Aeryx's face, he couldn't feel it, for his skin felt like flames would erupt at any moment. Fury burned its way through him. His jaw clenched, and his eyebrows dipped inward as he stormed away toward the barracks.

A few moments were like an eternity for him. By the time he approached the barracks, he'd opted to run and didn't slow down as he shoved the door open and charged into the infirmary.

Horned heads popped up from a few other beds, but it was the attending krampi who eyed Aeryx dryly that rankled him most.

"Where is she?" he blurted through panting breaths.

"You'll have to be more specific than that…"

Just as he was about to snarl, Lyra limped through the opposite doorway, gingerly placing a hand along her bandaged side.

"I think he means me."

She was *alive.* He rushed up to Lyra, assessing her for himself. Injured but not dead. He could live with that. "What happened?" He offered his arm to her, letting her use his frame to help her back to the cot she'd been on.

"I had the bastard, bound and ready to go, but as I was conjuring the portal, out of nowhere, several others attacked me. I don't know how many, but it was like they were waiting for me, Aeryx." She drew in a sharp breath as she settled back down again, carefully situating herself. "They tried their best to gut me right there. I was able to pull myself onto my reindeer, who knew what to do from there."

Aeryx dragged a hand down his face. "You're alive, though."

Lyra smiled sardonically. "Guess I'll be the one tending to your tomte."

Aeryx rolled his eyes, shaking his head. "Fuck the bet, Lyra."

"Listen to me, Aeryx, I know that look."

"What look?" He feigned an air of confusion. "I have no look." Oh, but he did, and he knew he did. His father had told him as much, and Aeryx had been reprimanded for it in the past, too. The calculating expression that he assumed when a plan was forming in his head, *that look.*

"The one that says you're going to charge back into the mortal realm and drag that horde back to Frosteria."

She was right, of course.

Aeryx chuckled darkly, then knelt by her. "Oh, that." He flicked his gaze upward and cocked his head. "I *will* do that, and nothing you say will change my mind. I will flay them until they are rasping for their useless lives, begging me to stop. Do you hear me?" His eyes searched hers before taking note of the mess of tangled curls around her horns. He opted to lighten the mood by dropping the topic.

"You should comb your hair. I'm surprised a raven hasn't taken up nesting on your head yet."

"Aeryx," Lyra whispered.

He offered her a hint of a smile. "Rest, and I'll check in on you soon." Just as he stood, a horn blared from the fortress. It was a high-pitched keening, differentiating from the alarm for battle. This meant all krampi warriors were to assemble into the main fortress yard.

Pushing his way out of the barracks, Aeryx jogged to where he'd left Tika and Xavi. Both of which were still there, peering up at the podium against the fortress' structure.

Krampi filed in by droves, all staring ahead at the same face: his father. Moments ticked by, but when most were standing in front, the captain leaped down from the podium. His lip curled in disgust as his icy blue eyes locked onto a writhing changeling.

"Warriors. We have received some troubling news. It appears the changelings planned ambushes in the mortal realm. A few of your brothers and sisters have fallen, some have returned. But what this means is that a select handful of you will venture out to apprehend these bastards, while the others will prepare to advance on the nests here." Captain Korreth walked through the parting crowd, and he didn't stop until he stood before Aeryx. "I've chosen who will return to the mortal realm when the next moon rises and they settle in for the night."

Aeryx bowed his head, pounding his right fist against his chest. "Captain, wherever you send me—"

"You're going to the mortal realm." Korreth's tone was an

icy mallet slamming down on the pulpit. Such finality in his words, but truth be told, Aeryx almost wanted to run into the nests and tear the fuckers apart before they even emerged from their home.

"Of course, my captain." He shifted his jaw, watching as his father walked away. Just because he was the son of the captain didn't mean Aeryx received special treatment. He was a warrior, as any other, and because he'd trained so young, more was expected out of him, too.

He was a youngling when his father started showing him basic footwork, then, as he perfected those, he learned simple defense blocks. Captain Korreth had been so pleased with how well Aeryx had taken to the training, he didn't stop at self-defense. No, the captain pushed his son as far as he was willing to go.

And Aeryx was glad for it.

Anything that would ensure he could protect those he loved because there was nothing worse than that helpless feeling that threatened to pull him under every time the image of his slain mother flashed in his mind.

"If I call your name, you'll be heading to the mortal realm. Everyone else, begin your preparations for battle in Frosteria." Captain Korreth's voice faded into the din of murmurs as he called out several names. It wasn't until he raised his voice that Aeryx's attention focused once more. "You're all dismissed."

Except Aeryx didn't walk away. He stood, waiting for his father to approach him.

Korreth sauntered up to him, needing to tilt his head back since Aeryx had grown taller than him. "Be careful. They're more agitated than I've ever seen them."

"I know. Lyra told me…"

Korreth frowned, shaking his head. "When I saw Efraun earlier, he couldn't pinpoint all of them. It's strange, like they've been waiting all this time…"

What did that even mean, if their cousin couldn't locate all of them? There must have been hundreds, thousands even, in the mortal realm. Aeryx folded his arms. "Why now?"

Korreth sighed. "Why ever?" His eyebrows drew together in what seemed to be a perpetual frown. Aeryx knew he was much like his father, but there was so much difference between the two. Although Korreth tried, he lacked a playful air that could lighten the mood. Maybe that was why fate had chosen Zira for him, because she could do that for his father.

"Good point." Aeryx dropped his hands to his sides and looked over at Xavi, who had one foot against the changeling's back. "I need to finish up, and then I'll prepare to leave."

Korreth clapped him on the back and offered him the faintest of smiles. "Be safe or I'll tear the mortal realm in half."

Aeryx didn't doubt it. Between his father and Zira, the changelings would suffer. Nodding to his father, he turned away and strode up to Xavi. "Time to make this fucker pay." Xavi stepped back as Aeryx bent over and yanked the writhing demon off the ground.

The changeling shrieked, kicking and wailing as Aeryx crossed the distance to the whipping pole. It was cold enough to see his breath, and as he tapped into his magic, clouds of air formed with each deep inhale he took.

Aeryx tossed the changeling to the ground. "Stand by, Xavi," he bit out.

Xavi only nodded.

As a youth, Aeryx had discovered his ability was much like his father's. Being able to create weapons from ice, but Aeryx only needed water, and water was nearly everywhere. All he had to do was picture it in his head and think the weapon into creation as he held onto his magic.

Aeryx shoved his hand into fresh snow, then made a pulling motion as if he were drawing something out of the depths of the earth. And he was. Link by link, a chain formed —but it wasn't snow, it was ice, and it was as flexible, as durable as anything crafted by a blacksmith. Instead of a normal chain, barbs covered its surface, all the better for ripping skin open.

"Time to let that poor child go," he barked at the changeling, then drew his arm back and slammed the fucker forward. The whip cut through the air with a wail of its own, then sliced through the back of the demon. With each motion, the skin tore away, and yellow vapor oozed out. The changeling's power was releasing into Frosteria.

Yellow slitted eyes, with no pupils, stared at him accusingly. Hate swirled within the depths.

"The loathing is mutual, you wretched fuck. Yet it looks like you're the one on the ground," he said with a smirk.

Blue blood spilled onto the snow, staining it a brilliant hue. "If you think for one moment I care whether or not I shred you into nothing, think again!" Aeryx drove the whip down harder, and this time, flecks of sinew came flying back at him. It slapped against his uniform, but he didn't slow his pace.

By the time the changeling shuddered, releasing its hold on the human child, Aeryx was panting.

"Grab the child," he ordered Xavi, then yanked the changeling up again. "You fucking rat." Aeryx sucked in a breath. Sweat trickled down his brow, into his eyes, and along his back. "Xavi, clean the child up, I'm dropping this one off myself." He spared a glance at the human, who swayed before collapsing into Xavi's arms. Despite the blood coating the child's clothing, his back was bare of any marks, but the demon who had emerged was covered in lashes.

The furnace was always blazing, and the smoke could be seen for leagues upon leagues away as it billowed from the fortress' peaks and shot upward. Embers occasionally jumped toward the cloudy night sky, tasting the air before they sizzled into nothingness.

Aeryx briskly walked up the stairwell, torches lighting the way, and turned toward the door into the inferno. A trail of blue blood followed them, dripping to the stone floor as the warrior stood in front of the iron door. Opening it, Aeryx thrust the wailing changeling into the flames, and the sound of claws scratching along the iron wall echoed.

Sneering, he slammed the door shut and locked it before returning to Tika. Moments later, Xavi sauntered his way with the sobbing child in his arms. The boy trembled violently, but the other krampi had done well to clean him up and wrap him in a fur blanket.

"What is your name?" Aeryx asked softly. Most didn't ask the children their names—because what was the point? The mortals wouldn't remember, and this boy was no different. He'd forget by sunrise that Aeryx had brought him home, tucked him into bed, and ensured he was safe.

"T-Trevor."

"I'm Aeryx, and I'm going to bring you back home."

"Please don't hurt me." The child's voice broke as he dissolved into tears again.

Aeryx didn't blame him. It was a traumatic experience.

"No one is going to hurt you. I'm going to pick you up now—is that all right?" Aeryx stepped forward, and the child held his hand out to stop him. He didn't try again, but he did motion for Tika to come closer. "Do you like horses, Trevor?"

"I-I don't know. I've never seen one in person." But his round eyes focused on Tika's reflective muzzle. "Why is it cold? And why do you have horns?"

"This is Tika, and she is quite special to me." Tika stretched her neck out, lipping the air near Trevor, yet not actually nipping him or even licking the boy. "As for the cold, this is a land of frost. And I'd like to believe I have horns because it enhances my appearance."

Trevor laughed. "They *are* cool, but horses can't be…"

Aeryx smirked at the compliment. "Ice? Most things are in Frosteria. You can touch her if you'd like."

And he did.

Trevor boldly reached out and brushed Tika's nose. Cold to the touch, smooth, and yet unlike any ice sculpture, it felt pliant, too. Like she was more than ice and perhaps a little flesh beneath the surface.

"Whoa," the little boy exclaimed, grinning to himself, then, as if he realized it, he sobered.

"We'll ride her to your home if that's all right with you?"

The boy's eyes lit up. "Oh! Yes."

Aeryx reached for him again, this time, the boy's arms wrapped around his neck as he walked him to the horse. First, he settled the boy into the saddle, then Aeryx mounted as well. "I won't let you fall, and you'll see your family again. I promise. But know, when we pass the barrier, you won't see me as I am—you'll see a beast. Don't be afraid." With a cluck of his tongue, they were off toward the cliffside he'd come from not long ago. The child plastered himself against Aeryx's chest, and his arms caged the boy in.

Once the mortal was back home, Aeryx was determined to catch as many changelings as possible and fill that furnace to the brim.

CHAPTER 7

NOEL

"Wake up, lovebug," a high-pitched voice sang from above Noel. She pried open her lids and met a pair of hazel eyes. Ivy shook a silver meditation ball in front of Noel's face, the light jangling sound echoing and soothing.

"Too early," Noel rasped groggily and pressed the pillow over her face to try and stop her head from throbbing.

"I've got the miracle cure for that," Ivy said, a smile in her tone.

Noel peeked out from the pillow, the light blinding her again. But Ivy's words rang true as she now held out two aspirin and pointed to the bottled water on the nightstand.

"You're like a fairy godmother." Noel grinned, taking the pills and swallowing them with the water. Her throat was still dry, so she emptied the bottle.

She was about to lay back down, hoping for her dream to take her to… wherever she'd been. Then an image of a tall muscular beast with dark curving horns, carrying a blond child, floated through her mind.

Noel straightened, her eyes widening. "What time is it?"

"Ten." Ivy shrugged.

"We were supposed to leave first thing in the morning," Noel groaned.

"About that," her friend drawled. "I did try to wake your lovely self hours ago, but you weren't having it."

That was probably true. Besides being hard to wake on a normal day, a tipsy Noel would've most likely been disastrous and moody. "You could've pushed me off the bed."

"Wouldn't want to risk your Greek god-like wrath." Ivy laughed, setting her meditation ball on the nightstand.

"Let me get ready, then we'll head out if you still want to come with me," Noel said, pushing the blankets back and getting a whiff of herself. She definitely needed a shower… and some deodorant.

"Of course I'm up for a good mystery, but I still think the answer involves one too many drinks."

"I'm not drinking *ever* again." Noel clutched her head while she opened the door. *Never. Ever.*

"That's what they all say," Ivy called as Noel entered the hallway.

Thankfully the bathroom was unoccupied, and she kicked a few damp towels on the linoleum to the side. She quickly brushed her teeth while the water in the shower ran. It always took forever to heat up, but sometimes the other girls had used every drop of the hot water.

Stripping off her costume from the night before, she stepped in the bathtub and let the water fully wake her. It might be pointless as fuck to go visit a street where she would most likely find nothing, but she needed to give herself some peace of mind.

After she finished bathing and dressing in her room, Noel headed downstairs, finding Ivy in the living room. She handed Noel a cup of coffee and a muffin, then sipped from her own drink. The caffeine in the coffee hit the right spot, and her headache had dulled after the shower.

The other girls were either asleep or lingering in their rooms. She bet they were still asleep—the only one who ever woke up early on the weekend was Ivy. Occasionally Noel would if she needed to crochet something for her Etsy shop, but she usually stayed up late to do that.

Outside, a cool gust of wind blew, but not enough to where she needed a jacket this time. She took a bite of the blueberry muffin, letting the delicious sweetness strike her very soul, as they walked down the sidewalk. The grassy area was empty except for a couple people on their cell phones.

"So, how did everything go with Jace?" Noel asked, breaking the comfortable silence. She'd wanted to talk to Ivy about the issue last night, but she'd been so distracted.

"It went as expected." Ivy sighed. "Jace gets it now. Or mostly gets it. He still believes we're meant to be, but maybe not right now, and possibly one day there will be a chance again."

Noel mentally rolled her eyes because of course he did. "And what did you tell him?" In the end, she would always support her friend no matter what she chose.

"I told him first loves don't make it most of the time and how we're just a part of that statistic. He then told me if I ever wanted to talk, to text or call him." Ivy bit her lip and stared at the bright blue sky like she was searching for something. He was the reason she'd chosen this college, the reason she'd come at all.

"I'm proud of you." Even though Noel rarely made the first touchy move, she wrapped her arm around Ivy's warm shoulders and drew her close. "Seriously. You're doing what's best for you. Not him."

The edges of Ivy's lips tilted upward, and she cocked her head. "After he left, I had a funeral for what we had. I should've done a miniature bonfire with all of our stuff, but a shredder and trash can worked just as well."

If Noel had been there, she would've handed Ivy the matches and taken her outside in the backyard to burn the nostalgic things. "Whether you stay single or decide to find a good beast in the future, you'll be successful."

"Thanks, Noel. With the good mood I'm in today, maybe I'll record a video with Winter and Holly."

Noel feigned a gasp. "Okay, where's the real Ivy at? What alien took over your body?"

Ivy laughed. "One of those wormy aliens that seeps inside your brain then slowly eats at it."

"I love how grim you can get."

They chatted the rest of the way and turned down the street where the party had been. Noel hadn't noticed last night, but most of the houses looked similar, only a few differentiations in the location of the garages. Each yard held pine trees and pristine gardens with plain green shrubbery. Apparently, no one was adventurous on this street.

As they continued down the sidewalk, she wasn't sure what the next step should be. Knock on each house and ask if they were missing a kid? That was exactly what she would do, but maybe word things a bit differently.

The party house stood out the most, with several red solo cups and beer bottles littering the yard. She remembered the passed-out guy from the night before, but he must've made an alive exit at some point.

A heavy sound drifted through the air from up ahead, and she watched as a yellow soccer ball appeared out of nowhere, sailing across a yard. It bounced on the sidewalk, then rolled out into the street.

Just before Noel was about to make a smart-aleck comment about a ghost being present, a young boy barreled out from the side of the house and grabbed the ball. Her eyes squinted as she studied the gangly kid while he kicked the ball around the yard. His long blond curls rippled in the wind against his pale skin. Familiar…

Snatching Ivy by the arm, Noel yanked her to her side. "That's the kid I saw last night," she hissed.

Ivy arched a brow as she exchanged a look between Noel and the young boy. "Are you sure? It was at night, and you were drunk. You even said you didn't see the kid's face clearly."

"I recognize the hair and the gangly build."

"But what if—"

Noel ignored the rest of what Ivy was saying and jogged up to the boy, who was maybe nine. "Hey!" she called.

The kid stopped kicking the soccer ball and glanced up at her. But he didn't say a word, just stared at her as if she were an idiot.

"Last night, were you with a guy dressed up as a beast?"

He wrinkled his nose. "I don't talk to strangers." That wasn't a no…

"You just did, but I'm going to ignore that," she said. "Were you? It's important."

He scratched his head and took a step back. "No, I was in my house."

"Do you have any brothers or sisters that are missing?" Ivy asked. Noel hadn't heard her approach, but maybe he did have a sibling who looked similar.

"No." He frowned, taking another step back.

"Are you sure?" Ivy prodded.

"Mom!" he screamed. "Dad!"

The door flew open. "Trevor, what is it?" a woman still wearing her pajama pants and a long sleeve shirt shouted, her eyes wild.

"Shit." Noel tugged Ivy. "Let's get outta here."

Ivy gave a quick apology to the kid's mom, and they hauled ass to the end of the street. Maybe they could've stayed behind and explained things to the kid's parents, but it would've been pointless and embarrassing.

"Well," Ivy started, her chest heaving, mirroring Noel's, "we either know he was returned and forgot, or you imagined it while drunk."

"There's no way he would've forgotten that." She drank in another gulp of air. "I probably imagined it, but I won't imagine cops being called on us by the kid's parents if we linger on this street looking suspicious."

They both busted out laughing and hurried back to the house. She'd done her good deed, and that had to be enough.

As they walked inside the sorority house, the scent of vanilla lattes caressed her nose. Winter yawned as she glanced back at them from the couch, her hair in a messy bun. A reality TV show was playing about coupon clipping.

"You guys missed out last night." Winter smacked the back of the couch. "Holly and I met a couple of hot guys."

She tilted her head. "I can't remember the guy's name I hooked up with, but I remember his moves damn well."

"Like Christian Bale's in *American Psycho*?" Ivy asked, grinning.

"Is that another movie I don't know?" Winter huffed.

"It is." Noel smirked. She had never seen it until Ivy showed it to her, and it was fucking great. "We'll make you watch it later today after *The Crow*."

"If the guys are as hot as my man from last night, then I'm in." Winter sank into the couch cushions and lifted her phone.

"I'm sure they're better." Noel laughed as she headed up the stairs beside Ivy. Her smile faded when she reached her door—something still nagged at her. Even though they'd checked the street and chatted briefly with the kid, she couldn't figure it out.

Ivy was lying on her stomach, lightly snoring. The lava lamp's purple glow crawled up and down the walls. Noel stayed on her back, staring up at the ceiling, unable to fall asleep. After packaging her Etsy orders and finishing her English assignment, she and Ivy had spent the day showing Winter and Holly movies. In return, they ended up doing *one* short video together. Clothing stayed *mostly* on.

With a sigh, Noel scooped up her phone to check the time. It was three-thirty in the morning. As though noticing the time, her stomach rumbled, craving something sugary. The donut shop wasn't too far away, and nothing else close by would be open yet. She glanced at Ivy, contemplating waking her to drive them, but Noel didn't want to disturb her.

She slipped on her Converse, not bothering to change out of her ratty T-shirt and plaid pajama pants, only adding her bra and a jacket. Grabbing her purse, she headed out of the sorority house into the chilly night. The lights were dimmed and she walked away from the campus, then crossed the empty street to take a shortcut through one of the neighborhoods. Several dogs barked from behind fences, ready to tear off her face, as she passed the houses.

The donut shop was at the end of the street, and she could practically taste the glazed pastries when she approached the building. But the lights were off, and her heart sank as she reached the door.

"Motherfucker." Noel lightly banged her head against the glass. They wouldn't open for another hour. *Well, what now…* She reached inside her purse to mess around on her phone, but she'd left it on her nightstand. *Could this night get any worse*? She was being dramatic, but fuck, she was hungry. If this had been her younger self, she may have attempted to pick the lock and help herself.

Noel turned to walk back home when she caught a large shadowy movement in the parking lot. It ran across the empty street. She gasped. *It* was a furred guy with long curving horns atop his head, his body draped in red and black clothing, chains swinging from his hips… Aeryx! But why the hell was he in his costume again when Halloween was over?

He pivoted to the side, his coat billowing in the wind, and Noel caught sight of a body over his shoulder, unmoving. A child? Noel cursed herself for leaving her phone at home when she could've taken a picture and called the police.

This was the worst fate ever.

Balling her fists, she didn't think about it before she

rushed after Aeryx to see where he was taking the kid. She kept as quiet as she could—she didn't want him to notice her because…

A. She was weaponless and B. He had a fucking chain weapon on him—and who knew what else.

By following him, she could at least know the location he was taking the kid, then report his sorry ass to the cops.

They weaved through neighborhoods and skirted around trees. She'd never been so damn stealthy in her life. It was like she was a fucking spy from a James Bond movie, only this was real life, and her heart was pounding in her chest, practically about to break open her rib cage.

But when Aeryx entered the woods, a sinking feeling coursed through her. What was he going to do? She grew up watching all sorts of crime shows, and her thoughts went in the worst possible direction. Holy hell, what kind of sick bastard was he?

A low, vicious sound escaped the kid's gagged mouth as he woke, his body bucking like wildfire.

"Shut the fuck up," Aeryx growled. "I'll be whipping the shit out of you soon enough."

Noel released a squeak, and she wanted to punch herself as Aeryx whirled around. At this shitty point, the choice was either run or help.

She chose to help and launched out from behind a tree, knocking Aeryx and the kid to the ground, just as something blue and fiery erupted from up ahead.

CHAPTER 8

AERYX

THE MOMENT AERYX'S GAZE LANDED ON THE FEMALE'S rounded pale face, he knew at once who had followed him. Noel. Her blue and green hair whipped across her features as a crisp breeze blew through the woods. In her eyes, Aeryx saw the reflection of the sputtering blue portal but wasn't prepared when she lunged for him.

She shoved him to the ground, then seethed, "Let go of that kid, you sick fuck!"

Surprised by the sudden attack, Aeryx fell onto the grass, his grip loosening on the changeling enough so it could wriggle away. Even bound, the demon inched across the ground while Aeryx dealt with Noel.

Fucking great. He didn't have time to deal with a mortal's delicate sensibilities. He had to bring the changeling back to Frosteria, and he had no intention of keeping the child overnight in a world it didn't belong in. While retaining them overnight happened often, it wasn't something any krampi enjoyed. Returning the child was always more difficult because the mortal parents needed to be influenced to believe whatever memory the krampi implanted in their minds. It was taxing, and not preferable by any means.

Noel was straddling him, poised to attack, but her focus wasn't on him. "What the fuck *is* that?" she whispered, then glanced around in confusion, perhaps in search of something —*what*, Aeryx hadn't a clue.

"What the fuck is wrong with you?" he roared.

"Me?" Noel laughed, but it lacked humor. She looked from him to the portal, then to him again before yanking her arm back and slamming her fist into the side of his face.

A burst of pain erupted at the same time his jaw cracked. "Fuck!" Aeryx should've seen it coming, but he hadn't. Rage burned beneath the surface. On one hand, he could understand what it seemed like to her, on the other, his face fucking hurt.

"You're going to tell me what the fuck that is." She pointed at the portal, then jabbed her finger into his chest. "Then you're going to tell me what the hell you *are*—because that magical glittering fire appeared out of nowhere!" Her body trembled as she looked at him.

The changeling had, unfortunately, rolled away from Aeryx, which irked him all the more. The demon would *not* escape him. "Actually, I don't have to tell you anything." He rose to his full height, dumping her on the ground and glaring at her. Drawing in a deep breath, Aeryx raked a hand through his hair, avoiding his horns. It was time to influence her.

Aeryx loomed forward and Noel backed up, her eyes lifting as he drew nearer, and she gave him a once over. "That's not really a costume, is it?"

"No. It isn't, *princess*." Aeryx's eyes connected with hers, and he reached for the deep well of magic within, felt as it stirred, and he drew on it. Noel's focus remained on him, but her face scrunched with impatience. *That isn't right. She should be in a trance, out of it, and waiting for new memories.*

"What the hell are you doing?" She leaned to the side, mouth opening. For a moment, Aeryx considered it to be a distraction, but rustling came from behind them, and he turned to see the changeling struggling. A muffled shriek emitted from it. "That's… not a kid."

Aeryx balled his hand into a fist and huffed. "*That* is a demon, and it *needs* to be dealt with." He sounded like he was talking a youngling down. His tone was a touch condescending like he was waiting to discipline her. And honestly, he had a few things in mind for Noel. If Aeryx wasn't on a mission, he'd consider the game of strip poker again. He was still curious, wanted her full lips pressed against his, and her body flush against him. But she was only a mortal—a pity.

"A demon?" she echoed. Her gaze settled on the creature again. Its form shuddered as it struggled to free itself from the child's body.

Noel had seen too much, and it'd been drilled into his mind that mortals couldn't endure this reality. Long ago, before the humans of Frosteria had become immortal because of the queen's magic, they could, since it was their home, but the mortals in this realm had grown too soft, too sensitive, and were unable to keep the knowledge without fracturing their minds.

At least, that was what the krampi warriors had been taught.

What was the point in withholding the truth any longer? A small amount of information could keep her safe. "A changeling, to be precise. Lesser demons from my world." He thumbed toward the portal.

"Your… world."

The swirling blue light flickered wildly before winking out entirely. Aeryx frowned. That had never happened, either, unless he'd commanded the portal to close. What the hell was going on? He'd summoned it prior to being pounced, but where was the damn stone? He glanced at the ground where Noel had tackled him.

Aeryx gritted his teeth, reeling in his frustration. "I don't have time for this." He turned his back to her and scooped the bucking changeling up into his arms. It had pulled the gag out of its mouth, and the shriek that spilled from the creature made Aeryx's ears pop.

"Oh, oh…" Noel stumbled back, her eyes wide with shock.

He grunted, tightening his arms around the writhing changeling. "Get back to your house, we're done here."

"Excuse me? I'm sorry, I'm not sure what the fuck is going on here exactly." She motioned toward the lesser demon. "But you want me to leave you with *that*?"

Aeryx chuckled despite his irritation. Was she worried about him? Or was it something else? "Yes, princess. Leave me alone with the demon so I can save the child."

Noel's body grew rigid, and her mouth clamped shut. Perhaps she realized her folly and that she'd thoroughly fucked up his mission, but Aeryx wouldn't have been that fortunate. "This is like the dream I had when I was little," she whispered. "He called me princess, too."

"A dream…?" Did that mean she was some kind of seer? Had she foretold the future and predicted Aeryx's arrival, or was she something else? A witch maybe? He couldn't even use his influence on her, so she was something…

"A boy beast, with two others, and we were in a sleigh, riding through the forest near my house… I remember riding with the boy beast on a mystical creature. He had me give him my torn nightgown…" She was rambling now.

Noel was so focused on recollecting the dream that she didn't notice Aeryx's face drop, his chest tighten. He remembered then, all of it. How he'd snuck into his father's sleigh when he should've been at his cousin's, meeting Zira for the first time, and watching the changeling leave the mortal girl's body. His father had been so gentle with the ash-blonde girl as he sat her on top of Dral's back, and Aeryx nestled in behind her, vowing to protect her.

Back then, he'd remarked on how beautiful he thought her hair was. He hadn't even known her name… But he remembered those bright green eyes, the ones that would still call to him at night sometimes, of a girl he'd wondered more about. This couldn't be happening. Not to him, and not when so many changelings were running amok, ambushing krampi.

However, when he looked at those piercing green irises now, those same haunting eyes, Noel… Noel was the girl he'd returned home all those years ago. He'd left his father and Zira to embark on the mission himself. It'd been the first one his father had trusted him to perform, and here the same mortal girl was, reciting the journey clearly, which meant she remembered it all.

And she wasn't supposed to recall anything. So, he'd say nothing about it being him and his family. "Great, so you dreamed about a *Krampus*," Aeryx grumbled impatiently, sarcasm lacing his tone. "Now, you can leave, because I need to get back *home.*" He shook his head, squeezing the demon in his grasp as it thrashed more violently. In the struggle, his gaze dropped to the broken stone in the decomposing leaves and pine needles, when it should've been smooth, unblemished even. But it was split in two pieces.

Noel sucked in a breath. "Krampus!" she gasped, as if she'd figured it all out. "Like the movie… You steal children… Except to help them…" she murmured, but Aeryx wasn't focused on whatever she was about to say, he was more concerned about the stone.

"Double fucking damn." He stepped forward, and as he did so, Noel scrambled backward. "Can you pick that up?" The demon in his arms shrieked again. When she obliged, Aeryx's heart plummeted. "The fucking stone is broken!" Anger bubbled within him, and as his eyes slowly lifted, Noel cocked her head.

"So?" She wrinkled her nose and waved her hand. "Get a new one."

Aeryx shot her a venomous look. "I can't *just get a new one.* This stone is from my world and it allows me to return there. I cannot just *find* one here." He squeezed his eyes shut. Noel didn't know—he had to keep reminding himself. *But doesn't she? She knows on some level.*

This wasn't just a matter of a failed mission, it was possible that there were other krampi suffering from changelings' planned attacks. "I need you to leave. Now."

"Absolutely not. You're a *real* Krampus."

He stared at her incredulously. "Morozko's teeth. Why the fuck would you stay?"

"In case you need backup."

Backup. He squinted, contemplating her words. Did this

tiny mortal truly believe she could stop a demon if she tried? "So, you're coming along in case *I* need assistance?"

"Something like that." She rolled her eyes, but despite the air of bravery she put on, Noel took a step back and peered down at the changeling in his arms. Maybe she was having second thoughts already.

She was brazen. Aeryx had to give her that. And foolish.

Still, he didn't want her alerting other changelings that he was here, especially since the stone was broken and he had no way of returning home.

He tilted his head back and sighed. "I'll allow you to follow, Noel, but you will listen to me."

"Fine."

It occurred to Aeryx that there was no rustling nearby. He'd left Tika here—where had his damn familiar gone? "Tika?" There was no returning nicker, no plodding of hooves in the crisp leaves.

His arms tightened around the thrashing changeling, and rather than shriek, it gnawed at the gag in front of its mouth.

"Who's Tika?" Noel sidled up beside him.

"My horse." It was easier than explaining what she actually was.

"You rode a horse here?" She drew her hair over her shoulder. "I'm not surprised. I mean, it is Vermont, and someone went through the Dunkin drive-through on a horse before."

Aeryx didn't know what the hell any of that meant, but he was certain none of them had ridden on an ice horse.

"I need to get rid of this creature, and you're not going to like how it's done." He'd have to collect sticks, build a fire, and whip the changeling here—or rather, deeper in the woods, so no one could hear the ear-splitting screams of agony.

As tall as he was, his boots scarcely made a sound on the leaf-littered ground. Noel, however, tromped through the leaves as if she were the size of a moose. How could one small mortal female make so much damn noise?

Aeryx opened his mouth, readying to warn Noel to remain close to him, but the changeling shifted in his grasp, and he realized the demon hadn't been gnawing at the gag, but the binding around its wrists. With its mouth and hands free, the changeling shoved at Aeryx's chest with enough force that he rocked back onto his heels.

Despite wearing the human child's flesh, the changeling's eyes glowed a brilliant hue of yellow. A low hiss came from the demon, then a chittering. An elbow connected with Aeryx's throat.

Noel screamed.

Instead of falling to the ground, Aeryx grappled with the changeling, its mouth open wide, baring the razor-sharp fangs as it phased between human and demon. It was determined to rip Aeryx's throat out, and he sure as hell was not in the mood to let it.

"Oh, my fuck," Noel shrieked. "That really is a demon!"

No shit. "Get out of here, Noel!" The changeling sank its claws into his neck, eliciting a sharp pain, before he pried them from his flesh. Blood trickled down his throat, and as anger seared through him, he jerked the demon from his chest, scruffing it like one would an angry cat.

The changeling's claws protruded from the tips of the human child's fingers, and it successfully swiped at Aeryx's face, cutting him while he was distracted by Noel.

"Shit. Aeryx!" She rushed forward, hands held out, and it was clear she wasn't sure what to do—or how she could help.

"Just get out of here!" he bellowed, struggling with the creature as it spun around in his grasp. It was quick and bent on escaping. Aeryx, half distracted by Noel still hovering, missed the subtle movement of the changeling's head dipping, then it chomped down on his hand, biting through the glove and piercing his skin.

He swore a blue streak.

Aeryx's grip weakened a fraction, but it was enough of a window for the changeling to break free of his hold, and much to the krampi warrior's dismay, the bastard had used one of his weapons to cut the remaining bindings.

Untethered, the changeling phased from the child's body, it's wax-yellow skin dull and naked. The demon dared to take one glance over its bony shoulder, the wisps of hairs on its head plastered in place, before bolting away into the night.

Aeryx was panting softly from grappling with the demon, but he caught the child as the boy fell into him, head lolled back against his body.

"Now, in case you didn't truly believe me before…" He turned to look at Noel, who was shaking, her mind fracturing.

CHAPTER 9

NOEL

WHAT IN THE EVER-LOVING NAME OF EXORCISMS JUST happened? The creepy-ass creature that scampered away had to be something straight from some sort of underworld. Noel hadn't been afraid of anything thus far. Not a mother-loving shimmering portal to another world, not Aeryx who, apparently, wasn't a human, and not even his talk about demons. But when that thing sprung out of the child's flesh, its claws sharp, its teeth protruding through a barely-there mouth... It was as though an alien had taken host of the kid—it was exactly that, except some kind of demon.

Noel's heart pounded as she studied the place where the creature had disappeared into the darkness, the limbs of the trees casting shadows across the ground. An owl hooted as if warning her to get the fuck out of the woods.

"Are you going to stand here for the rest of the night? You've made a perfect mess of things, and now I have to clean it up," Aeryx grumbled.

"That thing..." She spun to face him, his arms cradling the

passed-out little child. Dark hair slicked the boy's forehead, and his mouth hung open as he lightly snored.

"A changeling. A demon. It's been in control of this child for several days." He adjusted the kid and took a step toward her. "Some aren't so lucky. Now, go home."

Noel studied his face for a moment, one that would be considered monstrous to others, but she didn't hold any fear. Not as she watched the way he kept the child close, held protectively, the opposite of how he'd treated the changeling when the creature had been inside the boy.

"Where are you going?" Noel asked. She couldn't just go home and pretend this freakish night hadn't happened. Most of her roommates would've run for the hills, except for maybe Ivy. Even then, her friend would've been wary.

"Well," Aeryx drawled. "I need to bring the child home first before his parents wake. I was already running late from completing other missions tonight. Afterward, I need to hunt down the little shit that slithered off. And then, because of *you*, somehow, I need to fix my stone so I can get the fuck out of here and go home. The others aren't going to like this."

"The others?" Noel arched a brow. "There are more of you? I thought there was only one Krampus?" Even though there had been three in her dream when she was younger... Was there a possibility it had been real? It still felt like a dream, though...

He sighed. "We don't have time for a krampi history lesson at the moment."

"Fine, later," Noel said. "But I'm coming with you." Even though she didn't know this "krampi," she needed to make sure the child was returned home safely, regardless of how protective he seemed of the boy. If she had her phone, she would've called Ivy to come and pick them up. It would've made things faster—however, it was what it was.

Aeryx's wide nostrils flared, his lips pursed, his two elongated teeth stayed protruding—*real*—not a costume. He took another step toward her, his eyes narrowing, his pupils shining, performing the strange sort of dance he'd done before when he'd stared at her.

"Why do you keep doing that weird shit with your eyes while looking at me?" Noel wrinkled her nose and inched backward.

"I don't know what kind of spell you're doing, or how you're doing it, but you need to stop." He paused. "Are you a witch? Perhaps a descendant of Eirah?"

"What? Who?" Her voice went up an octave, her eyes bulging. If she were a witch, she would've done a lot of different things with her life in the past. Or now, for that matter.

"Never mind. If you want to come, then you better keep up, princess." He released a low growl and turned, jogging away.

Noel watched his muscles flex, his strong body briskly moving. Blinking, she reminded herself that he was not a guy in a costume, and she couldn't think of him as *sexy*. Especially not after everything she'd just witnessed.

She took off in a sprint, catching up to him after a few moments. "Cut the princess shit." Life would've been better in her past if she'd been one of those.

"Well, you're certainly acting like one with that attitude." One side of his lips pulled up into a smirk. "Now, move and stay close. I need to keep out of sight."

Noel didn't know how he could slink around wearing

bright-ass red clothing and looking like a beast... or Krampus. Halloween was one thing—this was another. If he was seen though, most people would believe he was wearing a costume, but the child in his arms wouldn't go over so well. She wouldn't have guessed him to be dressed like Krampus at the party because the one she'd seen in the movie had looked like a giant monster, and Aeryx's eyes were human. To her, he still looked more like the beast in *Beauty and the Beast*, although that character could appear vicious too. She'd believed *Krampus* was just a movie, and Hollywood, as usual, had gotten it wrong. The creature was a mythical being—she did know that—the legend said the beast stole naughty children, beat them, and who knew what else. As soon as she got home, she would research the shit out of it.

The moon's light guided their way to the edge of the street, where lampposts illuminated the road. Aeryx stayed behind a tree while a white car sped past, then booked it across the street. Noel dashed after him, staying hot on his heels. For someone so big, his feet remained light, and his body nimble as he ducked and weaved around trees through the neighborhoods.

A few early risers were getting in their cars, most likely heading into work. Aeryx lunged toward the side of a house with vinyl siding, and Noel planted herself beside him, her chest heaving while her heart beat wildly. He hadn't even broken a sweat, his breathing remaining steady.

She had questions—lots of questions, a whole mountain of them—and for a moment, she wondered if this was like the dream she'd had when she was younger. Aeryx had asked if she was a seer before mentioning the witch nonsense. But maybe, she did have a vision in her past. It was possible and would explain why it had felt like a dream. Psychics claimed to see things, yet she'd always believed they'd just been trying to make a quick buck.

The car in the driveway backed out and headed down the empty street. Aeryx didn't even warn her he was taking off again as he pushed off the side of the house and hauled ass down the road. She grunted, trying to keep up the pace, but she hadn't ever run this much in her life. At least not since maybe her younger days back in school.

The donut shop she'd gone to was now open—light illuminated from the windows, and a few cars lined up in the drive-thru.

Aeryx cursed and took a longer route around the shop, staying in the shadows of the back fence surrounding it. Weeds, in desperate need to be ripped out, grew as big as bushes along the ground near the wood.

All of this had happened because she'd just wanted a damn donut. Noel wouldn't lie and say she wasn't tempted to stop following him to go into the shop and grab a tasty dessert along with a cold bottle of water. She pushed away the temptation because that wouldn't be happening any time soon.

The streetlamps guided their way down the road she'd come from earlier. He slinked around the side of a one-story house covered in light gray brick. Several lawn ornaments decorated the garden, including birds, their bright wings spinning from the wind.

Aeryx slowed and opened the wooden gate. She followed him inside, and they stopped at the first window, where curtains, printed with different cars, hung behind the glass. The dark screen was propped up against the house below the window.

Noel's lungs were ragged and desperate for the oxygen she drank in. Her thighs burned, and her eyes widened in delight at the water hose crumpled in the grass. She turned on the water and lifted the hose. Her gaze drifted to Aeryx, who glared at her as she drank the cool liquid.

"What? I'm thirsty." She motioned him forward. "Continue with your business."

Shaking his head, he pushed open the window. She turned off the water while he crawled inside with the kid. As she peered through the open space, she couldn't see much in the room's darkness except for the outline of Aeryx taking the boy to a bed, where he gently laid him down, then placed the blankets over his thin frame. The boy didn't stir, only let out a soft sigh.

"Put the screen back on and meet me on the porch," he said, closing the window and locking it.

Noel furrowed her brow but placed the screen on the window before trekking around to the front, just as Aeryx shut the door. "We have to be careful when entering and exiting homes. If a window isn't unlocked already, like this one wasn't originally when I tried it, we use a special key that will open any door."

That thrilled her thieving side, which still lingered deep down inside of her, but it also was a bit creepy to think about how a krampi could just waltz on into any house they wanted.

"So that's not weird at all," Noel said sarcastically. "I don't understand how the kid didn't wake up from all that running."

"Their bodies are drained after having those leeches inside them." He shrugged. "Some wake in Frosteria, others a little

after, and some, hours later. But none of them remember
having a demon inside them."

Noel shivered at his words. That was a scary thought—not
knowing a demonic creature was living beneath one's flesh.
"Is he going to be all right, though?"

"He'll be fine." Aeryx raked a hand through his hair, her
gaze catching on his long curving horns. Again, *real*.

"Can I touch them?" She couldn't hold her tongue as she
stared.

"Touch what?" he whispered, incredulous.

"Your horns."

Aeryx shook his head. "I think that would create a whole
new problem for us." His voice came out gruff.

"Like what?"

He laughed. "Like my cock getting hard. Now go home."

Her eyes widened at his words. *Oh… Oh! His horns are a
sexy zone!* Noel couldn't keep her gaze from dropping to his
package. She now wondered if his cock was like a human's or
if it was covered in fur… Was it even shaped normally?

Get control of yourself, Noel! "Stop telling me to go
home," she hissed. "I'm not a child."

"You're being a nuisance, and we're wasting precious
time by chatting on this porch."

"I'm *helping* you."

A soft chuckle escaped his mouth, then he cleared his
throat as though he was doing something wrong. "If that's the
case, don't fall behind." Then he took off.

Bastard. She grunted and darted after him. They stayed
just as stealthy, or at least Aeryx did. She wanted to pass out
somewhere on the ground, catch her breath and *sleep*, but she
ignored the aches in her body until they reached the woods.

Just as they crossed the tree line, the sun peeked through the darkness, casting its light across the green and brown foliage. Dead leaves littered the ground, and a small furry animal scurried up one of the trees. The snap of a twig echoed —Noel grabbed onto Aeryx, causing them to both halt.

Aeryx shoved Noel behind him, and she wanted to roll her eyes, but she didn't have any sort of weapon if it was the changeling.

A pale blue horse with black hooves appeared from between two large tree trunks. No, not a regular horse. The creature was entirely made of ice, its bright blue eyes blazing, the sun's morning glow making it look even more ethereal than it already was. Even though the horse was ice, its tail swished from side-to-side, creating a clinking noise while its mane made the same sound as the wind blew through it. The horse was the most beautiful thing she'd ever seen, its movements graceful. A saddle rested on its back, as did several brown bags that looked like potato sacks at its sides.

"Tika, where have you been?" Aeryx asked, his tone annoyed. "I could've used your help earlier."

"You said you had a horse." Noel shifted out from behind his back and pointed at him. "Not an *ice* horse."

"A horse is a horse."

"Maybe in *your* world." Wherever that was exactly. It apparently wasn't here, at the North Pole, or wherever the history of Krampus was supposed to have taken place. Her thoughts turned to the changeling… As much as her brain was yelling at her to go home now, she was already in this too deep. "Are we going to hunt down that sick demon bastard now?"

CHAPTER 10

AERYX

AERYX GRITTED HIS TEETH. A SLIVER OF LIGHT PEEKED through the canopy of trees. The damn sun was coming up *already*. He couldn't very well trek through the woods in search of a changeling, possibly alerting and alarming nearby mortals.

He stared at Noel as she asked her question. "In the daylight? Surely you can see the flaw in that idea." When she didn't reply, he motioned to himself. "We hunt at night."

"Oh, right. Fangs, hair, giant-ass beast traipsing through the streets."

Aeryx mouthed the words *giant-ass beast* and squinted. He wasn't certain if he should've been amused or offended, but he chuckled, opting for the former. "Yes, well, this *beast* will be camping out in the woods until the moon rises again." She could continue believing this was what Aeryx truly looked like because she wasn't supposed to remember him in the first place. But, truthfully, it was almost like a private jest at this point.

Noel glanced around the woods. "But not by yourself."

He grinned, folding his arms across his chest. "Aww, are you worried about me?"

Color rushed into her cheeks, and she rolled her eyes. "No…" she drawled. "I just mean… you don't even have a tent. I suppose you do have a horse made of *ice,* though."

"Why would I need a tent?" His brow furrowed in genuine confusion. He'd packed a bedroll, weapons, and provisions. What else did he need? *A kiss goodnight.* Aeryx didn't have time for intrusive thoughts, especially since he hadn't *won* said kiss—*yet.*

Noel's lips pursed as confusion scrunched her features. "You just sleep on the ground?"

"Yes. It's far milder here than it is back home. Krampi are demons of winter—we don't feel the cold like a mortal does." Anything more than his leather uniform was extra and perhaps a touch vain on his end.

But, another intrusive thought of a shivering Noel, with her arms wrapped around his neck, flooded his mind, and he inwardly cursed. It would benefit neither himself nor Noel since she wasn't immortal, and her mortal life was so fleeting.

She arched a brow. "Of course." Her gaze dropped to his chest, and her lips twisted like another question was on the verge of slipping out, yet nothing came. "I need to head back to the house, but I'll return at… what time do you want me here?"

Time? He rubbed his hand against his cheek. Mortals and their concrete time, with their watches and clocks. "When most mortals are asleep." He shrugged, lifting his hands, so his palms faced upward. "I'll be here—or I won't—I suppose you'll find out." Aeryx was mid-laugh when a pinecone hit him in the head. He frowned. "Why would you do that?"

"Because you were being an asshole." Noel huffed. "Wait for me, *please*?"

Why would—or *should*—he? Noel could get grievously injured while he subdued the changeling, but the way she cocked her head and looked up at him with those brilliant, expectant green eyes... Fuck. She wasn't even trying to manipulate him with an exaggerated pout. In fact, she was almost scowling at him.

"Fine." He turned away from her and sauntered toward Tika. "But I'm not waiting for you all night." Aeryx pulled the buckle loose on his pack and yanked out his bedroll. "So, be here on time." He laid the blanket on the ground, then peeled his gloves off, followed by his jacket, tossing them into a pile.

"You didn't give me one, remember?" She put a hand on her hip.

He rolled his eyes and shooed her away with a hand, chuckling. "I remember, princess. Go back home." Aeryx leaned against Tika, slanting Noel a mischievous look.

She scoffed and turned her back to him. "Just... don't try leaving without me."

Her voice gave him pause. Vulnerability—and something he couldn't put his finger on—laced her tone. He pushed away from his horse and watched as she walked away. "I'll wait as long as I can, but no more than that." She turned to glance at him and his gaze locked on her beautiful green eyes. "And Noel, don't tell anyone about me." It was as good as he could do. With the stone broken, Aeryx wasn't certain of anything. It would take time to find the demon again, but how long would it take for Aeryx to repair the stone—if he could at all?

Noel didn't say a word as she disappeared through the overgrowth. A part of him wanted to reassure her he'd wait, and it was that piece of him he wanted to gag. Aeryx loosed a breath and stomped a foot into the ground once Noel was out of sight. A complex array of emotions rose within him.

Somehow, all those years ago, he'd fucked up influencing her, and now, it seemed he still couldn't. If it hadn't been for all the successful times he *had* wiped the memories of mortals away, perhaps he'd consider it had to do with his abilities, but it wasn't him at all.

It was Noel.

Sometimes, he'd thought about the girl he brought back home. Of how he safely tucked her in, then listened as she told *him* a story of a beast prince. She'd been the only one to look past the glamour of the mortal world and talk to him as though he were just a boy.

He dragged his hands down his face and closed his eyes. If he could reach Zira, she'd know what to do, and it'd spare his father from getting involved. Or better yet, Efraun. His cousin wouldn't tell anyone a damn thing if it meant an adventure. But there was no way of contacting anyone.

One thing was certain, now that Noel was gone, exhaustion washed over him, dragging his shoulders down. He knelt on the blanket, pulled his jacket toward him, and shaped it into a makeshift pillow. Prior to being trapped in the mortal realm, he'd collected as many changelings as he could find. Aeryx needed sleep.

As he closed his eyes, Noel entered his mind—the playful

glint in her gaze and her full lips, which begged to be captured, teased even.

Stop thinking about her and just go the fuck to bed.

It was hard, though. *He* was hard.

Eventually, he'd fallen asleep and only roused when his stomach growled in protest. It was loud enough that Tika sighed and nudged the pack full of jerky.

The sun shone through the branches, casting shadows of elongated fingers onto the forest floor. If he had to guess, it was late afternoon, and still, there was so much time to waste. He grumbled, then his stomach followed suit—*again*.

Tika snorted.

"I get the point." Aeryx rolled forward and reached for a handful of jerky. While waiting for the day to pass, he could make himself useful.

Shoving a few pieces of the strips of meat into his mouth, he balanced the rest on his knee, then dipped his hand into the pocket of his jacket and pulled out the two pieces of the stone. How was he supposed to fix this? Frowning, he pushed one edge against another, then let his magic course within him before sending his power into it. Clouds of icy air rose from the stone, and in between them, ice formed, but it didn't adhere to the stone.

"Well, fuck!" His outburst sent a flock of small songbirds fluttering away from a nearby tree. Glowering, he jabbed one of the broken pieces of the stone and sighed.

He'd have to wait until someone came searching for him. All krampi were given a deadline of a maximum of seven days. An entire week in the mortal world before they'd send a scout to check on the situation. All Aeryx could hope for was that his father grew impatient, sent for their cousin, and came for him.

Fuck. If only I had Efraun's tracking ability, then I could hunt more fucking changelings down. But it still didn't solve the issue of opening the portal.

With no book to read and unable to train—lest a mortal find him rustling around in the woods—Aeryx forced himself back to sleep.

Zira's dark eyes darted from Ryken's lifeless body to a throng of approaching changelings. They released loud, hooting snarls that shook the strands of sinew on their lips.

No. Not his brother. The sight of him was a knife to his heart.

Blood poured down the changelings' bodies, but the red blood told him it didn't belong to them since theirs was blue.

Zira wailed and picked up a discarded sword near Ryken's body before charging toward the approaching horde.

Aeryx couldn't move from where he stood. His limbs were frozen in place, and his lips wouldn't part to release a growl of frustration. All he could do was watch as Zira collided with the changelings, their claws tearing ribbons of flesh away. When her blood painted the snow, the mob of changelings turned toward him, racing forward with their claws readied.

One grabbed him by the shoulder, the bite of its nails digging in.

"Aeryx!" a familiar voice called out, filling him with worry. Noel couldn't be here—she'd die. The mere thought was enough to twist his heart with agony. He wasn't certain

why he cared, but the urge to protect and defend her rose like a wave within him.

The changeling's slitted eyes filled with delight as fear oozed from Aeryx. It tore its nails through his uniform…

Aeryx bolted upward, his hands immediately capturing the threat above him by their shoulders. He growled lowly, glaring at it.

"It's just me!" Noel shouted. Her eyebrows shot up to her hairline, and she looked like a doe caught in a snare, instantly sobering Aeryx.

He loosened his hold, blinking away the nightmare. "I'm sorry." Aeryx scanned where he'd grabbed her, wondering if she would bruise. Frowning, he rubbed at his eyes.

"A nightmare?" she asked softly from where she crouched on the blanket.

That was the simple answer, he supposed, but what plagued Aeryx was a mixture of reality and nightmare. He'd seen what the changelings could do first hand and on a personal level. One of his greatest fears was it happening again.

"Yes, something like that…" It was the easiest way to respond without the gritty details. Aeryx pulled his knees to his chest, then looked to the canopy of branches above. A crescent moon offered little light, which was just as well since he was in the mortal realm. He could see with or without the help of the full moon.

As it was, it was pitch black, except for a glowing flash-light on the ground.

She shrugged. "Everyone has them." Noel puffed out a breath, and her body seemed to sag at the same time. "Is it time to go hunting for that fucker?"

Aeryx scratched his temple. He'd nearly scared the life out of her, and she was ready to hunt down a changeling already? He couldn't help but smirk. "I'm going to be truthful, hunting a changeling down here without that stone is going to be nearly impossible."

Noel grabbed her flashlight and stood. "So, what you're saying is… unless you're attacked by one, you won't be able to find the changeling?"

"There is that, but also… it couldn't have gotten far from here. Not when there are so many children around." He just hoped they weren't too late yet, and that it hadn't found a new child to possess.

Aeryx moved off of the blanket, then rolled it up. Rather than putting his jacket back on, he tossed it onto his saddle—which lay in a heap on the ground.

Tika trotted from a cluster of small pine trees and stopped in front of Noel. She whuffled the air around her, then dragged her clear tongue along Noel's cheek.

"That wasn't weird or anything…" Noel touched where Tika had licked. "It's cold."

"Tika is made of ice, what did you expect?" Aeryx quipped playfully. He motioned for his horse to come to him. She complied, and he saddled her, then shoved everything back into his pack.

"Have you ever ridden a horse before?" He sauntered up to Noel, smirking.

She looked from him to the horse. "Once, but not a magical one…"

Aeryx chuckled, thinking of the time his father helped her onto Dral, the demon reindeer. "Well, today is your lucky day." Tika took a step forward, waiting patiently. Her ears flicked to attention, and her glowing, blue eyes focused on Noel, who shifted closer to the horse. With ease, Aeryx lifted her into the saddle, then he joined her, nestling in against the curve of her ass, sending a rush of heat through him.

Morozko's blood, give me strength.

Noel steadied herself by placing her hands on Tika's mane, but her bottom shoved into Aeryx's lap.

Perhaps it wasn't his best idea. Noel's body leaned into him, and her scent filled his nostrils. She smelled of fresh air and a sweetness that was wholly her own. Her ass pressed harder into him, teasing him, and threatened to harden his cock.

If they didn't have an important task, he might have devised a game of his own—it had little to do with cards and everything to do with removing articles of clothing.

Tika took a step forward, and as soon as she did, Noel gripped onto Aeryx's thigh. *Morozko's teeth, she's going to make this impossible.*

"I better not fall and break my neck." She turned her head to the side, and he firmly wrapped one arm around her.

"I will not let you fall," he murmured against her temple. When she settled enough, he pushed the horse onward, slowly at first, and Noel leaned against Aeryx's chest.

Tika's pace quickened. The horse's black hooves struck the dried leaves on the ground, kicking them up in her wake. Holly trees boasted bright red berries against their dark green leaves, and pinecones collected at the base of trunks on the ground.

Thankfully, Noel didn't shift against him repeatedly, nor did she require him to talk. Not that he would've been overly chatty, considering they were on a mission. He always grew quiet as he focused on the task at hand.

They must have been traversing the woods for a half-hour when Aeryx's skin prickled. He quieted Tika, slowing her pace to a walk.

Noel twisted in the saddle, peering up at him. "Wh—"

He shushed her with a finger to her lips. A low chittering echoed in the clearing. Whether it was *the* changeling he was looking for or simply another one running around, he wasn't certain. At the end of the day, it didn't matter.

"Noel—" He was readying to tell her to remain on Tika when a body crashed into his, sending him flying from the saddle. His horse, Morozko bless her, didn't bolt. She scooted to the side as the changeling screeched, grappling with Aeryx.

"Aeryx!" Noel cried.

"Stay on Tika!" Aeryx huffed, swiping a dagger from his side. It wouldn't kill the changeling, only distract it. He twisted the blade in his grasp, then lodged it into the demon's neck. A cry of fury melded with one of pain. Sometimes, despite his father telling him years ago to not think of them as humans—because they weren't—guilt washed over him for the violence against the child. But when they were in their true state, like this one, there was nothing but hatred aimed toward them.

Aeryx used his size to his advantage and pinned the demon to the ground, ignoring the creature as it swiped at his uncovered hands. Blood seeped out from the cuts, and he brushed off the sting as he stayed bent on securing the creature.

"Noel!" he ground out. "I need the chain in my bag. Grab it and bring it to me." The changeling bucked beneath him, screeching as it attempted to unbalance him. Its legs flailed, and claws raked over Aeryx's sleeves, hands, and thighs. Aeryx didn't dare look away for too long, but he glanced in Noel's direction, who was taking her sweet time, clumsily rifling through his bag. "Now would be good."

She hopped down from Tika, her eyes wide as she stepped near them, but not too close. "What now?"

"Now I bind the changeling, and then we're going to burn it here."

CHAPTER 11

NOEL

Burn the fucker.

That would be the final task in this screwed-up situation Noel had found herself in. Out of all the past circumstances she'd experienced in her entire twenty-one years, there'd been plenty of fucked-up ones. But nothing like this. Nope. This was absolutely *numero uno*. A murderous date with a beast from another world. Not a *date*, though. It was whatever the hell this was.

However, she had known that burning the demon was the plan.

As Noel handed Aeryx one of the chains from his pack, a gust of wind tousled his brown locks. The wriggling creature arched its back beneath Aeryx, its body curving as though it was possessed. But no, *this* was a demon itself, freakier than any Hollywood made-up bullshit. Well, maybe not *creepier* since some of the alien movie creations could open their mouths and do some sick shit with their tongues, but it was fucking up there. Because this was *real*.

The nerves crawling beneath her skin hadn't truly hit her the night before, not until she'd gone home, sat in her room, went to class as if all things were fine and dandy, and her thoughts had settled. Aeryx had asked her not to tell anyone about him when that was exactly what she'd wanted to shout from the rooftop all day. Once he was back in "his world," then she would continue to keep this secret, besides confessing it to Ivy. The thoughts had pounded more and more in her head—how many of these creatures were there? Were there people out there that she passed every day trapped with a changeling inside them?

As she stared at the squirming demon, she wasn't sure how she *should* feel about it. Animals did vicious acts because of their nature. But these things' natures were going around and implanting themselves inside human kids like they were parasitic aliens or some shit. If burning the demons prevented them from snatching innocent kids' bodies, then all right...

"Should I have brought a can of gasoline and matches?" Noel asked, taking a step back if she needed to sprint to the nearest gas station.

"What?" Aeryx jerked his head up, his sharp teeth poking out from his lips as he bound a gag around the changeling's mouth. Or at least what was supposed to be considered a mouth—there was practically not one at all. "I'm no fool. I carry a flint everywhere I journey to."

That saved her a trip then, but she didn't want to stand there feeling useless. "Let me bind its ankles together." Without waiting for his answer, she took out another chain and knelt in the dirt. She grasped the creature's ankles, its skin soft—too soft—and squishy like a jellyfish. A scent of decay and dirty laundry struck her nose as she hovered over it.

Holding back the urge to vomit, she looped the chain around its kicking feet while her heart raced.

"Tighter, princess," Aeryx grunted, pressing down beside her. He shooed her hands away and gripped the chain with his bloodied palms. Not to tighten it, but to unravel and redo the *entire* thing.

Noel rolled her eyes and stood. "That was a bit drastic."

"Not with these fuckers. You can't be too careful with them." He gave the chain a hard tug, but it didn't budge. *Damn.*

"Are your hands going to be okay?"

"I've been through much worse. Besides, I heal fast." He smirked.

Heals fast? She shouldn't have even been surprised by that answer after everything.

Noel scooped up her flashlight and searched the area. The night was darker than the previous one, the moon mostly hidden behind clouds. All was quiet except for a few noises coming from insects. "Now we make a bonfire, I'm assuming?"

"A pyre, yes."

"Fancy wording you have there." She grinned, trying to ignore the changeling's grunting and jerking as it attempted to roll to its side.

Aeryx chuckled. "Just grab enough kindling so we can throw the body onto it."

Throw, not place. Got it. She nodded, then went to gather fallen branches, pine needles, and leaves. She added every-thing she collected to the pile Aeryx had started beside the changeling. Its yellow eyes glowed with hatred as they bored into her, seeming to uncover every one of her secrets and sending a shiver down her spine.

Tika's light clinking sounds echoed through the air when she came up beside Noel. She dropped a large tree branch onto the collection of tinder, and even while doing that, the horse's movements were graceful.

"Couldn't have burned the bastard without that, Tika," Aeryx said, tossing a clump of brown pine needles on top of the branch. He ran a furred hand along Tika's jaw, and the horse released a low nicker.

He stepped close to Noel, so close his wintry scent enveloped her, just as it had when he'd been behind her while riding on Tika. She studied him for a beat too long, thinking about how he'd felt like a man pressed against her, his warmth cocooning her. But he wasn't. He was something else. She liked the way he'd felt—maybe a bit too much. And all she could think was how it was too damn bad as he bent down, his muscles flexing beneath his tight clothing while he easily lifted the changeling and tossed it onto the middle of the pyre.

Noel, he's not human… He's covered in fucking fur. He has fucking fangs for crying out loud. Not a costume.

The changeling's muffled hisses continued, and even without understanding the creature's language, she was pretty sure the bastard was spewing curses at them. Aeryx struck the flint with a loud swipe, and a spark ignited, its brilliant flecks of orange dancing across the first branch. Aeryx blew softly, then the sparks leaped onto the dried pine needles. The changeling bucked and writhed, attempting to roll itself out from the pyre.

Aeryx booked it to the other side, stomping his boot on the creature's shoulder as the first flame caught on the changeling's bare foot. Noel's stomach churned at the sight, and she closed her eyes for a moment before forcing them back open.

"You don't have to watch," Aeryx said, his voice soft as he studied her, even though his boot was still planted on the changeling's body.

Noel was tempted, *incredibly* tempted, to whirl around, leave this clusterfuck of a situation behind and slide into bed as if nothing ever happened. But she couldn't—she knew this existed, and she wouldn't pretend otherwise.

The flames snaked and crawled up the changeling's body, melting it, licking away its flesh from bone. As the fire drifted to its chest, Aeryx finally removed his boot. The creature thrashed harder, even more possessed, until its movements weakened, until not a single bone was left behind. The fire had completely consumed the demon, only leaving the pyre's ashes in its wake.

"Well, what now?" Noel asked, not exactly sure how to react after experiencing a changeling killing ritual. Aeryx was too busy fiddling with the broken stone that had been tucked away in his pocket, acting as if none of *this* had just happened.

Pressing the stone's pieces together, he glanced up, his brow furrowed. "I need to get this back together so I can go home. Without its magic, I'm useless to search for any more changelings."

Noel lifted her flashlight over the stone, peering at its bluish-gray color and smooth texture. "Do you want me to try gluing it for you?"

"I wish that would work." He sighed. "I'm attempting to

fuse it together with my magic—it has to be whole. Even if you glued it, there would still be a visible crack."

"Maybe we can go back to my place and glue it so it'll at least stay together while you work on it?" It was a stupid suggestion but it seemed a little less stressful if it were together somewhat.

"You want to take me back to your place?" A grin spread across his face, and she hoped he wasn't thinking it was an innuendo. But her gaze was fixated on his horns where he'd mentioned that just touching them could get him *hard.*

"Um, yeah?" Noel cleared her throat and looked away from those *long,* curving horns. "What else are you going to do? Sit out here until someone finds you?"

"Precisely that. My cousin Efraun can track other krampi, so if my father can't find me, they'll send him. But my father will wait the full seven days before searching for me."

"Seven days? You can't hang out in the woods for that long!" Noel glanced at the ice horse, who watched her curiously with flickering blue eyes. "You can bring Tika." She wasn't sure how she could sneak an ice horse across the street, let alone into a sorority house, though. At least with Aeryx, she could claim he was in costume if spotted.

He rubbed the back of his neck, then glanced at his horse. "Tika would be safer here and can survive off the water from the stream."

Noel remembered her dream, her vision, whatever it was, when she'd ridden a unique creature with a young krampi. They'd stopped at the edge of the forest, and he'd walked her the remainder of the way home, his small comforting hand pressed to her back. "We have a basement that no one uses.

You'll be fine, and I can come back to check on Tika whenever you want."

"I suppose…" he drawled. "But after the seven days, I'll have to stay out here to keep a lookout for krampi warriors."

"That sounds fair. On the way back, if we get stopped, we'll—"

"I'll influence them to forget." He batted a hand in the air as if he had it all figured out, which she guessed he did if he could easily make people not remember things. Well, except for her.

"Or that." She laughed.

Aeryx gathered his pack and said goodbye to Tika before they headed back toward the sorority house. Just as they reached the edge of the woods, Noel caught sight of bright headlights, and a car slammed its brakes. The tires squealed as it came to a stop just past them.

A young guy, maybe a few years older than her, threw open the door. "What the fuck?" he shouted, his voice shaky.

"Haven't you ever seen someone filming a movie in costume before?" Noel answered, keeping her voice casual as if he were an idiot.

The guy shook his head, and Noel yanked on Aeryx's hand, hauling him across the street. They hurried down each of the quiet neighborhoods to hopefully avoid more unnecessary drama.

The campus was silent, and the low lighting guided them to the sorority house. When she opened the door, the lights were already off. Earlier, Winter and Holly had both still been up with a few of the other girls.

Flicking on the light, heart slamming against her chest, she motioned Aeryx down the hall. Even with his tall and bulky stature, he didn't make a single sound, but he was probably used to sneaking into plenty of houses.

They passed several strange metal art pieces that Holly had decorated the hallway with, then stopped at the door leading to the basement. She opened it and gestured him inside after turning on the light. "Go to the bottom. I'll meet you down there soon."

Aeryx's brows shot up, his expression skeptical.

"Don't worry, no one ever goes down here unless it's laundry day."

Nodding, a hopeful glimmer lit his eyes. "Do you have any venison stew?"

Venison? Well, isn't he the fancy one. "I don't even know how to fry an egg, so don't get your hopes up."

As Aeryx walked inside, he seemed to pucker his lips at her even though his sharp teeth still protruded. She smiled and closed the door before dashing up the stairs to grab him some blankets.

Noel found Ivy on the bed, watching a movie in the dark.

"Finally back? I think you went to more than just the store." Ivy grinned.

"Um, I met a guy." It wasn't a total lie—he was a guy… of sorts.

Ivy perked up and leaned forward. "Do tell."

"Not much *to* tell," Noel said as she gathered a few spare blankets from the closet and her pillows on the bed. "He's staying in the basement for a few days."

"What the *hell*?" Ivy's eyes widened. "And you just met him in the past couple of hours?"

She should've just said she would be doing some sort of experiment in the basement for the next few days. But no—

that sounded even fucking stupider. "Please don't tell the others. He's… shy."

"Hold on." Ivy got off the bed and folded her arms. "This isn't making a lick of sense, Noel. Coming from Holly and Winter, this would make *perfect* sense. But not you."

This was a good and bad thing, all rolled up into one. Noel had always believed no one could ever know her so well, but Ivy did, causing her heart to swell at the thought. "Okay, I know him. He's the guy from the party."

"The one you thought kidnapped the kid?" Ivy's brows shot up. "The one you thought might be a *murderer*? Worse than horror movie style, remember?"

This wasn't going to work, and Noel knew she wasn't supposed to talk about Aeryx, but Ivy was her best friend so he would just have to deal with it. "You're going to think I'm completely psycho, but trust me. Please."

"You're not pregnant with his baby, are you?"

"What? I didn't *fuck* him." Noel didn't even know if they were compatible in that sense anyway. She didn't even know what the hell his dick looked like.

"I'm not one to judge, but go on."

How was she even going to word this without sounding like a lunatic? "He's, well, he's a demon from another world."

Ivy laughed, the high-pitched sound bouncing off the walls. "Noel, come on. Tell me what's really going on."

"He's a demon, a krampi, to be more precise. You know who Krampus is, right?"

Ivy's eyes lit up as though she'd just been given the crow she'd always wanted as a pet. "Hell *yes*, I do. I love that mythology and—"

Noel placed a hand on her friend's shoulder to calm her

down. "They apparently got it wrong, so forget any of that nonsense."

Ivy furrowed her brow, and Noel continued, confessing to her everything that had happened over the last twenty-four hours, including the kid Aeryx had taken. How a changeling had been within the boy... a demon they'd just watched burn. When she was finished, Ivy held up a finger, her lips set in a tight line. "Hold on. Give me one moment."

Noel watched her friend's fingers dance over the tablet as she typed something, then she turned the screen to face Noel. It was a picture of Krampus dragging a child in chains, but it looked more like a demon straight from hell with hooved feet, blazing yellow eyes, and a long, forked tongue.

"Does he look like this?" Ivy asked, tapping the screen.

She needed to have Aeryx poke out his tongue to see if it was forked to make an accurate assessment... "Um, no. Not really a goat-man... More similar to the beast from *Beauty and the Beast,* like I said the other night. If you still don't believe me, trust me, I understand. I wouldn't believe me either."

Ivy seemed to mull it over for a few seconds. "I mean, mythology had to have come from somewhere, right? Can I meet him? I don't know if I trust him, and I'd like to see him for myself."

"He's nice. I promise. No predator vibes. Let me butter him up and see if you can come to the basement, though. Just please don't tell anyone else."

"I promise I won't. But if you don't respond to my texts, I'm coming in with a baseball bat."

"Make it a sword." Noel grinned.

"Deal."

Cradling her things, she was heading downstairs when her stomach growled. After dropping everything off, she could go back and make them peanut butter and jelly sandwiches. Had he ever even *eaten* one of those before?

Shaking off the thought, Noel opened the door and descended the steps. She blew a lock of hair from her face, the coolness of the basement chilling her skin. As her foot hit the bottom, she stilled when her gaze connected with Aeryx's.

What the fuck was he doing?

"What the hell?" she blurted.

CHAPTER 12

AERYX

THE BASEMENT WAS UNLIKE THE CELLARS IN FROSTERIA. Lined against the wall were containers, filled with what, Aeryx didn't know. But there were no chains and no cells to hold prisoners.

He crossed the floor, heading toward a pile of clothing, and out of curiosity, he lifted up a piece—not that he'd call it more than a scrap. Black lace slipped through his fingers, snaking along his skin. Did it belong to Noel? Aeryx rubbed the fabric between his digits and held it up to his chest. It would hardly cover him, but Noel was smaller. Still, her breasts were full and would no doubt fill his palms. Squinting, he held the lace up to his eyes and peered through the holes. It wouldn't conceal a damn thing. So what was the point in it?

Never one to lack an imagination, his mind worked over the visual of the see-through top against Noel's curvy figure, breasts straining against the lace and her nipples teasing him through it. He groaned—what he wouldn't give to see her in it, his hands sliding up her torso…

Noel's voice disrupted his fantasy.

With a grin, he held up the piece. "Is this yours?"

She narrowed her eyes at him. "And if it is?"

Aeryx quirked a brow. "Then, perhaps a demonstration of how it works is in order?"

Noel yanked the lace from him and tossed it aside, balancing the blankets and pillows precariously in one arm. "We're not fancy enough to have venison stew. But hey, you're in luck, how about a peanut butter and jelly?"

He squinted. Mortals and their strange foods. "Peanut butter and jelly?" Confusion drew his brows inward. "I don't know what that is, but do you have bread and meat? Freshly squeezed juice?"

Noel blinked at him. She dragged her top teeth along her bottom lip, as if struggling not to laugh at him. "I don't know what food you're used to, but it's peanut butter and jelly here. No, we don't have freshly squeezed, but we do have juice… in a box, with a pre-packaged straw." She smiled and tossed the bedding at him. He caught it before the bedding collided with his face. "Will that suffice, beast?"

"Beggars cannot be choosers." He was hungry enough to eat anything put in front of him, and as if to prove a point, his stomach growled. While he had brought provisions, it wasn't a meal. Aeryx sucked his bottom lip into his mouth and sauntered forward, the bedding still in his grasp. "You know, if you keep calling me a beast, I'm going to start acting like one." His lips curled into a grin. Sadly, in the mortal realm, his charm would be lost on her—at least he assumed so. How many mortal females swooned at the sight of a hairy, fanged beast?

Noel scoffed and glanced up at him. "Is prince better?"

He winced. The very idea of even lying about being a true son of Morozko was enough to unsettle Aeryx. For although Morozko was, in a way, a grandsire of several generations back, no krampi laid claim to the throne. "I'm no prince. I'm a warrior in the Frost King's Immortal Army." His tone was void of malice, but there was an edge to it.

Aeryx was no noble.

He was a weapon crafted from blood and ice.

Noel arched a brow. "The Frost King? Sounds like a made-up name."

Aeryx took a step back and laid out the bedding. He glanced up at her and chuckled. "I assure you, he is very real and doesn't take kindly to insults." Quieting for a moment, he searched for words carefully. "Morozko is brutal, but he is fair."

Noel tipped a bucket over and plopped down on it, her eyes never leaving his. "I don't understand why the changelings are such twisted fucks then."

The muscle in Aeryx's jaw tensed. "Those *twisted fucks* are pure evil. And we have to kill them to protect children like you—"

Noel perked up at his slip. Her back straightened, and her hands pressed against her thighs as she leaned forward. "What were you going to say?"

Fucking hell. Aeryx didn't want to have this discussion with her, not when she wasn't even supposed to remember any of it. But, here he was, sitting with her in the basement of a house. When his father, or Zira, came, she'd be influenced then, and forget him, forget it all, right? Since he couldn't wipe her memories, his father would have to do it, or whoever came for him.

He rubbed the back of his neck and sighed. "Remember the dream you had? Well, it wasn't a dream. You've been to Frosteria before, and I tucked you into bed, listened to your story."

Noel's brow furrowed, her eyes narrowing. "What are you talking about? I told you about my dream, and you didn't mention any of this."

Aeryx shouldn't have said anything, but his memories lingered on the tip of his tongue. Eager to recount the past with her—and yet—unable to, until this damnable moment. "A changeling was inside of you. I helped save your life."

Her face paled, her lips parting as though she was truly realizing that it hadn't been a dream and she hadn't been taken to Frosteria for pleasure but for something much darker. "Prove it," she whispered. "Tell me something about my house."

That was more than a decade ago, and he was supposed to recall minute details of her house? "Your wallpaper was white with green and blue flowers."

She sucked in a breath. "Something else."

Aeryx lifted a hand and pinched the bridge of his nose. "Your parents decorated the front lawn with candy canes, but one broke because I used it to subdue the changeling."

"You… hit me with a *candy cane*?" Noel's face reddened. Aeryx couldn't tell if she was trying not to laugh, lunge at him, or cry.

Aeryx rose and crossed the distance between them. "It wasn't *you,* and I had no choice. The demon was going to hurt my father." His shoulders slumped as Noel turned away from him and her hands dragged through her hair.

"Are you fucking serious? I was possessed by one of those demonic things we just set on fire? One of those sick little bastards went around parading my skin, pretending to be me?" Her voice rose an octave, and her green eyes locked onto him.

He'd anticipated fear, even disbelief, but he didn't think she'd be angry. Not enough to turn on him and glare. Aeryx didn't move from where he rooted himself, not even as Noel strode up to him and gave his chest a shove. "If this is true, you lied to me earlier then. You could have confessed all this lovely news as soon as I told you about my dream."

"I'm *not* lying." He sighed, almost annoyed with the situation. "Your hair is—was—naturally ash blonde, and in the light, it looked as though a ring of gold sat on it."

Noel covered her mouth, hardly concealing a gasp. "You! You're *him*? All this time…" Her hand shook as it hovered near her lips. "I never once thought it was real. And the others—"

"My father and Zira. They allowed me to bring you back home after we dealt with the changeling." Aeryx had insisted on returning her as part of his duty in helping. "Dral, he was the reindeer we rode on, and you fed him some grass."

She cocked her head and folded her arms. "The barbed antlers… his red eyes… He was hardly a reindeer."

Aeryx chuckled. "Not by your standards. He is my father's familiar—a bonded animal—they can communicate with one another. Like Tika and I can."

"I don't believe this," she murmured. "Your ass should've told me this in the woods."

He shrugged. "You're not supposed to know any of this. Mortals have fragile minds, and they usually can't endure it, but perhaps you're different because you've already seen it, and you remember. You were a little girl then. Maybe that's why."

She started to pace in front of him and tugged on the ends of her hair. "I can't believe I had one of those fuckers inside me." She stopped and looked up at him, wide-eyed. "How *long* was it in me?"

Noel kept surprising him with how she was handling the revelations. Her mind was proving to be strong and fierce. "Not long. Zira and my father took care of that for you."

"By *whipping* it out of me?" Her voice came out shrill as she took a step forward. "And you? You were there when that happened?"

He wasn't supposed to be, but he had snuck along for the journey, and he didn't regret any of it. The thrill of hunting down the changeling, saving the girl—Noel—from a life in darkness. "I was, but you can thank my stealth for that." Aeryx scratched at his temple, screwing his nose up. "Although, it doesn't seem like I was very stealthy this go around... You saw me."

The edges of her lips curled up, and her shoulders relaxed. It pleased Aeryx, and her smile warmed him to the core.

"Maybe I was supposed to. Fate and all." She lifted her hands and wiggled her fingers.

Most would shrug off the statement, laugh even, but there was something in her words that unfurled dread in him.

Fate.

He gritted his teeth and looked away from her. Aeryx wouldn't let himself dwell on the possibilities. Even if it would have been a sensible thing to do. From the time he was young, Aeryx had always wanted to be in control of every situation, to never not have a choice in the matter of his immortal life, and yet here he was. Completely unable to command the situation. With a damn mortal.

"Don't you krampi believe in fate?" She tilted her head, trying to meet his eyes.

"Can we discuss this after I eat?" It was a sad attempt to avoid the conversation. An excuse, but Aeryx was hungry and hadn't eaten more than jerky in almost two days. It was time he had whole food, and he was going to need it if he expected to go hunting for a changeling again.

How, he wasn't certain since his stone was broken, but if the changelings were gathering, building their forces in the mortal realm, maybe he could find a nest here.

Noel rolled her eyes. "Oh, right. Food is much more important than this turn of events." She studied him for a long moment, seeming to mull over something besides food —most likely all that had been confessed to her. A hint of a smile then played at the edges of her lips before she turned away from him and darted up the stairs, leaving Aeryx alone.

Above, footsteps shuffled across the floor. Back and forth, until the basement door opened again and Noel came down with a plate full of food.

She swayed toward him, purposely putting on a show, and offered the bread to him with a bow of her head. "To my hero," Noel said, peering up at him through her lashes. He didn't miss the sarcasm lacing her tone.

As he lowered his head, enough so he could whisper against her ear, desire tugged at him. "Thank you, Noel."

Aeryx grinned, taking the plate and glass, then sauntered away.

It was a bad choice coming to the house. Even worse being this close to a mortal. Something was off with her—and he wasn't sure what it was. He couldn't wipe her memory, couldn't even influence her, as hard as he tried. It set his nerves on edge, called to the *beast* within him.

What is she?

CHAPTER 13

NOEL

"MORE," AERYX SAID, TAKING THE LAST BITE OF *ANOTHER* sandwich. How much could he eat? His stomach seemed to be a bottomless pit. She'd gone back to the kitchen earlier, grabbing jars of peanut butter and jelly and the remainder of the bread.

Noel held up the empty bread sack. "Looks like you ate it all. Winter's going to be pissed when she goes to make herself a sandwich tomorrow for lunch." She smiled at how Winter would overreact as she always did when someone ate or drank the last of something.

"Who's Winter?" he asked while downing a glass of milk, his gaze growing suspicious. "In my world, Winter is a witch name."

"She's definitely not a witch, but you don't want to get on her bad side." Noel unscrewed the lid from the jars of peanut butter and jelly, then slid them across the floor. "Have at it, beast."

Aeryx ignored the jelly, as well as the spoon beside him, and dipped his hand straight into the jar.

Noel wrinkled her nose. "Winter's now going to be pissed about the peanut butter, too. It's all yours now."

"I'd already claimed it." He grinned, his long tongue slowly flicking up his hand. "We don't have this in Frosteria. What a shame." She hadn't been sure if his tongue would be forked like the mythological Krampus, but she had her answer now. It was forked but not grotesquely long. The tip was split into two, maybe half an inch long, and the rest looked pink and human. She couldn't tear her eyes away from him as he continued to dip his hand in the peanut butter and lick it clean as if he was in heaven.

A low growl rumbled from his throat, deep and sensual, when he tasted a chunk collected in the crevice of his fingers. It was like he was having a fucking orgasm while swallowing, his eyes fluttering. A heated sensation warmed in her chest, drifting lower and lower, forming an ache between her legs. *Get a grip.* She blinked and looked away.

"I'm going to take a shower, then I'll get the glue for your stone." Her voice came out breathier than usual, and she cleared her throat.

Aeryx didn't seem to notice as he peered inside the jar, his brow furrowed. "More peanut butter?"

Was he experiencing gluttony? While she was experiencing damn lust? "Sure, I think there's one left." Taking a swallow, while trying to push her strange arousal away, Noel bolted up the stairs. She turned her focus to something else as she walked through the low-lit hallway to the next set of stairs, except something came to mind she'd tried not to think about since she'd learned it. About Aeryx's "confession."

The dream that wasn't a dream or a vision, but a *real* memory.

Noel opened the door to her room and was going to discuss this new turn of events with Ivy, but her friend was already fast asleep. She lay on her stomach, her head at the opposite end of the bed, the TV still on. Taking the knit blanket from the floor, Noel placed it over Ivy and grabbed a pair of pajamas from the top drawer.

Then she remembered the lacy bra in Aeryx's hand, *her* lacy bra, and how he hadn't known what the hell it was. Had he ever touched a breast before? By the way he expertly tasted that peanut butter, he would know what the hell he was doing if he put that forked tongue to good use. She normally didn't wear a bra to bed, but hell, she might need to wear two to hide how hard her nipples were.

As she headed toward the bathroom, the memories from when she was a child came back in a rush. If it really hadn't happened, and she'd been some sort of oracle, that would have been amazing. But this, this was… There were very few things that frightened her. Meeting a magical krampi warrior from another realm? *Nope.* Seeing a flaming portal that could take her to this other world? *No way.* Watching a freaky demon slide its way out of a child, then helping a krampi warrior set fire to it? That had mostly been easy peasy.

But… But… *Big* but. Having one of those *Invasion of the Body Snatcher* things inside her... *Holy hell full of demons.*

Shutting the bathroom door behind her, Noel started the water and peeled off her clothes. She'd seen the changeling slip out of the child, but how did the demons get inside? Had she been sleeping, and the thing slithered like a snake toward her and molded into her flesh? Had she been awake and it put a spell on her to forget? She couldn't remember. Even though pieces of her winter wonderland experience had faded over the years, she still remembered the three krampi clearly. Especially one in particular.

Aeryx... He'd been the first one she'd seen when she'd woken from... apparently getting a little shit beaten out of her in Frosteria. But she hadn't been awake in that world, at least not as herself.

Noel opened her eyes when a chilly wind brushed her skin. Her gaze connected with something furry. Dark brown hair, small horns, and sharp teeth. Familiar... *"What are you?" Noel whispered. Something rocked beneath her—they were moving. Were they in a car? No, they were in something without a roof.*

"I'm bringing you back home," the little beast said, not answering her question.

Noel blinked, squinting, focusing intensely on him. Ah-ha! I know why he looks so familiar! *"You look like the Beast in* Beauty and the Beast, *only your fur is darker, and your horns are shorter."*

"You're not afraid?" he asked, wrinkling his nose.

She blinked again and shook her head. What a silly question. Why would she be afraid? He hadn't tried to attack her.

Aeryx had then taken her home after his father helped them onto a *reindeer*, holding her close on the short journey, protecting her. When the reindeer could go no farther, Aeryx had walked her the rest of the way home after she'd fed the creature grass.

Noel laughed softly—he needed to get his definition straight on what a reindeer was. *Familiar* or not. There was also the issue with the broken candy cane... She'd been beaten with a damn plastic stick? It was like one of those cheesy low-budget horror movies that centered around Christmas time. Maybe not beaten—knocked out. But no, she would've had to be beaten to rid herself of the demon. Had she bled? How did she not have any scarring? More magic? Spells?

There was nothing that could be done now. The shitshow had happened, and, luckily, Aeryx and his family had saved her. But what if they hadn't?

Don't go down shitty memory lane and imagine all the what-ifs. But of course, she did. One thing was for sure if she'd ever questioned it, which she hadn't, the victim didn't hold memories of the changeling. There wasn't a single gap in her memory. It was as if she'd always been in control of herself, so she didn't have an answer to when the demon had hopped on board and taken a train to live her life to its fullest.

Enough of that. She finally stepped inside the shower and let the warm water softly pelt her back, allowing it to soothe her. Sometimes being alone with one's thoughts wasn't a good thing. And she kind of wanted to go back to thinking about the changeling instead of what was coming—a much bigger Aeryx crept into her mind. One who was built like he could easily handle a woman and bring her to ecstasy multiple times.

Then there were his long curving horns, and if she touched one, it would make him— She shook that away. What the fuck was wrong with her? Why the hell did her parents ever allow her to watch *Beauty and the Beast* when she was a child? Now she'd developed this weird fascination that she couldn't get rid of.

Aeryx's forked tongue gliding up his fingers, the way he

expertly slid it in and out between them. He didn't leave a single area dry. "Holy shit, he's not human," she whispered. But as the place between her legs throbbed, ached, *demanded* a touch from his long fingers, from that forked tongue of his, she pretended he was a human. *Mostly.*

Noel's lips parted as she pressed a hand in the valley of her breasts, running the pads of her fingers across her hard nipples. She imagined it was him caressing, sucking, nipping. Her digits trailed down her abdomen and she pretended it was his velvety tongue until he settled between her thighs.

She gasped as her fingers drifted to her clit, then she circled and stroked while she rested her head against the tiled wall. It was his tongue slowly lapping up her center, tasting all she had to offer. She grasped the grab bar, imagining it was his horn she was gripping, making his cock harden.

Her movements picked up, her pace growing faster, rougher. She then slipped two fingers inside her entrance, grinding herself against her hand, wishing it was his tongue, his fingers, his cock. Thunder rocketed through her, and she released a soft moan, his name spilling from her lips on the final note of bliss.

She kept her head pressed against the wall as her chest heaved. *It's fine. People have screwed-up daydreams all the time. It isn't as if I actually had sex with him.* But a part of her wanted to know if it would feel just as good, or better, if he slammed his beastly cock deep inside her.

Once her body didn't feel like jelly any longer, she toweled off and got dressed. She still wasn't tired, so she had an idea of what they could do once she glued his stone together. With a smile, she slipped back into her room and snagged her portable DVD player, a movie, and the glue.

Noel made one more pit stop and took the last jar of peanut butter. As she headed down the steps, she hoped she didn't discover him playing around with undergarments again. Instead, she found him hunched over, toying around with the broken stone.

"I come bearing gifts," she sang.

He glanced over, his eyes lighting up like a kid on Christmas as he peered at the jar of peanut butter.

"This is for tomorrow." Noel tossed it to him, and he easily caught it with one hand. She couldn't help but eye those long fingers for a beat too long. Setting down the DVD player, she then held up the glue. "And this is for now. Let me see the pieces."

He hesitantly handed them to her as if she was going to flee with them and never come back. She rolled her eyes while taking a seat beside him. He inched nearer, so close that she could smell his wintry scent. Her heart fluttered in her chest as the piney aroma surrounded her.

Taking the glue, she drew a thin line on the broken edge of one, then pushed the pieces together and counted to sixty.

"Still be careful with it, but try again," Noel said, placing the stone in his palm.

Aeryx grunted and closed his eyes, focusing, his lips pursed with his sharp teeth protruding. A blue light sparked to life from the stone, then died out.

"I'll try it tomorrow." He smiled softly. "But thank you for trying. It's better than it was."

"I mean, any idiot would've suggested using glue." She grinned while shrugging a shoulder. "Are you tired at all?"

He studied her for a moment, his expression unreadable before he finally drawled, "No."

"I thought we'd watch a movie. Have you ever watched one?"

His dark eyes widened in disbelief. "No, I haven't."

"All right, it's a date night, then. Let me make the area comfortable first." Noel took one of the blankets and spread it out across the floor, then propped the two pillows against the wall. "Lay down."

"Is that a command, princess?"

"A direct one." She laughed, spreading the other blanket over his muscular form before slipping in beside him and placing the DVD player in front of them.

Aeryx shifted, his arm brushing hers as he took a deep inhale.

"Are you *smelling* me?" She snorted.

"Um, no. I don't need to take a deep breath to smell you. Your scent is potent as it is."

"What the fuck ever." Noel was trying her damnedest not to inhale his enticing wintry smell. "I brought *Star Wars*. Figured you should know who Chewbacca is after I mistook you for him at the party. I'm also almost certain ninety-five percent of the human race likes *Star Wars*."

"I'm not human."

Noel took in the tight shirt across his arms and chest, where she could see defined muscles. "No, you definitely aren't." She thought about her moment in the shower, her hand between her slick folds while thinking of him, and she hurried to start the film.

About halfway through the movie, light snores escaped Aeryx's mouth. She supposed he was one of those five percent, minus the human aspect. As she was about to turn off the DVD player, his arm wrapped around her, his nose nuzzling into her neck.

Her heart raced as her gaze drifted to his horns, finding them only centimeters from brushing her flesh. In this lighting, with his features softened and his eyes closed, he looked a little closer to human. Except for the fur... the teeth... and the horns. But in that moment, she didn't really care. "I suppose I'll stay for the sake of your comfort, beast."

CHAPTER 14

AERYX

A<small>N ENTIRE DAY HAD COME AND GONE</small>. T<small>HE SCENT OF</small> N<small>OEL</small> still lingered on him from hours prior, and Aeryx wished he could bury his nose into her hair and draw in the fresh smell again. The previous night, she'd spent it plastered against him, and her body pressed to his soothed him in a way he'd never thought possible. He'd certainly tumbled with another, and even a few had spent the night at his cottage, but none made him feel entirely... drawn to them. *It doesn't matter. She's mortal,* he reminded himself. Humans were fleeting fancies to any immortal, and even if one didn't mind how a krampi appeared, anything with them would end in heartbreak.

No light spilled in through the small windows into the space, and without a timepiece to decipher what hour it was, Aeryx could only guess it was late enough that he could venture out into the woods.

Aeryx frowned at himself—he was foolish to waste precious time, yet the feel of Noel against him, her head tucked beneath his chin… sent an odd fluttering to his chest. She was beautiful, but it was her tongue sharpened by wit that he wanted to experience more. On him, in his mouth, his cock *sliding* between her lips, thrusting… *Fuck!*

But she would never consider it while he was in the mortal realm. Not while the glamour made him appear like a hairy, overgrown beast.

Noel would feel what her mind told her to. His fangs gliding along her abdomen, instead of his soft, full lips, and coarse chest hair instead of his smooth skin pressing into her.

Aeryx raked his hand through his hair, combing through the tangles. Above him, floorboards creaked, and he stilled, listening to the progression of footsteps venturing closer to the door.

He leaped into a crouch, inching away from where the bedroll lay and closer toward the machines in the back. It was darker there.

The door squealed open and heavy footsteps landed on the first few stairs.

Shit. Shit. Shit. Shit.

This was a terrible idea. Why had he agreed to come to a house full of mortal females? What if he couldn't influence *anyone?* He hadn't tried since Noel, but what if it didn't have anything to do with her, and everything to do with *him.*

Balling his hands into fists, he waited.

"Beast?" Noel's voice called to him.

Aeryx relaxed and stepped forward, only pausing as a second individual hopped down the stairs.

"Noel—" the female sang her name, but froze as soon as her eyes met Aeryx's. She screamed, then slapped a hand over her mouth and looked to Noel for support.

"Shh, no, shh. Be quiet, I told you not to scream when you saw him!"

Aeryx shot Noel a baleful glare. She was running around telling humans about him after he'd asked her not to? He dragged his hands down his face, groaning.

"For Pete's sake, it's not that, but he growls, Noel!" The female's tone grew more hysterical as she got into a fighting stance. "What are we supposed to do in this *Island of Dr. Moreau* situation? We didn't create him, but he literally looks like he's ready to attack."

Aeryx watched as the human didn't waver her gaze away from his. What could *she* do?

"Chill out. You wanted to meet him, remember?" Noel said. "He isn't going to attack anyone so get out of the Bruce Lee stance."

Both perplexed and amused by the exchange, Aeryx folded his arms across his chest, realizing there was no threat of a broom or other object being hurled at him. "You're not supposed to be telling other humans about me, Noel." He growled her name and homed in on the red-haired female, her hazel eyes widening as he moved closer.

She lifted her hands back up, balling them into fists.

Noel waved her hand in front of him. "Hey. Let's not do that, got it?"

Her words rankled him, insinuating *she* knew best when it came to mortals knowing about him—a krampi—didn't settle well with him. "She cannot know, Noel. I need to wipe her."

"Um, no. You're not wiping Ivy. I told her everything, and outside of seeing you for the first time, she's *fine*." Noel spun to face the female called Ivy, who was still assessing Aeryx in a mixture of horror and fascination, her arms falling to her sides. Mostly fascination.

He planted his hands on his hips and tilted his head back. Fluorescent lights washed over him, and the smell of clean laundry hung in the air. This would never have happened if Noel didn't break his stone. *None* of this would've happened.

"Is he going to roar? That may alert the other girls." Ivy cocked her head, her gaze sweeping over him more curiously.

Aeryx's head dropped forward and he laughed. Small at first, then breathless and loud. The oddity of the situation struck him, two mortals casually talking to Aeryx, debating on what he would do next. This entire ordeal was against the krampi's set laws and for a reason—it kept the balance in check and the mortals safe.

"He's not going to roar." Noel paused, then glanced at him, as if unsure.

Aeryx squinted. "I don't *roar*." But the thought of him opening his mouth and roaring as loud as Efraun's snow lion familiar brought on another bout of laughter. His shoulders shook, and he hissed as he composed himself. "She cannot keep her memories," he said, once he'd stopped laughing.

Noel cocked an eyebrow. "Why can't she? Aside from your rules."

"They're not *my* rules. It is Morozko's law, and disobeying is a punishable offense."

Noel's lips twisted. "Punishable how?"

"Do they imprison you?" Ivy piped in, her interest piqued.

Aeryx rubbed the back of his neck. "When you break a law in Frosteria, imprisonment is the least of your worries. Most of the time death is your reward after the punishments you receive."

Frosteria law was fairly simple.

Obey the king, for he kept the land safe.

Do not insult the queen, or the king would kill the offender.

Other than that, it was a wild and free world—anyone could run rampant if they braved the harsh landscape where snow coated the ground, and changelings lurked in the shadows, waiting to tear into a victim.

Noel paled and looked over at Ivy, who stepped closer to her. "No one ever has to know…"

Somehow, someone always found out. Then there was the fact that his father would be here in less than a week, and he'd ensure they didn't remember a thing.

A loud, nasally laugh caught Aeryx's attention. He pointed to the stairs, expecting Noel or Ivy to dash toward them and slam the door shut, but neither did, then the laugh came again.

"That's wicked lame," the female announced as she traipsed down the stairs.

Noel bolted forward, Ivy following suit to stop the new guest from descending the stairs. Aeryx rounded the back of them, crouching in the shadows.

"What? Were you two making out down here?" The dark-haired female scoffed. "Why hide? Be loud and proud of yourselves. Even if it's just experimenting." She clutched her phone and waved it around. "I've had my fair share of experimentation." The mortal sighed, almost wistfully.

"Wow, thank you for that, Winter. We totally appreciate it," Ivy cut in, climbing the stairs and pushing the female back up them.

Aeryx remained as still as he could, but Winter wasn't

about to be pushed back. She brushed past the two mortals and eyed them suspiciously.

As she drew nearer, Aeryx noted her black hair piled on top of her head in a messy clump. He scrunched his nose, but as his eyes roved along her figure, he noticed she was scarcely wearing trousers. The bright pink fabric barely covered her thighs, and her shirt was so tight that her ample bosom begged to spill over the top.

He blinked, wondering if he should look away. Was she in her underthings?

"What's up with you two?" Winter shook her head and rounded the corner toward the machines. At least, Aeryx thought it was where she was heading. But, she turned and moved straight toward him.

Unable to hide in the scarce shadows any longer, Aeryx froze and waited for the inevitable: screaming and panic.

Winter's gaze settled on him, and she raked her gaze up and down his form as though trying to piece together if he was real or not. Every muscle in her face tensed, then she screamed loud enough that Aeryx nearly covered his ears.

And here we go.

"Dammit, Winter!" Noel rushed forward, as did Ivy.

"What the fuck is *that*?" Winter shrieked, pawing at Ivy and Noel's hands as she stumbled backward, then tripped, falling. She shook violently and slid her hands along her sides as if searching for something.

The laws, as he'd stated, were in place for a reason. And this was one of them. Not all mortals could withstand the knowledge of *others* among them. Sometimes, it broke their mind. Fracturing reality and fantasy.

Aeryx noted her phone on the floor and scooped it up. He

approached her slowly, offering it to her. She didn't take it, only continued to back away from him, her chest heaving.

"She cannot retain her memories. Your friend can't handle them." Aeryx frowned as he turned to Noel and Ivy. It was remarkable to see the difference between them and this mortal. Although each had their initial moment of shock, they didn't continue to quake for long.

Noel pushed past Aeryx and ran her hand along her friend's forehead. "Winter, it's okay. We're here, and Aeryx isn't going to hurt you." Worry creased her brow, and he could see how her friend's current state bothered her.

Winter's eyes bulged, and she gasped for precious air.

If she kept this up, she was going to pass out.

Aeryx lifted his eyebrows expectantly, then Noel nodded. "Do it."

He leaned forward, and to ensure the mortal didn't inch away, he gently took her face in his hands. She clawed at his forearms, digging her nails into them, but her mind was weak and easy to enter.

"Winter, you never saw me. The last thing you remember is stumbling on Ivy and Noel in the basement, washing your clothing. You will venture upstairs and go to sleep." His fingers gently stroked her hair when he spoke, and as she roused, the influence taking over, Winter stood, wiping the tears from her eyes.

Aeryx slowly righted himself and watched her continue upstairs, leaving him alone with Ivy and Noel. They both remained silent, their eyes wide and mouths gaping. It occurred to him that his influence worked on *her* but not Noel, which further drove the idea that she wasn't what she appeared to be, but something more. He kept revisiting the notion she was a witch, yet she had no abilities that he'd seen so far, and she certainly wasn't confessing to them.

"What. Was. *That?*" Noel blurted and clutched Ivy's arm.

"That, princess, was what should've worked on you and didn't." He reached into his pocket and pulled out the glued-together stone. It glowed dimly, and he wondered if it would be enough to hunt down a changeling...

He may have been stuck in the mortal realm, but he still needed to move forward with the mission as much as possible.

Now, if only Ivy and Noel would remain behind—

"We're coming with you," Noel confirmed his suspicions. It was a statement, not a question. Noel's boldness, he'd grown used to already, but Ivy, although quieter, was still as belligerent.

"We can help. I'm a black belt in karate." Ivy bowed at the waist and placed her fist into an open palm. "No mercy, sensei."

He stared down at Ivy, his brow furrowing in question, but laughter bubbled up his throat. The little mite of a human speaking of no mercy when it came to a changeling, although laughable, he agreed. *No mercy.*

"I'm unsure what a sensei is, but no need to bow to me." He patted Ivy on the head, and as she rose, he winked. "The two of you would follow if I denied you anyway. So, my word of advice is to stay out of my way. Noel knows how wicked a changeling is."

Noel nodded. "They are nasty little fuckers. And I apparently had one inside of me when I was younger." She glanced at Ivy's parted lips. "Oh yes, more on that later."

His thumb ran along the rough ridges of the stone.

Aeryx didn't want Ivy or Noel there, but they weren't

giving him a choice. Sighing, he jerked his head toward the stairs. "We don't have much time."

The trek to the woods took longer than Aeryx cared for. Not because his muscles were locked up from a lack of action, or that there were too many mortals running amok, but because there *weren't*. No, it took longer because he couldn't run the entire way like he wished to. As fit as Ivy and Noel appeared to be, they weren't up to long distances.

Once they were deep enough in the woods that Aeryx couldn't see the light from nearby houses, or hear the rushing of vehicles, he whistled softly for Tika. She didn't answer his call. Where was that blasted horse?

"Be on the lookout. Changelings don't typically bother grown humans, but that doesn't mean they won't."

"Why?" Ivy asked softly.

Why? Aeryx sneered, disgusted by the truth. "Because they need the adults to create children. Without them, they couldn't thrive in this world. Still, if desperate enough, they'll jump into an adult."

"They treat them like cattle…?"

An apt comparison, albeit a sickening one. "Exactly like cattle. A farmer wouldn't put down his livestock unless necessary." Aeryx took the stone out of his jacket pocket and focused on it as if he could will it to work—fortune was on his side, for it flickered to life again. Small, but it was there.

He continued to walk through the narrow pathway until it led to a creek. Every once in a while, he peered over his shoulder to look at Ivy and Noel, ensuring they were all right.

Aeryx knelt beside the water and dipped his fingers into the liquid. "You blasted mare," he murmured.

"What's he doing?" Ivy whispered.

Noel laughed. "His horse is apparently being stubborn."

"Horse?"

Droplets of water floated from the stream until, one by one, they formed an outline of a horse. Tika shook herself, solidifying as she did, and turned to inspect who had summoned her. As if there were any question as to who would do such a thing. Aeryx glowered at the mare, but just the same, he lifted his hands and stroked her smooth muzzle.

Ivy tilted her head. "Well, this is better than all the best movie creatures combined."

Aeryx chuckled and stood. "Just wait, Ivy." He stroked beneath his chin and surveyed the area. This was a decent enough spot for a changeling to live in its natural form. A water source meant animals to prey on and drain their lifeblood until they could find a child.

Noel placed a hand on her hip and bit her lip. "We'll stay close enough to you for backup—"

"To do what exactly?" He quirked a brow, recalling the last time. Noel *had* helped him, but it was still far too dangerous for them. If Aeryx's father knew he had not one, but two mortals accompanying him...

He concentrated, homing in on the beat of magic within the stone, and envisioned the portal home, but *nothing* happened.

Fuck. A mortal's glue cannot fix everything, so it seems.

Something chittered in the woods. No, not something, a *changeling.*

Aeryx lifted a finger to his lips as he crossed the stream.

"Stay close to Tika. If you need to, jump on her and get out of here."

An argument rested on Noel's lips—he could see in the way she chewed on them that she wanted to debate. But at the next high-pitched shriek, she took a step back, looked at Ivy, and nodded.

Magic pulsed in his palm, the stone humming softly. When he glanced up at the clearing, flecks of blue swirled around the portal, and the chittering changeling tentatively stepped onto the forest floor. As soon as it did, the portal closed. *Damn.*

One of the females gasped behind him.

He pocketed the stone and reached into his jacket to pull out twin long daggers. This time, he wasn't going to wait for the fucker to attack him.

Aeryx lunged forward, and as the changeling sprung at him, gangly arms spread. The demon's mouth widened as much as it could, given the sinew sewing it mostly shut. Claws raked across Aeryx's thick leather jacket, tearing it.

Quickly, Aeryx maneuvered a blade beneath the demon and dragged the tip along its belly. An ear-splitting cry rang out, and one would assume the changeling would relent, but it only dug faster and harder at Aeryx's jacket.

Using the other blade, he jabbed it into the ribs of the changeling and skewered it with the second blade. Aeryx was heavier and thicker than the lesser demon, and as he lowered to the ground, he used it against the changeling. He pinned its legs down, its wriggling hands were next, and when the creature was mostly secured, Aeryx reached behind to grab manacles from his hip. He bound its hands, yanked the gag from his pocket, and strapped it on, muting the creature's wails.

Next, he secured the legs, and when he was done, he turned to find Ivy staring, her lips parted in fascination.

"I told you it wasn't what you'd expect…" He remained squatted near the thrashing changeling. "As much as I enjoyed our bonfire, Noel, do you know of anywhere that's private— that won't draw the attention of more changelings?" They had to make do with the bonfire from before, but it wasn't ideal, not in the mortal realm. His lips pressed into a grim line. "Krampi are being hunted, and I'd rather not be ambushed out in the open."

Ivy's eyes glimmered, her body perking up. "My aunt— she lives in a rad old house. The fireplace is *huge*, I mean, the hearth is basically as tall as you. She's not there right now, she's at Lake Tahoe… we could use it. The fireplace still works, and it gets *hot*. It's literally right next to the college."

It wasn't ideal, but it was better than drawing attention out in the woods, be it mortal, or approaching changelings.

Now, all he needed to do was carry the fucker back into the town, burn it, and perhaps indulge himself in another round of peanut butter.

CHAPTER 15

NOEL

"Hot damn, Noel. This is like a filmmaker's dream come true." Ivy beamed as Aeryx clutched the changeling, its body writhing over his shoulder beneath the moon's glow. "I mean, when you mentioned changelings, you didn't say they were creepier than the creature with the eyes in its hands in *Pan's Labyrinth*."

As Noel mulled that over for a second, it was a close call. From what Aeryx had said, changelings relished in eating lungs and other organs—besides the heart—while that particular movie creature bit the heads off of fairies in the scene. "Well, I didn't go into much detail since I didn't think we would go on another hunting mission so soon… or ever. Least of all with you in tow." Noel smirked, nudging her shoulder with Ivy's. "But I'm glad you're here to remind me that I'm not crazy or imagining this. Plus, I wouldn't have known of a place around here to burn the sick bastard." The fireplace at the sorority house wouldn't have been much help since it was broken.

Aeryx glanced over his shoulder and placed his long index finger over his lips as if they were waking the entire neighborhood. Noel rolled her eyes and gave him a salute. He rolled his eyes in return, but she could've sworn his lips twitched before he focused back on getting out of the forest.

Ivy arched a brow, her voice a whisper. "Are you *flirting*?"

"Oh, please. *No*," Noel rushed out, then took a deep swallow. Yes? *Fuck yes*, she realized. That was exactly what the hell she was doing.

"He does have a sexy little accent there." Ivy lightly hummed the dance song from *Beauty and the Beast*, and Noel gave her a soft shove. Her friend chuckled, then focused once they got to the edge of the forest. They waited for a few speeding cars to pass before darting across the street, Ivy now leading the way to her aunt's house.

Noel jogged beside Aeryx, her gaze staying glued to the changeling in case she needed to potentially do something. She didn't have Ivy's karate skills, and she sure didn't have Aeryx's warrior training, but she would do what she could… Throwing a shoe at it would have to be sufficient. She always considered it a good thing she'd never been in a physical fight in high school—apparently, that was a mark against her with changelings.

They hurried down dimly lit neighborhoods, keeping to the shadows until Ivy waved them down a dark street with looming old houses. Several of them were in need of repairs with dipped roofs, crooked foundations, chipped paint, and cracked windows. Noel swore one looked like the mirror twin of the house in *IT*. She didn't see any clowns lingering around, but she wouldn't be surprised if a changeling slithered out from inside.

Halfway down the street, the older homes became more pristine, and Ivy motioned at a blue and yellow one with a wide porch. A white swing dangled beside the door, creaking as it slowly swung from the wind. Green rhododendron plants were scattered across the garden, along with a few poodle-waxleaf shrubs.

Ivy tilted her head at the front door while drawing out her keys from her backpack purse. "Lucky Aunt Tilda gave me her keys before she left. I'm pretty sure she would've noticed the broken window I would've had to gift her."

"I would've had it handled." Aeryx's arm tensed as he held the changeling with one strong hand. He would've had it *handled* because of his handy-dandy magical key that could unlock any human door.

As Aeryx pushed open the door, a musty odor hit Noel's nose—mothballs combined with floral.

"Home sweet home," Ivy sang as she shut the door behind them, then flipped on a light switch.

They walked through a corridor filled with fruit paintings into what looked to be a living room straight from the seventies. A pea-green sofa covered in hideous printed flowers sat across from two bright yellow chairs that resembled eggs. Psychedelic artwork hung across the wood-paneled walls, and even the new flatscreen TV had a custom design surrounding it that made it appear vintage with its fake turn knobs.

"The basement's this way." Ivy led them across the room and turned down the hall, when a hissing shadow leaped forward.

Noel screamed and kicked her leg forward in a poor move that a sensei would agree was pitiful. A white cat stood in front of Aeryx, hissing, its back arched and tail straight up.

"Calm down, Geralt." Ivy huffed, kneeling in front of the cat and reaching her hand forward to stroke its back. Geralt peered at her friend, then booked it out of the room when a muffled cry escaped the changeling. "Scaredy cat," Ivy called and straightened. "Forgot to mention the cat would be here. I've been feeding him."

Ivy opened the door and flicked on the light before they followed her down a set of groaning wooden stairs to a large basement smelling of freshly-cut wood. Not much was down there besides the large hearth with logs, a washer and dryer, and rows and rows of wine bottles.

"Let's get this burning party started," Noel said, studying the fireplace. Aged gray and white bricks lined the wall, and soot covered them. On the stone floor, a worn iron grate sat. The space was large enough that Noel could stand in it comfortably. No fancy mantel hung above it, but beside it, against the wall, rested a poker.

Aeryx released a grunt in agreement.

"All right." Ivy nodded. "We don't get to burn a witch like Hansel and Gretel, but we do have a rather nasty little creature." She grabbed a few newspapers and a lighter in the corner of the room, then lit the paper on fire before throwing it on top of the logs. A moment later, bright orange flames ignited, licking across the logs, the heavy smoke tickling Noel's nose. The changeling's movements became fiercer, its bucking increasing, knowing it was about to meet its deserved demise. Aeryx didn't miss a beat as he hefted the demon from his shoulder, threw it into the fire, then grabbed the poker from the wall. He shoved the sharp tip into the changeling's stomach, holding it inside the hearth while it wailed, preventing the bastard from rolling out.

"Wow." Ivy released a low whistle as she took in the grim sight.

The hearth groaned and shook as the creature thrust its body against the walls. The demon's wails became louder— the gag over its mouth melted away, same as its skin was. But her stomach didn't churn at the sight as it should've—she was just relieved the sick fuck wouldn't take over a human child's life.

Once quiet filled the room, except for the light crackling of the fire, Aeryx turned to face them. He drew out his stone, his brow furrowed as he concentrated on it, seeming to hope it would spark to life with magic again. No blue light came. "The magic still isn't working, so I can't search for another changeling." He sighed.

"I guess we'll go back to the sorority house then," Noel said, disappointed she couldn't help him out more.

"I think I have a better option," Ivy started, running a finger across her bottom lip as she smiled. "Since my aunt will be gone for two more weeks, you can stay here. The sofa in the living room folds out into a bed. Much better than the hard floor of the basement or our cramped room."

Noel thought about it for a split second. That would defi- nitely be better for Aeryx. He wouldn't have to worry about someone coming downstairs to wash clothes, and she wouldn't have to worry about him having to wipe anyone's memories as he'd done with Winter. Seeing her friend like that was a thousand times worse than watching a changeling burn.

"It will do." Aeryx shrugged, cleaning the blade of his dagger across his shirt.

"All right, I'm going to grab some things from the house,

then I'll come back." She paused, her gaze locking on his. "Will you be all right here alone?"

"Aww, are you worried about me, princess?" he teased.

"Maybe," Noel lied—she was totally worried.

"I'll be fine."

"See you soon then, beast."

Once the cool breeze hit them, Ivy gave Noel a grin. "You don't have to stay the night here. He seems like a big boy."

"Well," Noel drawled, thinking. She really didn't need to come back, but she wanted to. "I need to make sure he keeps your aunt's place intact."

"Mm-hmm." Ivy's grin grew wider. "Among other things."

"Whatever." Noel rolled her eyes. "It's not like that, and he isn't even human."

"You've seen *The Shape of Water*, right?" Ivy brought her hands together, pointing her index fingers forward. She then mimicked the scene from the movie, bringing her fingers up as if a cock was waking up for some hot action.

"You have a nasty mind, Ivy." Noel snorted.

Ivy laughed, the sound coming out high-pitched. "Don't worry, I'll keep your secrets, *princess*."

Of course, Ivy hadn't missed Aeryx calling her that. But something about when she heard it from his mouth now thrilled her.

After they got back to the sorority house, Noel avoided chatting with Winter. She still felt awful about what Aeryx had done to her, but it was necessary based on Winter's reaction. Noel packed a bag full of several days' worth of stuff, then stopped by the store on the way back to buy some snacks.

As she opened the door to Ivy's aunt's house, a soothing melody drifted through the air. It was one of the most beautiful sounds she'd ever heard, light and gentle. The door shut behind her, and she followed the melody into the living room, where she found Aeryx relaxed on the carpet, his jacket and shirt off. She avoided studying his strong arms and back for too long. His hand was holding something as his fingers rotated a small lever on the side. A music box that he was playing for... the cat.

Her lips tilted up in amusement as she took a step forward. Geralt was curled up against Aeryx's stomach, nestling its head against him.

"I suppose the cat likes you now that the changeling is gone," she said.

Aeryx lifted his head, his dark eyes pinning to hers as though he'd known she was there the entire time. "All animals like me. I'm likable."

"Hmm. Maybe." Noel removed her backpack and sank down across from him.

"What do you mean *maybe*?" He sat up, snapping the music box shut in mock offense. Geralt's eyes opened, then shut again.

She smirked. "You can be quite demanding." As he held up a finger, she drew out a jar of peanut butter from the grocery bag. "I got this for you."

His finger fell, and a sexy as hell low growl emanated up his throat. It sent a warmth coursing through her, rushing straight to her core. How did he do that *again*? And did he make that sound when he fucked? Shit. She needed to focus on something else, but all she could think about was *The Shape of Water* nonsense Ivy had planted in her mind. Her gaze fell to the music box at his side, and she said the first thing that popped into her head. "Where did you get that?"

"It was a gift I received when I was a child."

He opened the jar of peanut butter, and she grabbed his hand, placing a spoon in it before he could lick his fingers all seductively again. "Use this." She stared at the box once more, the light wooden color, the unique swirling designs engraved in it. "The music box must be special then."

"Very much." Aeryx ran his fingers across the cat's head, and it purred in delight as he spoke. "When you were a child, the female who you met that day was Zira. She was the one who gifted it to me after she became my father's mate, and she's not only like a mother to me but also my best friend. The box was special to her and belonged to her sisters, who were killed by changelings. Her entire village had been massacred. Once my brother was born, she continued to treat us equally, both as her sons. Although I love my brother, he can be a little tyrant. But I believe he'll grow out of it one day."

Noel laughed. "I always wanted siblings, but my parents couldn't have any more kids after me. Then my mom passed away, and my dad became a spiteful bastard. I sometimes blame him for things I did, but they were still my actions, my choices."

"We both have mothers who are gone," he whispered. Her heart sank at his words, wondering how she'd died. Was it an illness like how her mom had passed from cancer? Or something much worse from his world… But then his fingers left Geralt's head and settled on her knee, changing the subject to something else. "What were your choices?"

Her breathing hitched at the heat of his fingers on her

flesh, making her hotter. There wasn't an inch of hair on his palms, and it felt... damn good. She swallowed, focusing. "Oh God, what *didn't* I do? I was a thief, did drugs, and screwed a bunch of loser guys. Pretty much acted like an idiot."

Aeryx sucked his bottom lip in, then released it. "You don't have a male now?"

"No." She bit the inside of her cheek, not sure if she wanted to know the answer. "Do you have a girl?"

He waved the spoon around. "No, I never wanted a mate, so I steer clear of possibilities."

"A mate?"

"We krampi have a mate chosen for us by destiny. They are to be our perfect match, our equal. I don't believe in not having a choice, and who is to say that *fate* knows what is best for me?"

"Interesting." Her chest deflated. It was a stupid response, but that meant there was someone in his world destined for him. It seemed easier to know who one was meant to be with versus the human world where people met loser after loser. Maybe it was better this way and would help her to quit having these weird emotions.

"So how old is the box then?" she finally asked, fracturing the silence.

"Old." He lifted the box, turning it around and around in his hands. "It was crafted by Queen Eirah, herself."

"The Queen made that?" Noel asked, surprised. It was so detailed and had sounded so exquisite.

"Before Eirah became queen and gained magic, she was a human. Not only that, she was a toymaker. She didn't leave her craft behind once she became Morozko's wife—she continued to gift villages her creations over the years."

"Did you say *humans?*" His world had people like her?

"There aren't humans anymore. It's a long story, but they were offered a choice once Eirah became Morozko's queen. They chose immortality, and after that, she was no longer able to gift immortality again."

Noel couldn't quite wrap her mind around that, but it shouldn't have been that much of a surprise after everything.

Aeryx placed a scoop of peanut butter in between his lips, then went back for more and held it out for her to take a bite. She leaned forward, the movement strangely intimate as she licked the peanut butter from where his tongue had just been on the spoon, his eyes never leaving hers.

"What do you want to do now?" Noel asked, her voice breathier than usual. "I brought a few DVDs."

"Sounds perfect," he rasped, his voice deep. "Where do you want to lay together?"

Together. Her heart leaped at the word as she pointed toward the couch. She took off the cushions and unfolded the bed. As he lowered himself onto the lumpy mattress, she put in a DVD and turned back around to find his arm open for her.

Noel removed her shoes, then settled on the hard mattress. She scooted back to relax into the crook of his arm and inhaled his addicting wintry scent, her breathing increasing.

Over the next few days, Noel went to school, then came home to Ivy's aunt's house, where she would curl up with Aeryx to watch movies. It became a routine—them sharing peanut butter, him telling her more about Frosteria, her confessing more of her stupid past. She discovered that the third krampi from when she was a child wasn't only Aeryx's father, but his name was Korreth, and he was captain of Morozko's Immortal Army. He learned more about her mom, who she didn't usually talk about to anyone. Noel then found out about his mother, who was slaughtered by changelings. She understood his loathing even more for them now.

And after she popped in another movie, she shifted closer to Aeryx, her hand resting on his stomach, close to the waistband of his pants. The thought of dipping her fingers inside, to touch, to stroke, to see if that growling sound would escape his lips as he came coursed through her... harder... harder... harder... Her heart beat faster, something blooming inside of there, and she shoved it away. But it boomeranged back because she couldn't deny that she had a hardcore ridiculous crush on the beast.

CHAPTER 16

AERYX

THANKFULLY, NOEL HAD LEFT FOR HER CLASSES, LEAVING Aeryx alone with a purring Geralt. He was relieved she'd gone, but it wasn't because he wished for it. While staying in the mortal world, he'd grown used to her company, and in the evenings, when she'd lay next to him, his arm wrapped around her… it stirred something within him. A delicate emotion that he wasn't accustomed to. Even he wasn't certain what it was entirely, however, there was something more than just wanting to fuck around. But then, there were his basic instincts, of wanting to taste her and discover what sounds she made at the peak of her pleasure. Did she sigh after she came? Would she scream his name while she came undone?

Sauntering across the living room floor, he peeked out a window and frowned. Soft, orange rays of light painted the white house across the street. It was almost evening. Another day was gone, and he'd *tried* venturing into the woods again, attempted to use the broken stone, but no light had spilled from the cracks. Aeryx was stuck, and he was useless in the mortal realm.

Geralt yowled from his perch on the couch as if echoing his dismay. The cat...

A tiny beast of a thing. While the feline was fond of Aeryx, he'd witnessed a bout of violence as it lunged for a mouse that had dared to not only stare at them both but dart into their space.

That had been the only fruitful accomplishment since taking out the changeling in the fireplace. Aeryx hadn't achieved close to anything he wanted to when he'd set off to hunt down the changelings nesting in the mortal world. He wondered how Lyra was healing and if any of his other comrades had fallen. How was Ryken? Likely pleased Aeryx had failed in some respect. Did his father and Zira worry for his safety? And what, if any, new developments had occurred while he was stuck in the mortal realm? Had Efraun been dragged to the barracks to hunt the changelings? Or maybe his father had prompted their cousin to search for him already. Efraun would only shrug off the urgency, knowing—thanks to his abilities—that Aeryx was alive and well.

He dragged his hands down his face as he turned away from the window and strode into the kitchen. Noel had shown him where the pantry was before she left and had even pointed out what was good to eat. Unfortunately, Ivy's aunt didn't have any peanut butter, but when Aeryx opened the door, he caught sight of blue. He picked up the contents and squinted at it. *Oreos.* Tearing back the top, he examined one and placed the rest on the kitchen table. A flat circle with white in the middle. It seemed simple enough. He popped one into his mouth and chewed. A rush of sweetness overtook his senses, and he kept chewing.

"Where is the chocolate?" he mumbled around a mouthful of cookie. It wasn't horrible, but it wasn't *good* either. Still, he shoved another into his mouth. He regretted it as the door creaked and keys clanged onto an end table.

Noel.

Aeryx gathered up the Oreos but didn't have time to put them away as she walked into the kitchen.

"What, no milk with them?" She eyed the package, rummaged around in a cupboard to pull out two cups, then reached inside the refrigerator, as she called it, and pulled out a white jug. "Milk and Oreos." She poured two cups worth and handed him one. "It'll help wash the cookie down, but also, it's fucking divine together."

He swallowed roughly. "You mortals are strange."

She arched a brow. "No stranger than you, who eats peanut butter like it's a meal."

Aeryx took the cup and chuckled. "And those are neither cookies nor chocolate. I'd rather eat peanut butter than *those.*" He motioned toward the Oreos, then took a sip of the milk and eyed where his torn jacket hung along the wall. It'd been too long since he'd peeled his clothing off, and he was in dire need of a proper bath. His attire needed to be burned at this point.

Noel drank down the rest of her milk, dribbling a little on her chin. Aeryx had the urge to lick it off, but she turned around and walked to the sink. "You managed to survive another day? Slay any dust bunnies with Geralt while I was gone?" She coyly looked over her shoulder and grinned at him.

"A rather devious mouse eyed me with contempt while I ate the sandwich you made for me." She'd left it on the table with a few other things that tasted like salted sawdust, but he'd forced them down anyway since he'd been famished. He hadn't had a proper meal since arriving in the mortal realm, and he missed the Frosterian food. Stewed venison, roasted boar, all of the heavy meals that sated his appetite. Still, the peanut butter was fucking delicious.

"Sounds like a better day than mine."

Aeryx snorted. When he lifted an arm, he caught a whiff of himself. Far too earthy to smell pleasant. "Noel." He paused, scratching the back of his neck. "Is there a bathtub in this house... I didn't notice one in the washroom—"

She blinked at him. "Oh. No, just a shower. When was the last time you actually took a *bath*?"

"Too long." The morning he'd left Frosteria was the last time he'd bathed. Aeryx grimaced. *Too long indeed.* He polished off the milk, and Noel grabbed his cup, washed it, then motioned for him to follow.

She drew her hair over one shoulder. "You don't smell bad yet, or I definitely would've told you. Go ahead and take a shower."

Yet? He lifted his arm and sniffed. Leather, musk, and the smell of the outdoors. Still, it wasn't about how he smelled but how his skin hadn't had a chance to breathe in bloody days. "A shower...?"

Noel laughed, waving her hand around. "Yeah, like it sprinkles down on you. I'll show you." She led him down a hallway and opened the second door on the left. It was the same washroom he'd been using but hadn't bothered to inspect it. Noel pulled the tan curtain aside to reveal a cubby with a drain.

He eyed it as she proceeded to turn the water on. It wasn't unlike a tub with a faucet, but this one had a knob that was twisted. Immediately, a torrent of rain poured down onto the shower floor. "It's like the rain." He reached out, touching its warmth, then, smirking, he flicked it at her.

Noel yelped. She hip-checked him before turning away. "Let me grab a towel for you." She went to a small closet against the wall and grumbled. "Nothing. Guess I'll find you *something* to use and be right back."

Aeryx unbuttoned his uniform and slid it off. He sighed in relief as air brushed his skin. While he waited for her to return, he wiped away the steam from the mirror above the sink. His reflection showed what he knew was beneath the glamour—him—the true Aeryx. No fangs, no fur. Just obsidian horns, deep brown eyes, sharp angles, and brunette waves that were in dire need of washing.

Noel hadn't rushed back. So, he took off his boots and breeches before stepping into the shower. Disappointment bloomed in his chest that she wasn't back yet, and he wondered if she'd dare to join him. The thought of water cascading down her bare form brought his cock to life. Grumbling, he yanked the privacy curtain across in case she chose that moment to walk back in.

While he wasn't certain what was in the bottles, he squirted some of the contents in his palm and sniffed. *Flowers*, he mused. Curiously, he dragged his tongue along the small pile of cream and gagged. "That is horrid!" Aeryx spit whatever was left in his mouth out. He slapped the remainder from his palm into his hair, lathered and washed it, avoiding his horns, then coated his body.

It was *so damn* difficult not thinking about Noel in the shower. Especially as he thought of how her body would nestle against him, his hand a precious distance away from her mound. His cock twitched in response, knowing exactly what *it* wanted.

Oh, but if he could let go, follow his instincts and what Noel wished for…

First, he would kiss her full lips that had taunted him since he'd first seen her. He would savor the taste of them until they were both breathless. Then, he would remove each article of her clothing, torturously slow until she was ready to rip them off herself.

And he would graze her bare flesh with the pads of his fingers, committing every inch, every dip of her body to memory, then he would taste her. His tongue would plunge into her center, drawing out pleasure until she tumbled over the precipice.

Fuck, he was hard, and he wanted her so damn badly. He wrenched his eyes shut. "Enough. No good will come of that."

When he finished cleaning up, and Noel still hadn't returned, Aeryx stepped out of the shower and padded forward, just as she quickly rounded the corner. The door was still wide open, the same as she'd left it. She must have registered what she was seeing because when her shoe stepped onto the bathroom tile, she yelped and tilted forward as she slipped.

Aeryx closed what little distance there was between them so he could catch her, but her writhing figure sent him off balance, and he slid backward, fumbling to right himself.

Inevitably, he crashed to the floor with a grunt, ensuring she was on top, so he didn't crush her.

"Are you okay?" he rushed, lifting his head. Concern melted away as she shifted on top of him, then straddled him fully. If he thought the shower was difficult, this was easily ten times worse. He would not, he told himself, think of her soft curves or what her mouth would feel like taking him in…

"Shit." Her fingers scraped against his chest, and while she may have felt fur, it wasn't—it was his bare flesh. "I'm okay." Noel's eyes dragged along his form, and what he wouldn't give to be back home so she could truly see him, the real him. A male capable of holding, kissing, and pulling cries of pleasure from her.

Instead of scraping her nails against his flesh, her fingers tentatively explored his chest, his neck, just below his jaw, and Aeryx swallowed roughly. He was not inexperienced in the least, but he also knew it would make his departure all the more bittersweet if they tangled with one another. But Morozko's bloody teeth did he *want* to. And she had to know that by now, since she had a front row seat to *him*.

No other human had ever looked at him this way, seeing beyond what they believed was before them—a monster.

"I—I should probably move, so you can get dressed…" Her voice was thick, sultry to his ears, and he wanted to argue. Wanted desperately to disagree with that very notion, but to what end? *Being sensible is for the fucking birds.*

Noel rolled to the side, grabbed one of her dropped towels, and without looking, draped it over him.

Aeryx sat up, chuckling over the entire situation. He grinned. "Did you like—"

"Aeryx," she hissed, but it was mixed with laughter.

He grinned and reached forward, tucking a strand of blue hair behind her ear. "I won't lie. I'm a little disappointed you've now seen me bare, and we haven't even had a chance to play strip poker." And no kiss, which was likely for the best.

Noel leaned forward, and before Aeryx knew what she was doing, her lips were against his cheek. Warm, tender, and lingering.

"Is that better?" she whispered.

Why couldn't we be in Frosteria?

She wouldn't kiss him on the mouth in her world. She didn't know she *could.* The glamour showed her fangs, thin lips, and the harsh lines of his face while in the mortal world —a beast. Not someone she could care enough for to kiss.

But fuck if he didn't want to…

"A little," he answered roughly.

Aeryx's arm snaked around her shoulders and pulled her against him. His nose dragged along her neck to where it met her shoulder, and his lips pressed against her skin. She shivered at his delicate touch, her breath hitching.

"What is it like with a lover in Frosteria?" Her question was simple enough, and yet it twisted his gut. He didn't want to tell her. He wanted to show her exactly what it was like being his lover until she was breathless and boneless beneath him. But he wouldn't because she was a human, and he was a krampi—*immortal.* In the end, he'd have to return home, and she would remain in her world. Yet, that notion didn't settle well with him.

However, he only shrugged at her question. She must have sensed the change in tension because she started to lift away from him.

So, he let her go.

THE SCHOOL DAY WAS TEDIOUS AS FUCK, AND FOR THE PAST couple of days, all Noel could focus on was how she'd been the first to lift herself away from Aeryx's warmth, leave him in that bathroom and act like nothing had happened, as though she hadn't seen him in all his naked glory. It hadn't mattered that most of his body was covered in fur because he was built like a damn man. If he'd had hooves, that might've caused her to second guess her arousal… *maybe*.

She shook away the images of the Krampus pictures Ivy had shown her as she unlocked the door. Evening had already swallowed the town—it was the one day of the week where her classes were all day.

The living room was empty, with no Aeryx in sight. She placed the peanut butter on the counter, then walked up the stairs, and the sound of the shower spilled out into the hallway. Geralt rested beside the door. *Me too, Geralt. Me too*.

Her thoughts turned to what she'd been doing in there every time she'd taken a shower since they'd been staying together. A heat stirred within her as she once again thought about Aeryx, his hard body beneath her. She imagined his large hand stroking his perfect cock, circling the tip, her on her knees in front of him— What all-mighty power was fucking with her? Couldn't Aeryx have taken a shower while she was at school? And why the fuck was she still standing outside the bathroom like a creeper?

Noel fled down the stairs and stepped back outside into the evening. "God, you're a moron," she whispered before pulling out her phone, needing to talk to Ivy.

"You're calling instead of texting? Something must be up," Ivy sang when she answered the phone after the second ring.

"I can't go into your aunt's house at the moment." Noel didn't trust herself to not go back up the stairs, so she sat on the porch swing, rocking it with her feet.

"What happened?" Ivy asked, her voice curious.

"I forgot to tell you that I fell on top of Aeryx the other day." She hadn't forgotten, just tried to pretend it had never occurred, which hadn't worked in her favor.

"I mean, it happens," Ivy deadpanned.

"While he was… naked." The image flashed in her head, her straddling him, *touching* him, *kissing* his cheek, *feeling* him beneath her.

Silence echoed between them for several beats before Ivy laughed and kept laughing.

"It's not funny." Noel rolled her gaze to the porch ceiling. *It was kind of funny…*

"So," Ivy cooed, "did you get a glimpse of his man bits?"

Noel released a heavy breath. "No doubt about it."

"And? Did it look human?"

That had been precisely one of the reasons that had made her stumble. His dick hadn't looked the least bit demon or otherworldly. Not that she knew how demon penises were supposed to look, but there wasn't an inch of fur on it, and it was fucking *big*. Maybe it *was* otherworldly... "Very human."

"So it wouldn't be that weird if you two... you know." Noel could hear the grin in Ivy's voice, and she wished she was at home to shove her friend.

It was just lust, even though she'd never experienced something quite like it. If she had to admit it to herself, this feeling was odd, but it wasn't only that, she liked him because he was sweet, different. "That's not happening. Besides, he's leaving soon."

"But he comes back all the time, right? Long-distance relationships are a thing."

Noel rolled her eyes. "Oh my God, I haven't even known him that long."

"So? My parents knew each other for a week and said I love you. Two months later, they were married, and nine months later, there I was."

"I gotta go... do something. I'll talk to you later." Noel laughed, needing to see if Aeryx had made it out of the shower.

"Excuses, excuses," Ivy shouted as Noel ended the call and headed back inside.

Aeryx still wasn't in the living room, but then his footsteps sounded as he sauntered down the stairs. He was fully dressed in an old baggy T-shirt she'd given him that was tight on his muscular frame, his hair damp yet his fur was dry.

"I got you more peanut butter," Noel said, sliding the jar across the counter.

He caught it with a lopsided grin. "You didn't have to do that. I now owe you food from my world."

Her heart thumped at his words, and she told it to calm the fuck down. "Did you try the stone while I was gone?" It was a better question than the one she wanted to ask, which was, *will you slide your precious cock into my mouth*?

"Still nothing." Aeryx fished the stone out from his pocket and briefly closed his eyes, but it didn't light up. "I think I'm going to try it in the woods again. Do you want to come with me?"

That was precisely what she needed—to get out of the house already. "Okay, but only if you show me how you shape things from water at the stream. I still haven't technically *seen* you do any of that."

"Are you going to get in the water with me?"

"You have to be in the water to do it?"

"No." Aeryx smirked and lifted his bag.

Oh. He wasn't making this easy on her in the slightest.

Once they finished sharing the jar of peanut butter, they headed out into the forest. She lifted her flashlight, listening for any strange noises. The last time she'd come here with Aeryx, a changeling had popped out, but only the familiar sounds of bugs and a few birds filled the air. She studied the stream and the trees, searching for Aeryx's ice horse. "Where's Tika?"

"She'll come back soon enough." He held up his stone, waiting, but not a single blue light flickered. "I'll try again in a bit."

Noel knelt at the stream, dipping her fingertips into the cool liquid. "So," she drawled, "what are you going to make me?"

"Hmm." Aeryx grinned, lowering himself beside her. He placed his hand in the water and brushed his pinky against hers. "What do you want me to make you?"

Noel thought about when they were children, riding on the reindeer. If he'd asked her what she'd wanted back then, she knew what her answer would've been. "A sword."

"How mundane." His grin grew wider, his sharp teeth protruding. Her heart accelerated as she watched a glittering blue magic drift from him and swirl with the wind, lifting droplets of water from the river. They halted in the air, then entwined, collecting with one another to shape a glistening object. As the sword hardened, Aeryx grasped the handle and placed it in her palm.

It was cold to the touch. "How long will it last?" she asked, studying the perfectly crafted blade in awe. The ice weapon was light in her grasp, and when she brought the blade down against the ground, not even a crack appeared. "It's strong."

"It won't melt." He paused, his dark eyes meeting hers. "Unless I will it to."

"I'm assuming you're experienced with a sword since you're a warrior. Show me how to use it." Her dad had collected a few antique swords that she'd fucked around with when he hadn't been home, but that was as far as that went.

"I would need one of my own." Aeryx cocked his head.

"Then make one, duh."

He rolled his eyes and chuckled. "You're such a brat."

Noel smirked as the magic poured out of him, the water droplets lifting, twisting in a familiar dance like they had with her weapon, creating a sword mirroring hers. She wished she had the ability to do what he could—it was magical, *fascinating*.

Spreading her legs apart, Noel settled into her stance while holding up her sword. "Show me what you got, beast."

"Mm-hmm." He placed a fist to his mouth as his shoulders shook.

"You're such a dick." She laughed and brought her sword forward. He easily swung his up, clashing it with hers. Her shoulders vibrated, the contact burning, but she didn't drop the sword.

"Damn, you're stronger than you look. You didn't drop it, princess."

"I mean, I'm sure if you swung again, my arms might rip off." The burn still pulsed through her, yet with practice, she was sure it would lessen. But when the hell would she be practicing with swords? "What else do you do as a warrior in Frosteria?"

"At the barracks, we also do combat training. Our magic doesn't work against changelings, so we have to learn other techniques."

Ivy would be good at the combat side of things. "The barracks?"

"It's where the trainees and most warriors sleep. It isn't far from the portal once you cross."

She wished she could see a picture of the barracks to compare it to the places where soldiers stayed in her world. "Since we have time while we wait for Tika to return, teach me something else."

Tossing his sword to the ground, he arched a brow and crossed his arms. "Run at me and hit my chest as hard as you can."

Noel rolled her eyes and dropped her sword. She then dipped into a lunge, preparing to do whatever it was she planned to do. Run, she supposed? She wouldn't be able to knock down his large frame. "Don't get lazy on me."

Aeryx swiped his tongue across his lower lip, then wiggled a finger at her, beckoning her forward.

Noel flicked her gaze from that long finger of his, taking a deep breath and focusing, then shot forward. The wind thrashed her hair, and when her hands struck his chest, Aeryx gripped her waist as she barreled him backward.

They hit the ground, making her gasp. Noel's chest heaved as she sat up, her legs straddling his waist. "Are you all right?"

"I'm good now." He chuckled.

Noel tapped his chest with her finger, her brow furrowed. "You did that on purpose, didn't you?"

"It's possible," he whispered, pushing a lock of hair behind her ear. "I was too busy thinking of strip poker."

"Whatever, I should have just brought cards instead." Noel laughed, then her expression grew serious as her gaze lifted from his face to his curving horns. "Can I touch one?"

He pulled her closer so her breath mingled with his. "Just the one, or both?"

"Whatever you want." At that moment she was like ice melting in his hands with the feel of his strong body against hers.

"Are you sure about that?" Aeryx's voice came out raspy as he tenderly grasped both of her wrists, his thumbs drawing light circles in the middle. She nodded, and he brought her hands to his horns. As soon as she made contact with their smoothness, she could feel him at her center, hardening against her softness. A low growl escaped his throat when she trailed her fingers across their curves, then louder as she gripped, stroking, his digits digging deliciously into her hips.

In that moment, she didn't care if it was right or if it was wrong. Maybe it was wrong for him because she was human, but he didn't seem to care. So why should she give a fuck? He was like her in all the ways that mattered. Noel rolled her hips forward, and he growled even deeper, his hands skimming down to her ass, gripping firmly while she moved against him. He guided her to grind harder into him, a low moan escaping her throat when his hardness brushed her nerves just right.

Touching the horns wasn't enough for her—she wanted to feel another part of him, *desperately*. Noel's hand drifted down between them, her heart pounding, anxious, *excited*. She unfastened the button of his pants when a tinkling sound filled the air. Her body froze at the same time Aeryx's did, then she hopped off him just as something trotted out from behind a tree. Noel's gaze connected with Tika's shining blue eyes and she sighed in relief.

"Payback," Aeryx mumbled as he pushed up from the ground.

"What?" Noel asked, her insides still burning hot from how good he'd felt beneath her.

"Just something that happened when I was younger before we found you." Aeryx ran a hand across the top of Tika's head. "Let's try the stone again."

After the night in the woods, and the stone doing nothing except staying a stone, Noel took a warm shower when she and Aeryx got home. She'd hoped the shower would distract her from the incident between them in the woods, but it hadn't —it had only intensified things. She and Aeryx had been quiet on the way back to the house, neither mentioning what happened between them. As she draped the towel around herself, she decided she would give him one thing.

As she walked into the living room, Aeryx glanced up from the TV, and his eyes widened at her, covered only by a towel. He lay on the sofa bed, wearing a pair of pants, the rest of him bare.

Noel swayed her hips before stopping in front of him, his lips parting. "I realize it wasn't fair when I saw you naked in the bathroom." She unraveled her towel and flashed him, then closed it and plopped down beside him on the bed with an amused smile.

"Did you just…" Aeryx paused and shook his head. "And you're going to lay beside me for the rest of the night in just a *towel*?"

"I mean, if you want the towel off, then it can go," Noel purred.

He stared at her for a long moment, to the point where she thought she may need to go ahead and put clothes back on, but then he answered in a gruff voice, "The towel off."

"You've got hands." Her smile returned, and she arched her back for him.

"That I do." Aeryx teased them both as he drew a line from just above her core over the fabric to the top. She swallowed in anticipation while he slowly loosened the towel, gently pulling it back. The cool air pebbled her nipples, and her heart kicked up. She'd never been this vulnerable with anyone. Sex had always been fast, clumsy, about getting off. But not whatever this was as his finger drifted to the valley between her breasts.

Heavy breaths escaped her mouth while she silently begged for him to touch, to do whatever he wished. He must've heard her quiet prayers because he drew circles around her nipples, then cradled her breast as he buried his face into her neck. Her eyes fluttered in bliss when his tongue tasted her flesh to just below her jaw, his hand trailing down over her belly button.

On instinct, her legs parted for him in invitation, and he didn't hesitate to cup her mound with his hand. She gasped as his fingers moved, rubbing at a perfect counter-clockwise pace around her clit, then his rhythm picked up, her breaths growing more rapid. His tongue flicked just below her ear, and she moaned, her body arching. Aeryx's hand circled, and circled and *circled*. That lovely tongue of his came again and the tightening within her unraveled as an earth-shattering orgasm rocketed through her, her body clenching and shaking in utter bliss.

Chest heaving, body a pile of liquid, Noel rolled to face him, wishing his mouth could mold to hers. Prayed it would, and she didn't fucking care that it wouldn't line up right.

She kissed his lips softly, then murmured, "Take off your pants."

"As you wish," Aeryx said gruffly, then unfastened his pants, freeing his glorious cock, and shoved them off. "I am at your mercy, princess."

Noel smirked, grasping his cock, the touch sending electric sparks through her. She stroked it with practiced motions until he made the growling sound she loved so damn much. And then she didn't want to touch it anymore, she wanted to *taste* it. So she crawled down his body, her gaze trained on his, even as she took the tip in between her lips, making him growl louder. She circled the tip with her tongue, his muscles flexing while she ran it up his base, bringing him all the way in.

Her pace picked up, her hand pumping as she sucked and glided her lips down his velvety skin, tasting every inch of it. His hands tangled in her hair while she worked him, made him feel good.

"Noel," he rasped. "I'm about to come." She didn't move, only continued devouring him until her name rolled from his lips with a satisfying groan. Her eyes widened as he spilled into her mouth—his flavor was like peppermint, like a damn good *dessert*.

Noel met his gaze once more, drawing the blanket over them both. "Were you ever disgusted that I am... furless?"

Aeryx's deep, beautiful rumble of laughter poured out from him. "Out of everything you could ask me, that's what you're questioning? Never." Then his voice grew serious. "The one thing that gave me pause is that I'm immortal and you aren't."

And that I'm not your mate. But she didn't say it out loud as the wonderful feeling she'd just felt dissipated.

CHAPTER 18

AERYX

Aeryx jolted awake. Remnants of a dream clung to his mind, melding with reality. He'd dreamed of Noel straddling him, his hands on her hips, pulling her down against him as she rode them both into bliss. Blood rushed to his cock, hardening it, wanting to bury himself deep inside of her.

He couldn't be having these dreams *now*. Not that reality was better. As much as his body yearned for her, Aeryx was leaving and she'd never see him again. Why couldn't she be immortal and venture to Frosteria with him? His chest shouldn't have ached, and yet, it did.

Noel rolled over in bed, facing him. She'd crawled beneath the covers with him, curled into his side, and turned the television on. Her breasts pressed against his back, and while she may have experienced the brush of fur, he most certainly did not. Noel's skin raked along his, only adding to his desire to pleasure her further.

Last night, Aeryx had been grateful for the distraction of *Thirteen Ghosts,* because, without it, he was certain things would've escalated. He was sure of it. He hadn't known the movie was supposed to frighten him. To Aeryx, it played out more humorous, then again, he'd witnessed true horror.

Still, her bare flesh made it difficult to focus on tragic memories. It surprised Aeryx that she didn't seem put off by his appearance, and when she took his length in her mouth, she did it willingly. Noel saw the beast, yet treated him as if he weren't one. While it was a relief, he was also conflicted about what that meant.

It was dark outside, but the moon offered enough light to paint the room in a soft blue glow.

Aeryx carefully slid out from under Noel's arm and sat on the edge of the bed. The glowing numbers on the clock read 4:25 AM, which meant it was early morning on his seventh day in the mortal realm. He needed to get to the woods and prepare for his father's arrival. He had no doubt Korreth would storm through a portal with tension oozing from him, readying for the worst outcome.

Noel groaned as she rolled again and bumped into his back. "Is it morning already?" she murmured and remained in a curled-up position.

He chuckled, shifting to look down at her. "If you want to say morning, it isn't quite dawn yet. But I should head into the woods in case—"

"I'm going with you." Noel lifted her head and slowly sat up. "You know, to say goodbye…"

Aeryx schooled his features, not allowing himself to frown. There was more than a hint of sadness in her tone, and while a part of him longed to tease her over missing him, he wasn't happy about leaving, either.

She's mortal, Aeryx. Nothing good would've come from tumbling with her. Not when you're immortal.

None of it mattered, of course. Once his father arrived, he'd wipe Noel, and any memories that involved them, stemming from the time they were children, would be gone. No stories of *Beauty and the Beast*, or the movies she'd forced him to watch.

But Aeryx would remember every damn thing. Every moment they'd ever shared would be seared into his mind, even burning the bloody changeling.

Noel poked his back. "Well?"

"Ah, yes, of course, you can come. Not that I'd be able to stop you." He shook his head, smirking. If he'd told her certain death awaited her in the forest, Noel likely would've tip-toed her way in, out of curiosity and defiance.

"Definitely not."

"There's a large chance my father will wipe your memories if he catches you. Humans aren't supposed to retain memories of us," Aeryx warned.

"I'll take my chances." She shrugged.

He stood and grabbed his washed uniform that had been cast aside for most of the week.

Noel shuffled behind him. "I'm going to get dressed." She padded out of the room, naked as the day she was born, and Aeryx stared at the curve of her ass. The blood rushed straight to his cock, tempting him to go after her. He let his warrior control take root, thinking of whipping changelings until his length turned flaccid once more.

When she left the room, he discarded the shirt Noel had given him and glowered. It was unfair for the krampi to retain memories, as far as he was concerned. Perhaps if her memory continued to haunt him, he could petition to see the queen in Frosteria and have her pluck the memories from his mind.

Then again, it could've been his cock talking. Imploring him to fuck Noel before he had to leave, but surely that wasn't just it. He'd done more with her than fuck around the entire week. He'd experienced life as a mortal, or as close as he'd get to it, and there was something to be said about that.

When he'd finished dressing, Aeryx walked into the living room and tilted his head as Geralt trilled at him. He'd miss the feline and the way the cat would curl up on his chest, purring so loudly it lulled him to sleep.

"Ready?" Noel sidled up beside him, offering a jar of peanut butter with a spoon.

No. "I suppose." He grabbed his utensil and dipped it into the open container.

By the time they reached the woods, golden light started to spread across the sky. Aeryx glanced around, half expecting a changeling to leap out at them, but when none did, his shoulders eased down.

"Tika," Aeryx murmured. It'd rained the prior night, and because of that, small puddles had formed. Particles of water lifted from them, suspending in the air until there was an outline of Tika. The droplets slid along an invisible body, shaping the horse until she was whole. This time, she hadn't made them wait. Perhaps she could sense through their bond that it was time to go.

He lifted his hands and rubbed the mare's smooth cheeks,

then turned to look at Noel. "Would you like to ride her while we have time?"

Noel's brows furrowed, then she stepped closer to Tika. "By *myself*?"

Aeryx chuckled. "It's all right. She'll take care of you." Noel inched closer, and he leaned forward, letting her step into his cupped hands. Tika didn't have a saddle or bridle on, but it didn't matter. She'd behave for Noel.

"Okay, now that I'm up here, what now, beast?" She smirked.

Aeryx turned away from her and rifled through a nearby bush until he found Tika's tack. Quickly, he put the bridle on and handed over the reins. "Hold on and have fun, princess."

"Aeryx! That's not hel—" Tika walked forward, silencing Noel as she visibly concentrated on how to stay on the horse.

"Would you prefer me up there with you?" He arched a brow.

Noel's lips twisted, but he wasn't sure if it was in concentration or because she was trying to decide whether she wanted him with her. "No, I got this."

Aeryx believed she could do it too. She just needed to relax.

"You know, when I was learning to ride, my father told me I needed to laugh. Laughing relaxes you," he offered, then stroked his chin as he considered their activities during the week. How was the mortal celebration only a *week* ago?

"Think of falling into my arms in the washroom."

"Into your arms?" Noel laughed. "You mean your *lap?*" She relaxed the more she spoke, and Tika continued to walk at a slower pace.

After a few beats of silence, Noel spoke again, her expression now serious. "So, are you ever going to come back here and visit?"

"Only for changelings." Aeryx rubbed his chest. A heaviness he wanted no part of settled there. Leaving the mortal world was one thing—he had no attachment to it, and his primary mission was to keep the human children safe. But leaving Noel weighed heavily on his mind—his heart. Not being able to listen to her smart mouth or see her vibrant green eyes light up in excitement.

Morozko's teeth.

"Not even to come by and say hello?" she asked, her brow furrowing.

"It's better this way. Easier. Even if it wasn't against krampi rules and your memories never got wiped, you're mortal, and I'm not..." His voice trailed off because if he said anymore, he'd change his damn mind.

Noel nodded, not giving into the fight as she always did about things. Perhaps she could easily move on from him. That would be better, even though he would spend the rest of his life thinking about her.

"Uh, whoa, what the fuck is that? Whoa, Tika!" Noel's voice shook as she stared forward.

Aeryx flicked his gaze toward his mare, to Noel, who gaped at a spot in front of her. When he followed her line of sight, blue flecks swirled, then grew until a full circle formed. His muscles tensed, unsure of whether it was a changeling portaling or his father. Holding up a hand, Aeryx signaled for Noel to remain where she was. Then, as the portal widened further, his father emerged on foot, hair mussed by the wind and brows pinched. Aeryx noted the scowl on his father's face and how his fingers twitched toward his side as if he was readying to unleash his sword.

Tightening his fists, Aeryx gritted his teeth together with enough force that he thought they'd snap. In a few moments, Noel would likely be wiped, and there was a fierce urge to spirit her away on Tika.

His father's lips parted as he hissed. When he finally registered Aeryx standing there, he charged forward and embraced him. Grown or not, he couldn't express how good it was to know his father was alive and here. No matter if he would be pleased with the circumstance or not.

And he wouldn't be pleased.

Aeryx's gaze flicked to the portal, then back to his father.

"Morozko's fucking teeth, Aeryx. What happened?" His eyes searched him over, assessing him.

Aeryx pressed his lips together, clearing his throat. "A complication." He glanced to the side, adding, "Something broke my stone, and I'm unable to conjure any magic to it."

"Hello." Noel waved. She'd been quiet up until now. "I'm the complication."

Aeryx slanted her a sideward glance, but inwardly, he growled at her. He generally played by the rules but would also push them to their boundaries. His father? He hardly ever toed the line, let alone broke the rules. The fact that Noel knew about them wouldn't go over well.

"Excuse me?" Korreth tilted his head and focused on Noel, who still sat on top of Tika. "What are you doing with a mortal, Aeryx?"

"And here we thought there was an emergency in the mortal realm," a feminine voice called from behind. Aeryx twisted to see Zira stepping through the portal, her blonde braid falling across one shoulder. She grinned at Aeryx. Dral, his father's reindeer, followed by her side. Her jaw was tense, the only sign that she was, in fact, not as relaxed as she seemed.

While his father's severity may have twisted his gut, like a child in trouble, Zira's energy was infectious, and it put Aeryx at ease, if only for a moment.

Aeryx could almost hear the lecture spilling from his father. Still, he hesitantly spoke, "This is Noel." He motioned to her, grimacing. He didn't want her in trouble, didn't want anger directed at Noel when she was only at fault for taking care of him. "She has been hiding me all week." *Among other things. Like helping me slay changelings, feeding me peanut butter... and pleasuring me.* None of which would've pleased his father to hear, he was certain.

"Dammit, Aeryx," Korreth growled. "You couldn't have wiped her and hid in the woods?"

"He tried," Noel spoke up, biting her lip. "But I'm immune, apparently."

Korreth turned away from him and sauntered toward Noel, who shrunk back. "Did he really?"

"You're his father, right? Captain Korreth?" Noel blinked down at him and held onto Tika's reins like they were a lifeline.

"I am."

"Thank you," Noel said softly.

It took Aeryx a moment to truly register what she'd said. But why? Was she thanking him for all those years ago? A protest lingered at the tip of his tongue. He wanted to distract Noel from what she was about to say because Aeryx wasn't sure what was worse. That he couldn't influence Noel at all, or that he'd failed his very first mission. Either way, he was a disappointment to his father.

Korreth slanted him a look over his shoulder, amplifying his humiliation.

"You saved me, the three of you. I had always believed it was a dream until I met Aeryx, but it wasn't. And I just want to say thank you."

There it was. The truth out in the open.

Surprise filtered into Korreth's eyes. "You remember that, or Aeryx told you?"

"I remember. He told me it was his first mission, and Zira's, but I remember everything about the short journey to my home."

Zira sidled up next to him. "This isn't a jest by any chance, is it?" She arched a brow. "Because he's not in the mood."

Aeryx jammed his fingers through his hair. "I wish it fucking was, Zira."

Zira's digits drummed against her thigh. "This is the least of our problems. We're just relieved you're alive and well. A mortal can be wiped, even if you experienced a fluke." She glanced at him, then cleared her throat. "This is fixable."

He felt the same about Zira, and his father too. They were alive, unharmed from a changeling attack. But the weight of the moment distracted him. "Is it?" But why didn't he *want* it to be fixed? He rubbed his knuckles over his heart.

Zira looked at him a little too closely. "I'll wipe her memories."

"There's no other way?" he asked quietly enough so his father couldn't hear.

Zira's dark eyes softened and she shook her head. "No… but answer this, do you care for her?"

He did. More than he'd cared for any other—and it just felt *wrong* leaving her behind. "I do."

Zira peered over at Korreth, then back to Aeryx. "This is the best for Noel."

He clenched his teeth and nodded, then strode forward, hearing the tail end of the conversation Noel was having with his father. It was part of the mission that she had to be influenced—she was a mortal after all, but it riddled him with apprehension. Aeryx didn't want her to forget any of their time spent together.

"That's the reindeer I remember." She pointed to Dral and his father's familiar lowed softly, shaking his fur out.

His father didn't so much as look at Aeryx as he came up beside him, and from his current position, he couldn't make out his father's face. He wasn't angry, but maybe that would've been preferred. His energy was impossible to read.

Korreth grunted. "We should get back to Frosteria. It's daylight now and we're all at risk."

Aeryx nodded and dragged his gaze to Noel. An array of emotions flashed in her eyes: dread, sadness, hurt. "Come on, princess." He helped her down from Tika, but didn't move away as she stood.

"I'll miss your stupid peanut butter habit…" She chewed on her bottom lip. "So you really won't be back?"

"It would be best not to." He dragged his fingers down her back and gazed into her eyes, committing the vibrant green depths to his memory. Aeryx would remember for both of them. "So, remember our time together fondly."

"Aeryx," Korreth ground out.

Ignoring his father, he wrapped his arms around her, squeezed, then whispered in her ear. "Thank you for taking care of me this week." He brushed a kiss to her temple, then withdrew.

"I'll always remember you, beast."

She wouldn't, though, and the more that became real, the more it shattered him.

"I'll stay behind and tend to things here." Zira motioned. "Gather your supplies and such, Aeryx. Ryken will be so pleased you're back."

Somehow, Aeryx doubted that. His brother likely awaited the glorious news that he'd succumbed to battle in the mortal realm, and for the day he'd assume ownership of Aeryx's cottage.

"Be well, Noel, and stay out of trouble." Aeryx laughed, but it sounded hollow. In truth, he hoped she remained as rebellious as ever, and stayed true to herself, because that was how he'd remember her.

CHAPTER 19

NOEL

KORRETH WAS HAVING A DISCUSSION WITH AERYX, AND NOEL couldn't tell what kind of mood it was, but she was sure it wasn't a happy one. The captain hadn't tried to use his influence to erase her memories—not yet anyway.

Zira walked toward her as Korreth lifted his stone, a circle of blue lighting up, but not even a crackling sounded from the flames. Aeryx gave her one final glance, and Noel's heart lodged in her throat as they both passed through the portal. Something that said he wished things could be different.

"What ever did you do to your lovely hair?" Zira smiled, pushing an emerald lock behind Noel's ear. The krampi's teeth protruded from her mouth the way Aeryx's had, the whitest of ivories. She wore a red and black uniform similar to Aeryx's, her dark leather pants hugging her thighs.

"I get bored a lot." Noel shrugged, amused that an other-worldly creature was asking about her hair. "You aren't going to try and wipe me, are you? Because if you are, I'm going to run like hell. *Fight* your magic like hell. I won't give up your secret. Who would believe me anyway?"

A stone like Aeryx's broken one rested in the krampi's hand and Zira shoved it into the pocket of her long fur coat. "You were the first mortal child I helped save when I became a warrior," Zira said, a smile tugging at her lips. "Over the years, there have been many human children I've rescued, but I remember you the most. I think because you were one of the few who weren't afraid."

Since realizing the past wasn't a dream at all, but real, it had been coming back to Noel in waves. Clearer and clearer. Korreth's reindeer, its flaming red eyes and razor-sharp antlers. "I remember you telling me I was safe, and I think it was the kindness in your voice that made me trust you." Also, she'd been a child, and children tended to be less aware of things, of the world. From what she could recall, Zira looked as she had years ago, with smaller curving horns than Korreth's, deep brown eyes, and dark fur that she knew from her fingers roaming over Aeryx's was soft to the touch.

A low sound escaped Zira's mouth as if she was warring with herself about something. Her serious gaze held Noel's as she whispered, "This once, I won't wipe your memories since you weren't a problem before. You seem to care about Aeryx, and I don't want you to forget him. Just don't make me regret it." Her tone left no room for argument.

Noel's eyebrows shot up in disbelief. "Thank you." Even then, she didn't know if the magic would've worked on her since Aeryx's sway hadn't done a damn thing. A dark thought passed through her mind of Zira sliding the stone inside her pocket and Noel "borrowing" it. She wouldn't technically be stealing it if she planned on returning it. Korreth had left the portal open for Zira as the blue flames continued to blaze. However, Zira would still eventually find out the stone was missing—the question was how soon. But maybe not *that* soon...

Her fingers itched to take it, and she hated herself after Zira's kindness, but what if Noel stumbled upon a changeling and needed to warn the krampi? It was an excuse, yet it was partly true as she gave into temptation and circled her arms around Zira's muscular body. This was the only way she could get close enough. Zira wrapped her arms around her—a lovely scent caressing her nose—and with nimble movements, Noel dipped her fingers into the krampi's coat pocket and brushed the stone. She quickly drew it out, then slid it into her jean pocket as she took a step back.

Zira's gaze locked with Noel's—her pupils not dilating the way Aeryx's had when he'd attempted to sway her. "Now, go home," the krampi instructed.

Noel nodded and smiled. "Maybe I'll run into you another time." Blowing out a breath, she pivoted on her heel, not once looking back as she trudged through the woods. Regardless of the fact that she'd confiscated Zira's stone, it could very well be the last time she saw Aeryx. He'd said it was best they not see each other anymore—he was immortal and she wasn't.

Maybe he was right.

Eventually, she would grow old and wither while he stayed beastly sexy as hell. Besides that, what if he left her behind after meeting his true mate? *Fuck that.* It was better this way.

The stone felt heavy in her pocket, and she rolled her eyes to the sky. Sometimes she hated having a conscience. She turned around and darted back toward Zira to return the stone, hoping she wouldn't attempt to actually sway her memories this time. But when she arrived, Zira was already gone.

Noel arrived at Ivy's aunt's house to collect her things and head home. For now, the stone was hers. She needed to get her priorities back in check and think about the future, a boring human existence. Yet, not boring because now she would wonder every time she passed someone if a little demon fucker resided inside their body.

She grabbed her backpack from upstairs, catching Aeryx's wintry scent in areas of the house. *Of course.*

As she rounded the corner of the stairs to put the bed back inside the couch, Geralt hopped up on the side table beside it. "Hungry again?" Noel smiled, then her gaze fell to what rested beside him. Aeryx's music box. The cat wanted to hear the song as he did every day when Aeryx would play it for him. *Shit.* She knew how important that damn box was to Aeryx.

"Thank you, Geralt." And now she could at least pat herself on the back for taking Zira's stone instead of feeling guilt. Her stomach sank at a thought, though—that she might not be able to use it. She wasn't a krampi, but did it matter? She wasn't sure, and Aeryx had never discussed how the stone worked per se.

Noel lifted the box and inspected its engravings, the memories of the night before coursing through her. Her hands sliding up Aeryx, his gliding down her, him in her mouth. The taste of lingering peppermint on her tongue. It was more than returning the box because he would eventually come to retrieve it—she wanted to risk seeing him again, tell him fuck being immortal. She wanted to get to know more about him and if he met his mate, then so be it. But this was now. She needed to admit to him what she was *really* starting to feel, that it was more than getting each other off.

Noel fished out her phone from her purse and called Ivy.

"Is Aeryx still there?" Ivy asked when she answered.

"No," Noel said. "But I need you to do something for me. Can you bring me my heaviest coat, snow boots, and some winter clothes, then drive me to the woods? I promise I'll explain it all when you get here."

"I don't like the sound of this," Ivy groaned. "But fine."

Noel ended the call and emptied out her backpack. She went to the pantry and stashed it with the rest of the food she'd bought for the week since she wouldn't be in Frosteria for long. A box of granola bars, a couple of bottled waters, and the last jar of peanut butter, then added a pocket knife and her cell phone.

Geralt purred beside her and Noel glanced down at his needy begging. "I can't forget about you now, can I?" She poured him food in his bowl, then finished folding up the couch and arranging the pillows when a car honked.

Ivy.

Noel stepped outside and locked the door behind her before sinking down into the passenger seat of Ivy's car and tossing her friend the house key.

"Clothes are in the back seat," Ivy said. "So can you tell me now why we need to go to the woods if Aeryx is gone? Please don't tell me you want to be some sort of changeling slayer now?"

"I mean, now that you said the word slayer..." Noel teased. "But seriously, Aeryx's family came for him, and I sort of stole one of their portal stones." She gave Ivy her most innocent look.

"Of course you did." Ivy grinned while backing out of the driveway.

"Aeryx left his music box at your aunt's house, and I know how important it is to him. I just wanted to give it to him in person, but I also need to give him a piece of my mind."

"You've got it bad for him," Ivy drawled, still smiling.

Ah, shit. She *did.* "Even if he doesn't want more, then why can't we still be friends? Why does it matter if he's immortal and I'm not for us to hang out or whatever?" Friends... She could do friends. Aeryx slowly unlacing his pants, freeing his velvety cock and taking her up against the wall, then slamming into her from behind. She would pretend she could do friends for the moment.

"I think he's trying to save himself from being hurt—mostly from you being hurt, though. But I think it's better to get everything out in the open, the way I had to with Jace. It's never good to go on without everything being confessed," Ivy said, then glanced at Noel.

"You're right." Her friend would be a damn good counselor.

"Let me come with you. You don't even know what's over there. Demons, Noel. *Demons.*"

Noel shook her head. It was stupid enough for her to cross into an unknown world like a moron—she wouldn't risk her friend. "No. From what he said, the barracks aren't far from the portal, so it shouldn't be hard to find them."

Minus the fact that she didn't know exactly what they looked like.

"But what if you don't come back? What if a changeling hurts you again?" Ivy's voice rose an octave, her eyes wide. "I'm not going to tell you what to do because you'll do it anyway, but what if?"

What if she didn't go, though? She would wonder her whole life what would've happened, and to her, that would be worse than death. Dramatic, she knew. "I don't have an answer to that."

"You will come back. That's final." Ivy pulled into a parking lot, and Noel took off her Converse to slip on her faux fur-lined snow boots, then packed a few pieces of the clothing into her backpack. Even though the air wasn't chilly, Noel put on a sweatshirt and her heavy coat. She then pressed her knife inside a pocket as they entered the woods across the street.

It didn't take long before they reached where Aeryx and his family had been earlier. A few snapped twigs littered the ground, but no other sign gave proof that anyone had been there.

Noel adjusted her backpack. "It's not guaranteed this will work."

"Have faith." Ivy circled an arm around her waist and rested her head on Noel's shoulder. "And if it does work, remember Sarah survived the Goblin King's labyrinth."

"That was a movie," Noel pointed out.

"Hey, we didn't believe Krampus existed the other week." Ivy lightly shook Noel. "Who's to say the Goblin King doesn't exist? Oh please, let him exist."

Noel laughed. "All right, let's try this." She fished the stone out from her pocket, lightly rubbing her thumb across its smooth surface. There wasn't a rule book to tell her how to do this, so she clutched it in her hand, silently begging the stone to open the portal for her.

"Should we have a séance to help nudge it?" Ivy murmured.

As though summoned by the word séance, blue flecks sparked to life before their very eyes, then bright cerulean flames licked at the edges. Noel gasped, her heart pounding, as the world within the circle became a different place than what she'd been seeing. A rolling landscape of ivory snow with alabaster trees in the distance stood before them.

"It worked!" Ivy shouted. She wrapped her arms around her friend once again, squeezing her tight. "Be careful."

"I will, and I'll try not to stay away long." Noel left her friend's arms and took a deep breath as she shuffled toward the portal. Clenching the stone, she stepped through, and a light sizzling sounded. She prayed the flames wouldn't burn her flesh, but they were cool to the touch instead of heated.

As her feet connected with soft snow, a crisp smell mixed with evergreens enveloped her when a strong gust of wind blew. She shivered and drew her hood up. It was cold as fuck here. Trembling, she took the gloves from her coat pockets and put them on while the portal faded, then disappeared.

Noel focused on the winter wonderland surrounding her— it didn't seem otherworldly in the least. Frosteria looked like any northern state during the winter months. Hell, it looked like *Vermont* during winter.

Tall mountains rose in the distance, snow capping their tops. Besides the mountains, only sky-scraping trees littered the area. No barracks, no sign of life. Nothing. This was a stupid idea, and maybe she should've had Ivy come. Noel homed in on the stone, telling it to open the portal back up.

After a few minutes passed, the flickering blue flames didn't come. Fear pulsed through her. Why the hell wasn't it lighting up? What if she really was stuck here and didn't find Aeryx? She was an idiot! Taking her phone from the front of her backpack, she glanced at it. No signal. Of course there wasn't. What was she going to do, anyway? Call Ivy and tell her to find another stone to open the portal?

Noel's hands shook as she shoved the phone into her backpack, quietly asking the stone one more time to open the portal for Ivy. Nothing. Noel studied the ground, noticing several lines of hoof prints in the snow.

Thank God. She blew out a relieved breath and took a step forward, hoping the barracks weren't far by foot, but by the look of no buildings in sight, it would be just her luck that the distance was far.

Noel trudged across the snow, and some sort of white bird soared above her, releasing a loud squawk. The first sign of life she'd seen, even then, the bird didn't seem out of the ordinary. One head, two wings. The wind blew harder, and she held her jacket tighter when a sloshing noise filled the air.

An outline of something red came into view from just past a cluster of trees. She squinted. It was a mother fucking sleigh being pulled by two elk. *Santa Claus*? But then she remembered the sleigh ride home when she'd been saved from a changeling.

As the red sleigh drew closer, with black lines swirling across the sides, a krampi wasn't seated up front. There was a boy with golden hair and... horns? They were similar to

Aeryx's, dark and curved, but not as long. The sleigh slowed to a stop beside her, and she met his ice-blue stare.

"What are you doing out here?" he asked in the same accent Aeryx and the two other krampi had. Even though his face looked young, and he could be no older than fourteen or fifteen, he was built like a man. Tall, muscular, his dark fur jacket tight across his build. If he wasn't krampi, what sort of demon was he?

"I'm looking for the barracks." Her teeth chattered as she said the words, hoping he could help her.

His gaze fastened on hers, a scowl forming on his face. "You're *human*."

Maybe not...

"Yes, and you're not." It came out snarkier than she'd meant it to. She reached into her pocket, gripping her knife.

"Humans don't exist here anymore." The boy hopped from his sleigh, and he was taller than her, but not by much.

Noel took a step back, preparing to run somewhere into the forest. "I'm not from here."

His eyes widened as he noticed the stone that was still clenched in her other hand. "You stole that!"

Noel lunged to the side, darting around him, but he was too quick and knocked her to the snow.

"You little shit, stop—" Her words were cut off as he gagged her mouth with something. She thrashed and bucked, but even though he was young—or *looked* young—he was stronger. She tried to scream yet the gag muffled the sound. The boy hoisted her up as if she weighed nothing and tossed her into the sled. She kicked him in the chest, but he flipped her face down, then roped her arms behind her back.

"Well now," he cooed. "You're a feisty one. I think my

parents will be pleased with what I caught. This time they will dote on me instead of my brother."

When she went to kick again, he was too fast, binding her ankles together. Panic set in then, her heart thundering. What the hell had she gotten herself into?

CHAPTER 20

AERYX

THE FAMILIAR COLD WIND OF FROSTERIA WHIPPED AGAINST Aeryx's face, drying his eyes. Behind him, the portal still swirled a brilliant blue, remaining open for Zira to pass once she was finished. In front of him, snow blanketed the landscape, and he squinted as the sun glinted off of it. The mortal realm hadn't been warm, but it wasn't as cold as home, and he had missed the snow. Somehow, the bite of the air was soothing. However, whatever comfort he'd found vanished as Korreth turned and faced Aeryx.

An unreadable expression formed on his face, then softened. "I am glad the mortal took care of you and that you are alive and well, but remaining amongst humans... that was reckless."

Heat pricked beneath his skin. Father or not, Aeryx didn't want him to disregard her in such a way. "Noel," Aeryx offered.

Korreth's brows lifted, surprise filtering in his gaze. "What?"

It wasn't a real question, but a trap instead, testing to see if Aeryx had the audacity to speak out against his father—his captain. "Her name is Noel," he reiterated, keeping his tone level.

Every muscle that had relaxed in Korreth's face had tensed again. "Now that you've returned, I thought you should know Lyra is on the mend from the assault a week ago, and the changelings' attacks have intensified. Efraun has been offering to track down the nests, but they're in large numbers everywhere."

That was his father's way of brushing off an argument, and he deemed the talk of Noel as unimportant. *But she is important*, a voice screamed inside him. However, this was the *right thing to do*, no matter how painful it was. Above all else, Noel's safety was in the forefront of his mind, and this was how he could ensure she remained safe.

Zira had likely wiped her by now. This would soon be a distant, fond memory, like the one from Aeryx's childhood. And he'd carry the memory with him for both himself and Noel. For eternity. For *always*.

Amid his conflicting emotions, he was relieved to hear news of Lyra, and it would've brightened his mood had his father not mentioned the changelings. "What do you mean?" His eyes shifted toward the mountain range in the distance. At the top, the castle remained hidden. Idly, Aeryx wondered what Morozko thought of all of this and why he sat on his hands while the krampi dealt with the changelings.

"They're pressing closer to the fortress and not just the villages."

Aeryx's stomach dropped. "Fuck. I was ambushed in the mortal realm. I burned two, but without my stone…"

Korreth growled. "Wretched creatures, their time is coming to an end." He paused, lifting his hand to run his fingers through Dral's fur.

His father's words set Aeryx's pulse to racing. "What do you mean?"

"Between you and I?" Korreth scanned the area as if anyone was out there, listening, but Aeryx supposed one could never be too careful. "The queen has found a way to seal off the changelings for good."

Aeryx's eyes shifted, and surprise contorted his features. His lips formed words he didn't utter. "I don't…"

"The less you know, the better, but their time is almost done—I hope." While Korreth sounded so certain, there was a hint of doubt too. "After Zira deals with Noel, she'll meet me at the barracks. Xavi is leading a patrol not far from here—make sure he's all set, then check on your brother for me. With the increase of attacks… I don't want to chance anything."

"Of course," he murmured and mounted Tika. Her mane chimed against her neck as she shook her head. The last thing Aeryx wanted was for his brother to come to harm, but if his comrade needed aid, he should be there.

His father mounted Dral, then with a cluck of his tongue, the reindeer galloped away.

Aeryx watched as his father disappeared down the snowy hillside. With a prodding of his heels, Tika bolted forward and glided across the terrain. Thick clusters of tall, green pines loomed above, with heaps of white clinging to their limbs.

He'd missed the freeing nature of riding through the open tundra. With no restrictions, no worrying about who would see him—his horns. And selfishly, he wanted Noel to experience Frosteria, wanted her to feel his flesh, not fur, and for him to touch her once more. To dine on one of their meals, and taste their delicacies. It was no peanut butter, but it was certainly better than those Oreos.

What would she think of the harsh world and of him in his true form? Would she be disappointed that he wasn't the furred beast she'd grown used to, or pleasantly pleased that, aside from his horns, he appeared no different than a mortal?

With his thoughts tumbling around in his head, Aeryx followed the trail Xavi's group left.

After hours of patrolling with the other warriors, and finding no threat in the area, Aeryx finally arrived at his father's cottage.

Stout bushes decorated the front of his former home, and red berries stood out against the dark green leaves. A giant pine shaded most of the structure and occasionally dumped snow on top of it. Aeryx recalled having to crawl out on top of the roof to shovel the snow off or else it would've caved in.

Movement from his peripheral halted his thoughts. He homed in on Ryken, who froze the moment he saw him. His blond hair fell into his eyes, but his piercing blue gaze remained on Aeryx. Relief registered on his younger brother's face, then it quickly changed into a scowl. He tugged on the sleeve of his black linen shirt and sniffed.

"You're alive, I see…" Ryken folded his arms and looked his brother up and down.

Aeryx smiled. "I'm so glad to see you as well, brother." But he was, and if Ryken allowed it, he would've trapped him in a bear hug, but they hadn't been that close for years. Not since Ryken aged, and why, Aeryx wasn't certain. He blamed it on the need to rut and the inability to join the army still, while Aeryx had joined when he was twelve.

"Where is Papa?" Ryken frowned, then glanced behind Aeryx. "Mama?"

"Papa is at the fortress, and Mama stayed behind to deal with a complication before meeting him." He kept his features schooled, but knowing Noel's memories were wiped left a gash on his heart, and while he wished he could tear the world apart to find a way to unite with her, he'd sworn an oath when he joined the army to uphold the laws and do what was best for Frosteria—and the king.

Ryken's shoulders relaxed, and he shifted his gaze toward the barn behind the house, instantly inspiring suspicion in Aeryx.

"Why? What did you do?" His voice hardened as he leaned forward, and when his brother didn't respond, he prompted again. "Ryken?"

He scowled. "Fine." Ryken smiled slowly, but it wasn't at all friendly—it reminded Aeryx of a snow lion, opening his maw and readying to devour its prey. "I caught a human in Frosteria. A *human.*"

Aeryx hopped down from Tika and swiftly crossed the distance between him and his brother. A human... in Frosteria? "What? Where are they?" His heart thudded in his chest. What did it mean if there was a human in Frosteria? "Was it a child who escaped?"

"What? No. I would've brought a child to the fortress. I'm not a fool! I know humans don't belong in Frosteria unless they're possessed," Ryken hissed. "She's in the barn. What a foul creature she is! Even if her hair is a pretty shade of blue and green."

Aeryx's throat bobbed as he swallowed roughly. What were the chances...?

Ryken must have seen the wheels turning in his eyes, for he rushed forward and slammed his palms against Aeryx's chest. "She's mine."

"*No one* is fucking yours, least of all a human." He stared down at Ryken, shaking his head before he shoved him aside and stomped his way to the barn.

"I found her!" Ryken hollered, his words escaping in a growl. "She had Mama's stone!" Ryken pulled it from his trouser pocket.

She what…? Of course she did. If the human were Noel, and he had a strong feeling it was, it didn't surprise him.

Aeryx continued to the barn and flung the wooden door open. He scanned the sawdust-covered floor. No human to be found, only a few tomte rummaging around with their tasks, humming to themselves. But as he looked down the rows of stalls, his heart plummeted. No human. Was this a twisted joke of Ryken's?

He frowned and glanced into the last one, only to find Noel bound and gagged on the floor. She shivered violently in the corner. Her eyes met his, and she scampered back into the corner. She didn't recognize him, not in this state. Not without his fur and fangs. But he recognized her, despite straw and shavings clinging to her tangled hair, plastered against her face.

"Noel," he said softly, opening the stall door. "It's all right." He peeled off his torn jacket and crouched as if she were a frightened child. What was she doing here? It occurred to him that he could explain who he was and that she was safe with him, but did she *know* who Aeryx was anymore?

"I'm going to undo your bindings."

"The hell you are!" Ryken rushed forward, but Aeryx stood quickly and pushed his brother to the ground. The younger krampi stared up at him with fury in his gaze.

"I suggest you remain where you are, or go back into the cottage. You will not touch her again," Aeryx spoke lowly, but the threat was there. The *or else* lay heavy in his tone.

Ryken's eyes widened, and his lips pressed together in a thin line. When he scurried out of the barn, Aeryx turned to Noel again and knelt before her. First, he removed the gag, then the rest of the bindings.

Noel opened and closed her mouth, shifting her jaw around as she eyed him suspiciously.

"I'm sorry about that," he said softly, bowing his head. And he was. If he could punish his brother for such an offense, he would've, but he was kin, and their father would've punished Aeryx, too. "My name's Aeryx."

He lifted his head and caught her staring at him. Her gaze flicked to his horns, then to his face. "Aeryx?" she whispered. "As in the Aeryx who just left the mortal world through a portal?"

Aeryx sucked in a breath. "You remember me?" His voice came out in barely a whisper.

Noel's eyes widened. "Of course I remember you, you idiot!" She didn't come any closer as her gaze raked up and down his body. "W-why do you look like this? Where the fuck is your fur?"

He grinned, clasping onto her wrists gently. "This is what I truly look like. The other form is a glamour in your world.

Do I disappoint you?" His heart thrummed wildly. Why he cared if she found him attractive or not, he wasn't certain, but he cared so damn much.

She blinked at him. "No."

Just no? Aeryx glanced to the side. "Well, that's good…"

"Why didn't you tell me you look like a fucking Greek *god*?" she hissed.

The mounting disappointment faded, and he helped her to her feet, chuckling. "Because you weren't supposed to remember, and you certainly weren't intended to be here." Aeryx bent to pick up his jacket and wrapped it around her. "Morozko's teeth, you must be freezing."

As if answering, Noel's teeth chattered. "Let's head back to my home." His brows furrowed as he frowned. "He… didn't hurt you, did he?" Aeryx didn't believe Ryken would willingly do something truly horrific, but with the mounting animosity bubbling within his younger brother, he was never certain.

"No, who is he?" She rubbed at her arms beneath the fur jacket.

"Ryken. My brother."

"Your *brother?*"

Aeryx nodded. "My younger brother. He's fourteen." He had a lot to discuss with Noel, and perhaps that was best for the ride back home. But something bothered him. If Zira had stayed behind to wipe her…

"Zira didn't wipe you?"

Noel pursed her lips. "No, she didn't. But do you think I would've just let her if she'd tried?" She glanced away and shrugged. "And I may have stolen her stone." Not that she *couldn't* wipe Noel, but she didn't go through with it.

Aeryx narrowed his eyes, wondering *why*. Zira knew how furious his father would be when he found out, and yet she still chose to keep Noel's memories intact. What was the reasoning? But it was a gift what Zira had done, and he would protect Noel at all costs, making sure no one—and nothing—would harm her again as his brother had just done. And no one would ever take a single memory from her. *Ever*.

To say he was overjoyed Noel remembered him was an understatement. Elation fluttered in his chest, and he knew, even if Zira had tried to eradicate the memories revolving around him, that Noel would've fought back.

Aeryx walked out of the barn, scratching the back of his head. "That sounds like something Zira would do." With one last glance around, he didn't notice Ryken lurking. If luck was on his side, Zira would find him first, and since she played a part in Noel's presence in Frosteria, she would silence Ryken's blabbering mouth.

His brother's grand lecture would have to wait—Aeryx wanted Noel safe and warm. He summoned Tika, who trotted around the side of the house, and snowflakes followed in her wake. Aeryx turned to face Noel. "Did you truly take Zira's stone?" He lifted a brow.

She sighed. "Yes, but for a good reason."

His lips twitched despite how dangerous it was to pass through the portal. A snow lion could've attacked her, and although changelings weren't typically aggressive to mortals, they were in an agitated state as of late and would still possess an adult. "You'll have to tell me your reasoning, princess." Winking, he lifted her onto Tika and hopped up behind Noel, his arms comfortably wrapping around her.

She pressed against him, her warmth heating his insides, stirring his desires.

What good would come from Noel being in Frosteria?

The trek back home wasn't a long one, and during the time, Noel relayed her interaction with Zira, and how she inquired as to what Noel was to him. If Noel *liked* him.

Rabbits darted from out behind the evergreen bushes in front of the log cabin, startling a hidden pair of bluebirds, and sending them flittering away.

Inwardly, Aeryx groaned. Why was Zira prodding Noel about any of it?

Noel, shivering, slid from Tika and cocked her head as she took in her surroundings. He lived down a beaten path, surrounded by looming evergreen trees that blotted out most of the moon's bright glow. Frosteria was a land of harsh beauty. Snow and ice didn't make for easy comfort for mortals, but for krampi, it was home.

"You live out here?" She spun around, clinging to the jacket. "It's beautiful."

"And you're freezing." He sighed, sparing a glance to his horse and then to Noel. She needed a fire first, then he'd settle his mare. Aeryx led the way up the pathway, covered in freshly fallen snow. He stomped his boots on the wooden stairs, loosening the packed snow off them, and opened the door.

The smell of smoky woods and spice struck him: a combination of the hearth, cinnamon, and clove drying on the table.

FROST CLAIM

His lodgings were quaint, a small dining space coupled with a
kitchen and a hall that led to two bedrooms and a washroom.

A massive antler chandelier, with several half-burned
candlesticks, hung from the center of the dining area.

Aeryx reached into his uniform's pocket, pulled out his
flint, then lit a lantern on the table. "We have no electricity
here. I'm afraid there will be no *binging,* as you say." When
he glanced over his shoulder at her, she was staring intently.

"Guess I'll have to manage."

"Are you sure you're all right? I still can't believe Ryken
would do something so foolish," Aeryx ground out.

"Seriously, I'm fine now. Besides *kidnapping* me and
tying me up, he didn't hurt me. I was more afraid of freezing
to death in the barn before I could talk to you." She arched a
brow. "Although, I may have to scare him back at some
point." A mischievous grin spread across her face.

Aeryx chuckled while crossing the room to the fireplace,
poured a small amount of oil onto some logs, and lit a fire.
Flames leaped high, then lowered to the dried wood. "It'll
warm up in no time." He pushed himself up and walked to
Noel—taking her hands, he rubbed them together. "Will you
drink winterberry tea? I'm afraid that is the extent of my
cupboard…"

"I've never had winterberry tea," Noel spoke through
chattering teeth and deposited her backpack by the couch.

"You can try it, and, worst case, you can sip warm water
until I can get warm milk." Aeryx sauntered into the small
kitchen and pulled a cup off a wooden shelf. He grabbed a
pitcher, poured the water into the iron kettle, then hung it over
the fire to warm.

When it was bubbling, he dropped a satchel of bundled tea into the pot. "It'll be ready soon."

Noel cleared her throat. "I came here to bring back this." She bit her lip and drew something rectangular out from her backpack. His music box. "You left it at the house."

He smirked as he took the trinket from her. "You came all this way, crossing worlds, to bring me my *music box*? You do know I could have easily come back and gotten it, right?"

Noel rolled her eyes. "That isn't all. I wanted to tell you there is a reason I keep not forgetting you, that there is a reason we met again. And I wanted to tell you fuck immortality. I want us to be in the here and the now."

She closed the distance between them and pulled his face to hers. At once, her lips were on his, tentatively at first, then the kiss intensified as her tongue grazed his. Aeryx pulled her against him, but she withdrew her lips, laughing breathlessly. "No fangs," she murmured, then threaded her fingers through his hair.

"Fuck immortality." His heart pounded wildly. Aeryx wanted her in the worst way. Her tongue grazing his had him recalling the feel of her mouth on his cock. "Tell me you want me as badly as I want you," he rasped against Noel's mouth.

"I assumed that was clear, and if not, *fuck yes* I do." She peeled his jacket off and clawed at the buttons of his uniform, nimbly undoing them until she could shove the leather fabric from his form. She sucked in a breath as her eyes hungrily drank in the sight of him.

"Not here." His lips twitched into a grin before he grabbed Noel and slung her over his shoulder. Her ass pressed against his face as she thrashed around in play.

"Aeryx!" She laughed. "Unhand me, you beast."

He stomped down the hallway and growled as she continued to wiggle, which only served to harden his cock even more. "Oh, I will, princess." He toed open his bedroom door and hurled her onto the fur blanket. Noel crawled backward, swiping her tongue along her top lip as he loomed forward. "I'm going to devour you piece by piece."

"Show me what you got." She bit her lip, her eyes meeting his. The same emotion swirling in her gaze, he knew was mirrored in his.

Aeryx methodically pulled off her shoes, then moved up the length of her body and unbuttoned the jeans that hugged her curves perfectly. Curves that he wanted to kiss and touch with a mounting need that begged him to quicken their tumbling. It didn't matter that she wasn't krampi, for one he didn't have to worry about the bond snapping into place, and for two, aside from the lack of horns, she looked no different from them.

No. I want this slow. I want her to feel me.

Next, he removed her top layers and that damn tricky undergarment with a clasp. He'd seen Noel naked before, but this was somehow different. She was laid out on his bed, her blue and green hair framing her face. And damn, she looked like a queen, a *goddess*. He moved his hand to her breast, caressing her nipple with his thumb until it hardened.

Aeryx pulled his hand away and lowered his head to her breasts, kissing the valley between before he dragged his tongue along the curve of it. In a purposefully slow motion, he flicked the hardened peak, then drew it into his mouth.

"Aeryx, I swear, don't you fucking tease me." She wriggled her hips, and his cock twitched in response. "We can take our time after, but right now I need you inside of me."

Morozko's teeth!

"Who am I to deny you?" he whispered hoarsely and slid his boots off, then his pants. Noel's eyes traced along his waist, his hips, and his length. She had no idea what she did to him. How she made his blood boil, his cock harden, but it was his chest that throbbed.

Noel scooted back on the bed, then moved onto her knees. "You're taking too fucking long."

Aeryx chuckled as he knelt on the mattress. "So impatient," he rumbled.

But apparently, Noel had enough of waiting. She crawled onto his lap and positioned herself above him. His tip grazed her seam, driving him mad.

"Oh fuck," he growled, grabbing her hips at the same time she drove herself down on him. Heat encompassed his length, searing him. But something more than desire drove his hips upward as she crashed down onto him. A primal urge to possess, to claim, to *bond*.

Aeryx captured her lips, his tongue plunging into her mouth, muting the cries of Noel's pleasure.

"God damn, you feel so good," Noel moaned, grasping onto his shoulders as she quickened her pace, grinding herself against him. His fingers dug into her ass cheeks as her inner muscles tightened on him. "Don't stop," she panted. "Fuck, I'm coming."

He didn't intend to stop, and yet, as she threw her head back, crying out in ecstasy, Aeryx's pleasure uncoiled. Pressure in his chest released at the same instant he came within her. Panting heavily, he carefully lowered Noel to the mattress, still connected to her.

She smiled lazily, sucking in precious air.

Aeryx trailed his lips from her perfect, round breast to her throat. His eyes opened and he caught the glimpse of a shadow on Noel's neck. Carefully, he brushed at the lines, but when they didn't come away, he rocked backward.

"Give me a moment, beast, and I'll be ready for you again. This time we can do it—" Noel's eyes met his, and he must have looked as stunned as he currently felt. "What?"

No, no, no, no.

Aeryx swiped his hand at her neck again, then flicked her hair off her shoulder, only to see the webbing of the mark spread. A mark he knew well, for every mated krampi bore one.

He hissed. This wasn't what was supposed to happen—he was supposed to have a choice, and his choice was to avoid the god-forsaken mating bond. How was it possible to create such a bond with a human?

Aeryx laughed mirthlessly. "It would seem fate has chosen for us both."

"What are you talking about?" She sat up, yanking the fur blanket to her. No doubt the cooler air of the cabin was sinking in now.

He motioned to her shoulder and neck, her gaze falling down to the area.

Noel gasped. "The fuck? What the hell is this, Aeryx?" She scooted as far back as she could until her back hit the headboard.

It struck him as humorous because, after everything, this was the drop of water that broke the dam.

And despite panic flaring within his chest, he spoke coolly, "We are mated."

CHAPTER 21

NOEL

"Fuck no. Fuck no. Fuck no," Aeryx grumbled while gripping his hair, his tight ass flexing as he paced the room.

"How many times are you going to say that?" Noel snapped. He halted his pacing and leaned against the wall, lightly hitting his head against it as his chest heaved. She kept her gaze trained on his face, even though he was still naked. "Are you hyperventilating?"

"No," he groaned, his cheeks flushed red.

"If anyone should be freaking out, it's me!" Noel shouted. "How the hell am I supposed to go home with this on my neck?" She pointed dramatically at the new addition permanently marked on her skin. A *mate* mark. "Say I got a shitty tattoo when I was drunk? Wear turtlenecks in the summer?"

Aeryx lifted from the wall, his eyes finally meeting hers. His face softened as he looked at her. "It's beautiful on you. But give me a fucking second." He sighed.

Noel studied his neck, his mark. It really was beautiful,

like lightning spider webbing across his tan flesh in thin pale white lines. "It's been more than a second," she finally said.

"I'm serious, Noel," he grunted. "The tea should be ready by now." Without another word, he left the room and didn't take long before returning with two porcelain cups. Aeryx stayed quiet as he handed her one and tossed his back like he was drinking a shot of whiskey. He then set the empty cup on the nightstand and sank down beside her on the bed while she drew the blanket tighter around her.

As she sipped the delicious winterberry tea, she glanced at his neck again. She thought about the moment the mark must've formed, when her orgasm had come, like a meteor colliding with earth, shaking, conquering, *owning*. There had been moments she'd been drawn to him from the beginning. Was it because of this bond? Even now, something pulsed within her, that raw need for him to be inside her again, for her to roll her hips on top of him, for her to claim that luscious mouth of his.

But her annoyance with his reaction won out on that because he'd known he would one day have a mate—*she* didn't. She wasn't from this world. *He* was. Given, it was supposed to be a krampi, or so he'd thought.

Noel held back from twiddling her thumbs as she waited on him to finish mulling over whatever he thought he needed to mull over. She glanced around the room that wasn't all that different from a human's. A bed with furred blankets, a tall wooden wardrobe, and paintings of stags and horses across the walls.

The entirety of the day came back to her in a rush, flooding her mind. She'd been *kidnapped* by Aeryx's jerk of a little brother in a sleigh of all places, then he'd thrown her into the barn like a sack of trash where she'd nearly froze to death while tied up, was saved by Aeryx, found out he wasn't a beast, fucked him, and now she was his mate? The only thing she'd planned on when coming to Frosteria was to give him his music box, discuss her feelings for him, and how she wanted to continue seeing him, not whatever *this* was. A mate! To the krampi that meant she was basically *married* to Aeryx!

Her heart thundered in her chest, and she peered at him beneath lowered lashes, observing him. He still hadn't covered his muscular body. All this time, he'd been practically human and he hadn't said a damn word while she'd worried over and over about her attraction to a beastly male. But those perfectly curving horns were still there, and they were all Aeryx, one of her favorite parts about him. The *Beauty and the Beast* movie was most definitely not accurate —the prince was hot as hell in this instance, even though Aeryx was a krampi warrior and not royalty.

She studied his square jaw, the angles of his face that could easily cut glass, his perfectly-shaped lips, his smooth broad chest and muscles that were rock hard. Hard as his… She shook the thought away as a rush of heat stormed through her, straight to her core. The way her body had aligned perfectly with his, the way he'd fit inside her, stretching her to the brink of pleasureful insanity.

"I can go home now, if you want," Noel rasped, shoving away her arousal. Maybe that would be better for them both, or at least for him since he still hadn't said another word.

"*What?*" His lips parted as a horrified expression formed on his face. "I don't want you to leave, princess."

She arched a brow. "You sure about that? Because the way you're acting suggests otherwise."

Aeryx leaned against the headboard, drawing his knees to his chest, making him appear younger than he was. "I just never wanted a mate and now, *now...*"

She knew what he was thinking, that he was immortal and she wasn't... "I've known you a week, Aeryx."

He bit his lip, sucking on it as he seemed to think about something. "My father and Zira knew each other about the same."

"You don't want a mate, though." Back in Vermont, he'd made that perfectly clear. He may have wanted to get to know her more, may have wanted to fuck her, but he didn't want this. Her shoulders sagged as she peered down at her hands.

He sighed and cupped her cheek so she could only look at him. "No, but I know I want you as I've never wanted anyone and perhaps that's the same. And no, that isn't just because of the bond."

"You live here, though, and I live in another world." Besides that, his family hated her. Zira didn't seem to before, but when she found out Noel had stolen her stone, she would. This was a place where she knew no one, only Aeryx. At home, she didn't have a lot either, but she had Ivy and the rest of her sorority sisters. Even then, they would all move on one day with their families, their lives. But the one person she couldn't leave behind would be Ivy.

"I won't force you to stay here if that's what you're thinking," Aeryx said softly. "But know that with the bond snapped in place, leaving will gnaw at the both of us. And if you do decide to stay and get to know me more, you can travel home as much as you wish. There are portals, remember?" He offered a weak smile. This, this right here, was the Aeryx she'd grown close to, the one who smiled and teased. Noel thought about living in a world of frost and snow, a world without technology, a world with monsters and beautiful, otherworldly creatures. It didn't seem as awful as it should've—to her, it was a challenge, the possibility of trying something new. *No, it's too soon to think about this.*

They stayed quiet for a long time until Aeryx's stomach rumbled. She grinned and pulled the blanket from her body as she moved to get up. "I brought you something else besides the music box."

He straightened, his eyes hooded as his tongue licked his lower lip. "Oh yeah?"

"Yeah." Noel stood from the bed, not bothering to put on her clothes. She could feel his blazing gaze on her ass as she swayed her hips to the other room for her backpack. With a smile, she fished out the jar of peanut butter and brought it back to him. "Thought you would want some of this in Frosteria."

His gaze lit up. "Thank you." He took the jar from her and set it on the nightstand. As she went to sit beside him on the bed, he pulled her on top of him in one easy motion. A squeak escaped her, but when his hard cock pressed against her softness, she moaned in delight.

"I think there's something else I want at this moment." His lips brushed hers in a soft kiss, igniting a spark within her. She ran a hand across his cheek and into his hair, gripping the wavy locks. Their lips caressed, slanting over one another. As their kiss deepened, their tongues toying with one another, she rolled her hips forward, tearing a growl from his throat.

"Can I taste you?" he purred, his hand kneading her breast, his thumb expertly rubbing her nipple.

"You are, aren't you?" She flicked her tongue across the seam of his lips.

"Not here." He pressed two digits to her mouth, tugging her lower lip before trailing them down the valley of her breasts, to between her legs, stroking her clit. "Here."

"*Hell yes.*" Another moan escaped her when his fingers circled the throbbing spot again.

Aeryx leaned forward, giving her a soft lick beneath her ear. His hot breath brushed her neck as he spoke in a gruff voice, "Grip the headboard."

Excitement and nervousness swirled inside her as he leaned back and hoisted her up to his face, her legs spread wide. She'd done a lot of foreplay in the past, but she'd never had a guy go down on her while in this position. A thrill shot through her as she lowered herself. Aeryx's hot tongue slowly glided up her center, and her eyes fluttered at the sexy move-ment. His fingers dug into her thighs, then her ass as he tasted and licked, drinking all of her in. His tongue worked as though it were still forked, as if it was made of some kind of damn magic itself. He sucked and nipped at her clit, his tongue plunging inside her while she arched her back in ecstasy. Her hips rocked as she rode his face, her fingers biting into the headboard.

That blissful sensation was stirring, flowing, whirling, then exploding. Her eyes shut, and she shouted his name, the sound echoing off the walls as her orgasm rocketed through her, like it was releasing a power of its own.

She smiled, her legs like jelly when she peeled open her eyelids. The smile on her face dropped as she peered at the headboard and gasped. "Aeryx!" The headboard was frozen over in pale blue ice.

"Don't ever stop saying my name, princess."

"No, look!" She cupped her mouth and crawled down his chest, away from the iced-over disaster. That *she'd* frozen.

Aeryx glanced over his shoulder, then at her, his eyes saucering. "Magic," he murmured, rolling to his side and running his hand across the ice. He faced her once more, blinking rapidly. "*Your* magic."

Noel looked down at her arms—the goosebumps from earlier were gone, and the chill in the air was no longer there. She hadn't noticed with everything going on, and she might have even chalked it up to the sex having warmed her body. But that wasn't it… "I don't feel cold anymore."

Aeryx frowned when his digits brushed her mate mark, sending another delightful sensation through her, deep into her blood. But fear was there, too, as the tingling flowing within her wasn't dissipating. "I feel something inside me, like prickling."

Aeryx inhaled sharply. "Besides us, only krampi have mates, but Eirah and Morozko still have something stronger. And she was human before…" He paused and took a dagger from on top of the nightstand. "Give me your hand."

She stared at the blade and furrowed her brow. "I'm not going to let you cut me."

Aeryx grasped her hand gently, his thumb brushing her flesh. "Let me try something this once. It will only be a prick —trust me."

Trust. Noel did trust him. "All right." She held her breath as he pricked the center of her palm. A slight sting radiated in the spot while blood bloomed to the surface.

Aeryx wiped the droplets away with the edge of the blanket. She watched as the skin sealed itself shut, healing.

The knife clattered to the floor. "You're not human anymore," he said.

Noel's head jerked up, her body trembling. "Then what am I?" She wasn't krampi—that was for sure—she hadn't sprouted horns.

"I think you're a witch, like Eirah, immortal, same as what the other humans became. And part of the reason the bond must've chosen you to be my mate is because of your potential to become one. I'm guessing the bond is also why I couldn't wipe your memories."

A witch? Immortal? Her body shook—it hadn't even done this when she found out they were mates. But now, she was something else. "Will Ivy and everyone else see me differently back home?" Ivy wouldn't be afraid of her if she looked beastly, but Winter…

"It's all right." Aeryx's strong, comforting arms circled her, pulling her close. "And no, only the krampi are seen differently. Stay the night with me at the very least, and if you wish to return home, I'll bring you back first thing in the morning. But there are things we will need to discuss, not now, but tomorrow. Things that will change everything."

She blinked, seeing the worry on his face, so she held him tightly, squeezing him maybe too much until her breaths were somewhat even. "I'll stay as long as you want for us to figure this out."

Noel woke to her face nuzzled against Aeryx's chest, and she inhaled his piney scent. They hadn't talked any more, only lay in the bed as he held her.

She could be a witch… When she imagined witches, she thought of *Hocus Pocus* or *Sabrina the Teenage Witch*—something silly. Not real. But this was real.

A fluttering stirred within her, caressing down to her fingertips. Magic. She concentrated on a painting of a stag hanging on the wall while holding up her finger—nothing. Squinting, focusing, letting the tingling flow harder, a small blast of blue escaped her finger. Pale blue ice spread across the picture, silently freezing it.

"Might want to watch where you point that thing." Noel heard the smile in Aeryx's voice as he tugged her back to his chest.

Horror filled her. "Holy shit. What if I accidentally freeze someone? What if I do it to you while you're asleep?"

"I'd live." He drew her close and whispered in her ear. "Although, if you wake me with a bolt of ice, I'll need to punish you, princess. Besides, knowing what you could do with your magic makes me want to take you right here." The fright within her dissipated as his fingers trailed up her side, a warmer sensation filling her.

"Does it?" She arched a brow, reaching down between them until her fingers brushed his hard cock, stroking him. "You're not the least bit scared?"

"Fuck no." He groaned.

Her hand stopped, a smile spreading across her face. "Is that a fuck no for me to stop?" she teased.

"Never." He bent his head down, flicking his tongue

across her nipple, then bringing it between his teeth. "Don't ever stop."

Noel grasped his length once more, stroking him harder this time. With a growl, he flipped her to her back, so he was on top of her. His hard body caged her in. "I need you now."

"Then quit wasting time." She released his cock, allowing his length to slide up and down her slickened folds. His tip came to her entrance, and he was about to bury himself inside her when a banging sounded at the front door, followed by a shrill squealing in the distance.

Aeryx didn't even pause as he jolted off of her and shoved on his pants, the warrior within him emerging. "Stay here."

Noel nodded and threw on her jeans and sweatshirt while he grabbed a large metal ice chain from beneath his bed and raced for the door.

Not one to go beneath the blankets and hide, Noel peered from the bedroom into the sitting room as Aeryx drew open the door. *Shit.* She held her breath at the sight of a krampi male, his tall frame, his scowl. Windblown brown locks brushed his chin, and his chiseled features were strong and beautiful like Aeryx's.

"Changelings are coming this way," Korreth's deep voice said hurriedly. "Prepare and come now." For a moment, she was confused that this male was the captain, that he wasn't a furred creature, but then she remembered, in this world, krampi were practically human looking except for their curled horns.

"What can I do to help?" Noel asked, stepping out of the room. She may not be skilled with magic, but she could do *something.*

Aeryx hissed under his breath.

"What the fuck is she doing here?" Korreth spat. As he turned back to Aeryx, his gaze settled on his son's neck and shoulder, seeming to finally notice the new mark.

"*She* is my mate." Aeryx squared his shoulders. "So, Captain, kindly refer to my mate as Noel."

CHAPTER 22

AERYX

Korreth's blue eyes remained on Aeryx, his scowl morphing into a snarl. "What have you *done*, Aeryx?"

If he were regarding anything else, Aeryx would've accepted the verbal lashing from his father, knowing that he'd been in the wrong, and deliberately disobeyed the order of Frosteria. But whatever snapped into place when he and Noel tumbled chased that notion away. A resounding need to bar his father's path to Noel urged him forward. In turn, Korreth's eyebrows shot up.

What had he done? *Nothing.* It'd been fate. If his father wanted to be rankled by someone, let it be the powers that created the mating bond. "I've done nothing that wasn't already set in place, Father." His words were low, spoken in a hiss.

When the words seemed to register, Korreth's shoulders relaxed. "A mortal?" he asked incredulously.

Aeryx glanced over his shoulder. "We didn't plan it per se, Captain." His lips twitched into a grin, and in turn, Korreth loosed an exasperated noise. "She's immortal now, and we can discuss it later." Noel caught sight of Aeryx's growing smirk and she released a breath. "You said changelings were coming. How many?" His attention was back on his father because although his new mate may have needed him, it was imperative that he became the warrior instead of the playful krampi she was used to dealing with. Her life depended on it.

With the shift of discussion back on the priority, Korreth frowned. "A swarm of them. Efraun is here—he tracked them, and Lyra was close behind."

Lyra? She'd been wounded a week ago, but given the fact that she was a krampi, she healed faster than a mortal would. Still. Should she be fighting? And Efraun... if he was caught in the middle of battle, he might not survive. He was no trained warrior. A hunter? Yes.

Aeryx grimaced. "I'll prepare."

Korreth's gaze lingered on Noel. "And find a safe place to hide." With that, he darted down the stairs and into the frozen snow, his boots crunching it.

Aeryx whirled around to face Noel, his heart thrumming wildly. "You have to stay in here." Even as the words left his lips, he could see an argument brewing. Noel lifted her chin. Now wasn't the time to be stubborn, now was the time to listen to him and *hide*.

Noel stepped closer to him. "I can help. Or at least try."

Aeryx avoided her eyes and shook his head. "This isn't like the woods in your world. There isn't just one... It's a swarm of them, Noel. You could die." The words left a bitter taste in his mouth. Flashes of his mother's shredded body rushed into the forefront of his mind. That wouldn't happen to Noel. "Trained krampi fall every day, let alone a newly immortal who has just discovered they're a…" A *witch*. She wasn't a krampi, so those abilities didn't come from the same blood coursing in his veins, but there was no doubt she was *something*. His mind kept returning to thoughts of Eirah and Morozko, how she was human *before*. "No, Noel."

A distant changeling shriek pulled Aeryx to attention. Without glancing at Noel, he stormed into his room and pulled out a fresh uniform, slid it on and quickly buttoned it.

"I can help," she argued again. "I don't want to be one of those cowards in the movies who did nothing when they should've done *something*."

Aeryx frowned as he approached her and cupped her face. "Please stay here. You're no coward, and I know that, but you're not of Frosteria. You're safer in here." He lowered his eyes and pressed a soft kiss to her lips, savoring the taste of them. It was a reality that it could be the last time. A swarm was no small number of changelings—it meant, even with the experienced krampi, they were still outnumbered.

She leaned into him, grabbing him by the lapels of his uniform. "Just don't fucking die." Noel slid her hands around his neck and brought her lips to his in a deeper kiss, her tongue gliding along his.

When they pulled away, Noel's green eyes seemed to glow in the dim lighting of the cottage. He wished there was more time to explore what she was capable of. Aeryx hoped there would be more opportunities later—not only of him taking her in ways he only dreamed of, but so they could have more conversations, learn more about one another, and explore the bond. Dare to live and love.

Frowning, he brushed his knuckles along her cheeks. "I'll be back." But he couldn't promise, so he wouldn't vow it.

With that said, he briskly exited his home out into the day's chill. Once in the snow, he bent to scoop up a handful of ice. Magic pulsed in his veins, and as he swept his fingers down, a long, gleaming blade formed.

"Tika, to me," he whispered. His familiar didn't need to hear him to feel the urgent need for her, the heavy thrum of his heart calling for her. In reply, her soft whinny carried over the growing wind, sending clouds of snow dancing over the frozen landscape.

Tika galloped toward Aeryx, the sound of her hooves thundering on the frozen ground, and every muscle in him readied for a flying leap at her back. She scarcely slowed, which was just as well, as he jumped and grabbed a hold of the saddle's horn. Tika didn't miss a beat when she circled around to face the approaching horde.

Wax-like bodies writhed, their mouths opening to release ear-piercing screeches. There were more than a dozen, and if Aeryx had to guess, it was closing in on forty demons. The odds weren't in their favor.

Snow dust kicked up from the battle down the hill, but it wasn't the sight of his father that gave him pause, nor was it Efraun or even Lyra. It was the flash of white hair against a blue uniform close enough to Korreth to shout an order if need be. The Frost Demon King. Morozko was amidst the battle, on top of his familiar. A white wolf, as tall as two krampi, bared its teeth at the nearby threats. Its fur rippled like a banner. Instead of armor, the wolf only wore a leather contraption on its back, a saddle of sorts.

A red cape whipped behind the king, like a battle standard, as he wielded his sword and leaped down from the wolf. With his weapon in hand, he landed on the back of a changeling, piercing the creature's blackened heart.

Aeryx urged Tika down the hill, and she barreled through a cluster of changelings. They were primed and ready for attack, to kill the krampi. Their claws scratched against Tika's legs, but her icy flesh prevented them from grasping onto her. The closest one to Aeryx screeched in fury, launching itself at him. Raising his sword, he brought it down on its back as it fought to clamber up his calf. Scratches, likely inflicted by its fellow demons, oozed blue blood. Dread filled Aeryx. They could fight the swarm and pierce their hearts, but none of it would keep them immobilized for long. They needed fire. And where would they get fire from on the tundra?

In his peripheral, Aeryx caught the movement of his father falling. Tika was already in motion, bounding across the distance to block a changeling from rushing onto him. Claws bit into Aeryx's leg, and he howled in pain before embedding his sword into the skull of the changeling with a sickening crunch. Blood burst from the wound, like a geyser of blue, as he yanked the weapon out.

Korreth rushed to his feet, swiping his blade at not one, but two attackers.

"You didn't tell me the king was also here," Aeryx panted the words out. Lyra was there, so was Efraun, but the king?

"No, I didn't." He grimaced, holding his side while blood seeped through his fingers. "But you seemed preoccupied." Korreth's icy eyes narrowed on a pouncing changeling, and he twisted his blade just in time as it jumped and impaled itself on it.

Soon, the pristine snow was coated in navy. Chunks of sinew, torsos, and heads littered the ground. Still, they were outnumbered. "Where is everyone? Why is the king with us?" Aeryx shouted over the melee. Morozko never entered the fray unless it was an absolute war. For him to be present had Aeryx wondering, *was* this war? The stirrup on his saddle gave way as a changeling snapped it in half, then worked its clawed hand up Aeryx's leg, yanking him down to the ground.

His sword loosened from his grasp, and Tika sidestepped to avoid stomping on him. Prone to the advances of the changelings, Aeryx forced himself to his feet and grimaced. He could very well fall right here and never see Noel's glittering gaze again. His chest tightened at the prospect, and, at the same time, a twinge that didn't belong to him pierced his heart. Through the bond, there was anguish, then fury.

As he resigned himself to the horde surrounding him, shards of ice rained down from the sky, impaling the lesser demons and trapping them against the ground. When he glanced up, he saw the king's familiar tearing into the remaining demons. The ice had been the king's doing.

"I am with you because I was scouting the area with the captain and the tracker," Morozko said, suddenly by Aeryx's side, then jerked his chin in Efraun's direction, who was prying a changeling off of his back "And you're welcome, warrior." The king's silken voice held a hint of humor to it, but his eyes, glowing a vibrant blue, were a contrast. The craze of battle and bloodlust filled them.

He'd seen the king a handful of times, but never in such close proximity, and Aeryx had never had the pleasure of fighting alongside him.

"Many thanks, Your Majesty." Aeryx bowed his head, but couldn't help glancing at the ice jutting from the ground that had been mere inches from impaling him.

Morozko grunted, then spun away into the fray, his white hair blowing across his face, shadowing his sneer.

"Aeryx, behind you!" Lyra shouted. Aeryx realized she'd gained ground behind him, and as he glanced her way, he noted her torn uniform and a new gash on her face.

It was good to hear her voice again—breathless and spurred on by a mutual hatred for the changelings.

Aeryx twisted his blade, so it pointed behind him. A spray of navy blood washed over him as the sword squelched into the flesh of the demon.

For every one they took down, two rose from the snow in their place. As battle-hardened as Aeryx was, exhaustion tugged at his muscles. For years, the changelings had attacked, but they'd grown quiet as of late. Now he knew why —his suspicions of a false lull had eased the army's offensive attacks. They'd been tricked. He saw it in the lines on his father's face, saw the tension in Lyra's. Even Efraun's jovial expression was grim.

The king couldn't fall. His magic was tied to the land and the land was tied to him. If he was slain, the entire realm would be in an upheaval, slowly but surely dying.

Morozko tore his cape from his neck and let it float away on the wind. His severe expression turned to Aeryx as if this was his doing. "Our time is running short, warrior. So, I suggest if you have any tricks up your sleeve, you best pull them out now." His familiar lurched forward, opened its mouth, baring its sharp teeth, and bit down on a cluster of writhing changelings. Blue blood dripped from its white fur, down its chin, and onto the snow.

Tricks? Since when was Aeryx known for tricks? He was playful, but never had he tricked anyone.

"Your Majesty, I'm afraid I'm not a trickster, but I am sworn to protect and serve you." He clenched a fist and pounded his chest. "It has been an honor."

Morozko nodded. "I suppose it's a good thing your king *is* a trickster." That was all he said before snow kicked up, shrouding his figure from the changelings.

Aeryx's arm throbbed from lifting and striking repeatedly. His lungs ached as he drank in deep breaths as if he'd swallowed a lungful of water.

He collapsed to his knees, driving his blade deep into the chest of a screaming changeling, but he didn't have the energy to stand again.

"Aeryx!"

Noel's voice had him lifting his head. Panic lanced through Aeryx, and he used his sword to pull himself to his feet. "Noel?" He shouted and stepped forward. "Tika, find her." His horse lowered her head and galloped forward, zigzagging through the throng of demons.

Why couldn't she listen for *once*? Stay behind and remain safe.

He trudged through the snow, slowly following Tika's trail until fire spread along his thigh. Aeryx howled in pain as the upper portion of a changeling embedded its claws into his flesh, digging in deep. Without a reserve of energy, he sank to the ground, allowing for another to hop onto his back and latch onto him.

Aeryx tried peeling the demons off, but it was no use, his muscles were shaking. With one last glance over at Noel, who was still a good distance away, he watched her eyes widen in horror.

"No! Aeryx!" Noel called, reaching her hand out as if she

could will the changelings off of him.

The air stilled, filling with the taste of magic. A magic Aeryx hadn't experienced firsthand. With a burst of energy, blue flames lapped at the ground, melting the snow on contact, but more importantly, they sought out the changelings. Angry tendrils of fire coiled around the changelings' bodies, like blazing manacles.

Instead of extinguishing against the ice, the fire snaked around the lesser demons, snuffing out their breath, twisting around them, binding until their bodies turned to dust.

Aeryx had never seen anything like it before. Fire, but ice. Frost fire? And it'd come from Noel? The smell of her magic hung in the air, crisp with a hint of spice that burned his nose.

Morozko rushed to Aeryx's side and speared the two changelings attacking him. He grabbed Aeryx by the collar and yanked him to his feet. The king's intense gaze flicked from him to Noel. "I thought you said you didn't have tricks? A witch is a trick." He loosed a breath that sounded more like a strained chuckle.

"She wasn't supposed to be here," Aeryx declared, but then his attention turned toward Noel, who was rushing toward him. He'd believed that was what she had to be, but he wasn't certain, not until he'd just heard it from Morozko's mouth.

She crashed into his chest, stealing what little breath he had away. "I thought you were going to fucking die!"

Aeryx ran his hand along Noel's back. "Still might, princess." He meant it as a joke, but the strain in his voice had it coming out a little more serious than he intended.

An unreadable expression passed over the king's face. He surveyed the area, and for the moment, quiet enveloped them.

ELLE BEAUMONT & CANDACE ROBINSON

The surviving changelings hadn't twitched back to life. Morozko lifted a pale brow as he glanced at Noel again. "She is a witch, and I know witches."

Noel turned to face the king. "So I truly am a witch?" She stared at Morozko with wide eyes and looked to Aeryx in question. He assumed she wanted to know who *this white-haired male* was. The notion she was speaking so boldly to the king amused him.

"I wouldn't have said so otherwise," Morozko countered and pointed to his neck and then to his shoulder, indicating her mark that matched Aeryx's. "You see, when your bond snapped into place, you became something other—"

"We could use some help over here!" Lyra shouted from behind Morozko, and sure enough, changelings were coming to life once more.

"Can you use that blue fire again?" Morozko pressed.

Noel shifted and glanced down at her hands. "I don't know. I fucked with it a little earlier, but it was nothing like this! I just screamed, and it shot out of my hands like I was Mr. Freeze!"

Aeryx cocked his head to the side, wondering who Mr. Freeze was, but considering it was Noel, he supposed it was someone from a movie.

Morozko stared at her, unblinking. "What if your mate's life depended on it?"

Noel looked him up and down. "Who the fuck are you?"

Aeryx inhaled sharply, his tired muscles twitching in anticipation of having to hurl Noel out of the way. Morozko wasn't known for his kindness, and when insulted, he enjoyed making examples out of the offender. Aeryx wasn't about to lose Noel because of her foul mouth.

The same energy as before flared to life. Aeryx reached out and touched her shoulder—he readied to explain who Morozko was and why it was in her best interest not to bait him into a fight.

Morozko stepped forward. "I am the king, witch. *Your* king."

Noel's eyes saucered. "Oh. Shit. Morozko? I heard about you. I'm sorry." She shot Aeryx a look, as if mentally reaming him.

"Try to use it," Aeryx murmured. "I cannot lift my sword anymore. The bastards got my wielding arm." Blood dripped down his fingers, and his uniform was shredded, exposing more of his wounded flesh.

"How?" Noel's gaze flicked between Morozko and him. "Tell me how?"

Aeryx shrugged. "I know nothing of witches except for—"

"Fortunately for all of us, I live with one." The king's lips twisted into a small smirk. "Now, witch, focus on that feeling of hopelessness—embrace it. Amplify it in your mind."

Noel closed her eyes, held out her hand, and did just as the king instructed, but nothing happened. She growled in frustration.

"Not like that." Morozko chided, then summoned a spear of ice in his hand. "What if I were to impale your lover? I wonder what that would inspire." He pressed the cold tip to Aeryx's throat.

Aeryx swallowed roughly, hoping it was just a ruse to help Noel's magic flare to life. But who could say for sure when they were on the lethal side of Morozko?

"You fucking asshole!" Noel rushed forward, a blue light

formed in the palm of her hand, spiraling.

Morozko inclined his head. "Good. Now, release it."

"But I'll hurt everyone!" Panic crept into her voice.

The weapon's pressure increased, causing Aeryx to wince. He wondered if her magic would hurt the krampi too. And *why* it was effective against the changelings.

"No, you won't," Morozko purred his words. "Just focus on the bastards you want to slay."

Aeryx relaxed a fraction and pushed the tip of the spear away.

Noel scowled at the king. She thrust her hand forward, but the light sputtered and fell to the bare ground with a sound much like flatulence. Color rushed into Noel's cheeks as she peered around the small gathering of krampi.

Morozko waved his hand, and a wall of fine snow appeared. It reminded Aeryx of when a strong wind kicked up the dust, blinding him temporarily. The snow shifted, dancing in the air as it served as a veil. "Now they're gone. Do it again, and focus on those fucking bastards."

This time as Noel focused on the energy circling in her palm, she turned her wrist so her palm faced outward, and the blue flames blasted forward. The privacy of snow fell away, and with it, the frost fire tore across the snow, melting it in its path. The blue flames licked and devoured the changelings, their shriveled bodies writhing in agony on the ground.

Aeryx's shoulders fell forward. If he'd been told a human girl from the mortal realm, a girl who he'd first helped save years ago, would one day help to defeat the most wicked of creatures in his world, he wouldn't have believed it. But now, there was more than a chance they would survive this ordeal.

Because of Noel.

CHAPTER 23

NOEL

Aftershocks from using her magic washed over Noel in waves and her hands trembled. This was nothing like when she'd used the little bit of power inside Aeryx's house. Fuck, she didn't even know she could *do* something this big! She'd just slaughtered forty changelings, and even though she'd spent the majority of her life being human, even though she'd been told murdering was wrong—this… this felt incredibly right. In this cold world, these were creatures who deserved it. She'd seen what they'd done to children, witnessed how they'd torn into Aeryx, and found out how one had taken over her young life for a time. If there was any question about her being a witch before, there sure as hell wasn't now. What she'd just done definitely proved she was one.

Gray dust swirled with the wind around her, the krampi, and the Frost King. No, not dust, but changeling ash from her frost fire. Noel peered out at more of the gray littered across the snow, a few light blue sparks from her magic still glittering across the remains. Aeryx stumbled toward her, cradling his wounded arm. Blood trickled down his torn flesh from where claws must've raked it open, but it was already starting to heal.

An uncomfortable feeling swam through Noel as the krampi turned to face her, their horns pointed toward the sky, their eyes focused on her, including Aeryx's and his father's. Korreth was no longer scowling at her like she was the scum of the earth. Blood marred the captain's pants, along with rips of fabric at his thighs and chest.

Noel took a deep swallow, folding her arms around Aeryx, wanting to shield herself from the prying eyes. She hated being front and center—it was like speaking in fucking speech class. Then their heads bowed at Noel, their fists coming to rest at their chests, and she was about to tell them to stop acting ridiculous when a soft feminine voice spoke from behind her, "Well done, little witch."

She withdrew from Aeryx and spun around to face a young woman shorter than her, her body lithe. Long, wild, black hair brushed her waist. The woman wore tight white leather pants with a matching corset over a long-sleeved silky shirt. Ivory feathers were sewn into the shoulders, and on her right one, a barn owl, paler than the snow, perched with its head cocked.

"You're late, my love," Morozko purred. His love? Eirah... This was *Eirah*, the first witch, the *queen*. Noel's magic, and all of the krampi's magic, had come from *them*. The queen didn't appear ethereal like Morozko with his other-worldly beauty, his white hair, his pointed ears, and the lightest blue eyes she'd ever seen. Eirah looked like a normal woman who wouldn't stand out in a crowd aside from the way she was dressed and the bird on her shoulder. Normal like a human… because she'd once been one too.

"Sorry, after dropping off the gifts I made, that mangy cat started to stir up trouble in the western lands." Eirah sighed. "The little nuisance escaped once again."

"Little? That cat is bigger than a house." Morozko smirked, then swaggered to his queen, trailing his index finger across his lower lip as though the sight of her made him want to fuck her right there. As if the other krampi weren't standing around watching them and he could easily ignore them. Morozko probably could.

"He's still sly." The queen arched a brow and grinned. "Let's see you catch him, darling. I'm tired from my flight."

"Flight?" Noel asked, because apparently, she couldn't keep her mouth shut. But there sure as hell wasn't an airplane around here.

"I can shift into an owl, like my familiar, Adair." Eirah shrugged and brought a hand to the owl at her shoulder, softly stroking its wing.

Noel's eyes widened, excitement stirring within her. "Holy shit, can I do that, too?"

"No, but you can do one thing I can't, and you just did it." Eirah's lips twitched, and Noel's excitement dwindled a fraction. "Now, it's my turn to finally break this changeling curse and seal the veil. You may not know this, little witch, but a curse was put in place here a long time ago, and together, I helped Morozko create the krampi to stop the destruction caused by the changelings. Once the changelings are burned, their souls go behind a veil, yet they always come back. This time after I seal the veil, they won't return when burned. It's something we've been trying to figure out for a very, *very* long time."

"How did you figure it out then?" Noel asked.

"You." Eirah smiled, a proud expression crossing her face. "A drop of your blood mixed with mine so I can start the spell. Your magic is from me, yes, but your witch blood also holds a different sort of power, one of another world that the changelings aren't born of, that they can't break free from." She reached out her hand. "Now, may I see a finger, please."

Noel's heart pounded, and she locked gazes with Aeryx, who gave her a comforting nod, to trust. Back at home, she would've told the person to fuck off if they'd asked for blood, but here in Frosteria was different—she trusted Aeryx, and he trusted them, so she would relent. She held out her hand, and Morozko drew an ivory dagger from his waist.

"Hold steady, you don't want to lose a finger, witch," Morozko said, his voice cool. And she couldn't tell if the king was joking, but by his serious expression, he definitely wasn't.

Eirah rolled her eyes at him, then focused on Noel. "Morozko had a vision of you, but we didn't know who you were or why. Then the images became clearer, and we learned from them that the curse could indeed be broken. For your help, you will be welcomed here, always protected. Now, tell me your name."

"Noel." Her heart beat faster, slamming against her ribs. "My name is Noel."

Morozko grunted, placing the cool steel of the dagger against her index finger. The prick was quick, the sting only lasting for a moment as a drop of red bloomed to the surface. Morozko then lifted Eirah's hand, kissing her digit before piercing her flesh. The queen swiped the blood from Noel's already-healing fingertip and gazed out toward the ashy graveyard of the dead changelings. Eirah brought up her arms, causing the ground to tremble beneath Noel's feet. Aeryx drew Noel close as the world shook harder. Ash and snow floated from the ground, circling the small gathering. The queen's dark eyes changed, glowing a bright blue as a burst of white magic unleashed from her, a boom penetrating Noel's ears.

Even though Noel wasn't practicing magic, the power inside her blood stirred while the queen used it. A cerulean color flashed before Noel's eyes, and she was no longer standing where she'd been. She was in another white land-scape with a blue barrier in front of her. Screeches and wails ignited behind a gelatin-like substance—appendages and bodies shoved against it, trying to escape. A skeletal gray hand broke through, only to be pushed back as stone after stone appeared on the barrier, building a wall, sealing it up so no one could escape.

Then as if it hadn't been there at all, the vision was gone, the krampi back in front of Noel. Snow and ash were no longer in the air but resting on the ground.

"It's done," Eirah gasped, her chest heaving, perspiration coating her forehead and upper lip. "One day soon, our world can permanently be rid of these destructive creatures."

"You did it." Morozko ran his knuckles gently across the queen's cheek, then turned to Noel, the edges of his lips pulled up. "With your help, of course, witch." He then looked on toward the others. "We will have a celebration in a fort-night. For now, the queen and I will have a celebration of our own." In answer, Morozko's giant-ass wolf bolted to his side, and he hopped on with one graceful movement, holding his hand out for his queen. The wolf's white body lowered a fraction, its yellow eyes glancing in Noel's direction.

Eirah's owl flew from her shoulder as she grasped Morozko's hand and mounted the wolf behind him, her arms circling his lean waist. The wolf took off, kicking up snow as it darted in the direction of the snow-covered mountains.

Aeryx tightened his grip on Noel, pressing his lips to her temple. "To think all of this might not have happened if you didn't stumble into my lap at that mortal party."

"You mean if you didn't stick around to watch me dance by myself." Noel laughed. She didn't want to think about what would've happened if they hadn't met, but it would've been her doing the same daily routine on her end.

"So, you have a mate?" a female krampi interrupted, her playful gaze zoned in on the tip of Aeryx's mate mark peeking out from his tunic. She then switched her stare to Noel's. "I didn't think I would ever see the day." The female laughed, clapping her hands together. "Good luck, Noel. Aeryx can be quite insufferable." She grinned and backed away to leave. "I'll see you two lovebirds later. We have much to discuss."

"You'll like Lyra, I promise," Aeryx said to Noel.

"Were you two ever—"

"In the past, but it was never serious."

She nodded, even though a hint of jealousy coursed through her, but how could it not? Lyra was beautiful. She seemed funny though, and Noel wanted to know more about her.

A large hand landed on Noel's shoulder, startling her. "So," a deep voice drawled, "you're the little squirt who was rescued years ago and now made a comeback."

"As for if you'll like my cousin, Efraun, I'm not so sure."
Aeryx chuckled. "He's a tracker for the krampi warriors."

"The *best* tracker." Efraun waggled his brows and lightly
elbowed Aeryx, who grunted in response.

Noel studied Aeryx's cousin, his shirt thrown over his
shoulder, the taut muscles of his firm and broad chest on
display. Efraun looked like a warrior too. He ran a hand
through his shoulder-length chestnut hair, his hazel eyes
dancing as they studied Aeryx. "You mated well, cousin."

"Go home, Efraun." Korreth's voice cut through the
banter and left no room for argument. He sauntered up behind
Aeryx, rolling his eyes at the other krampi.

"Where's Zira when I need her to deal with your grumpy
ass." Efraun laughed, tilting his head to the side. "But fine,
we'll eat a meal together tomorrow."

"Just no boar again." Korreth wrinkled his nose.

"Hey, there's nothing wrong with boar."

Korreth waved him away and turned to Noel, his heavy
stare locked on hers. A deep crease settled between his brows.
"I don't say this often, but I'm sorry for how I treated you."

"No, it's okay," Noel said in a low voice. She would've
treated herself the same way if she'd been a krampi warrior.
Aeryx's way home got screwed up because of her.

"It isn't." Korreth's gaze softened. "Frosteria hasn't been
safe for humans in a long time, and we have rules we are
meant to obey. When I found out you were the same girl we'd
saved years ago, that made it even more serious. As though
we failed our mission and put you in danger again."

He'd been worried about not only Aeryx, but her? "I'm all
right now."

The captain's dark eyebrow rose. "It will take time to

ELLE BEAUMONT & CANDACE ROBINSON

adjust. You have a lot to take in as an immortal now. But then again, I think we all do."

Being a witch? Being mated? It was a fuck ton to take in, but not shitty.

"What now, Captain?" Aeryx asked, his shoulders relaxing.

"You heard the king and queen. She's welcome here." Korreth paused, his lips pursing. "And if anyone disagrees, they will have to answer to me."

"Thank you. Where's Zira?"

"Zira was leading another scouting group with Ryken due to the increased activity."

"Did Ryken mention Noel?" Aeryx folded his arms, his voice hardening on his brother's name.

"No?" Korreth's gaze narrowed. "What did he do now?"

"Just returned something to Zira for me," Noel said before Aeryx could mention to him what had happened. Aeryx shot her a look, and she gave him one back that told him she would discuss it with him later. Noel still needed to have a chat with Ryken herself, though. She wondered what would've happened to her if Aeryx hadn't found her, and that part of her wanted to put Ryken in a time-out corner in the barn for a month since he was only fourteen.

Korreth gripped the back of his neck. "Get cleaned up, then meet Major Enox and I at the barracks in a few hours. We have a lot to discuss."

"Yes, Captain," Aeryx said.

"I'll see you two soon." Korreth let out a low whistle, and Dral dashed to his side, the reindeer's barbed antlers bobbing. The captain mounted him and stroked the creature's head, the familiar's red eyes blazing before taking off in what must've been the direction of the barracks.

"So," Aeryx drawled, backing Noel up against the nearest tree, his forehead pressing against hers. "You didn't listen to me about staying behind."

She couldn't—she'd *tried*, or maybe only for a few minutes before she'd gotten too antsy. "Your arm seems to be doing better?"

"We're not talking about my arm here, princess."

"You know I'm not the type to take orders." Noel tugged him closer. "Reckless is my middle name."

"We might need to do some training together on that." His mouth brushed hers in a soft kiss and his tongue flicked deliciously across her lips. She still had to take in that this was Aeryx. That he wasn't a beast—he was her *mate*. Beautiful and sexy and otherworldly.

"I think I'm understanding a bit more about why I need to stay," she whispered against his neck, making him shiver. "But what would really happen if I left?"

"That's why I always wanted to choose, regardless if it had been a krampi who had been my mate," Aeryx rushed the words out, his face pained. "So no one would feel like a prisoner. And I'm not worried about myself anymore because I feel the perfection of the bond—I feel *you*. I fully believe you are the one for me, but what if I'm not for you? What if you decide you don't want to stay here? The bond will let us be apart but not worlds away—for some, it can drive them mad—for others, it physically hurts. I can't let that happen to you, but I can't force you either."

"Stop being dramatic." Noel placed her hands on his warm cheeks, cradling them. "I was only curious. I want to stay, you idiot. I want to continue to be reckless with *you*. Because I feel it too, this bond, this burning brightness in me that I have for you is right. *We're* right. It may still feel weird as hell that I'm confessing this after a little over a week, but hey, look at the cool things I did today. We'll figure it out together, if the krampi will have me, that is."

Aeryx lifted her, a gasp falling from her lips and her legs automatically circled around his waist. "You're a pain in my ass, princess," he rasped in her ear, a heat rushing straight to her center. "A lovely pain I don't want to get rid of, and if anyone has anything against us, they'll have to answer to me."

"You mean *witch* princess." She grinned.

"Let's not get too cocky now." He chuckled. "But we do have a matter to settle with my devious little brother."

CHAPTER 24

AERYX

Aeryx was in no condition to hop on Tika and take off toward the barracks to join in hunting more changelings. There would be more changelings to battle after today, when he wasn't exhausted or injured. But there was something he and Noel needed to talk to Ryken about. Whether or not he thought abducting a human was the right thing to do or not, it was ultimately *wrong*.

Aeryx glanced down at Noel and offered her a smile. He still couldn't wrap his head around her being his mate, let alone a witch, and one who had a part in sealing the changelings off with the queen. A sense of pride thrummed within him. This stubborn, clever, and beautiful female was an essential piece of Eirah's plan. "Before we leave, I need to clean up. We don't need Ryken thinking you kicked my ass."

Noel snorted and lifted her hand as if she were about to blast him with magic. "Beware, beast. I'll force you into submission."

Aeryx's brows rose and he grinned. "Is that so?" He

brought his good hand up so he could stroke his chin. "It wouldn't take magic to bring me to my knees before you—all you need to do is ask." He leaned in closer, then dragged his lips along her temple. "Or say *please*.."

Noel sucked in a breath. "All right. You're hurt and we have to deal with your brother. Now isn't the time to fuck around."

He mock-pouted. "Isn't it?" Aeryx grunted and rubbed the back of his neck. "I know. But are you sure you don't want me to tell my father what he did so he receives punishment?" His playfulness faded, replaced by anger as he remembered Noel tied up and helpless. Ryken could be so foul, and his actions were often heartless. Why? He'd grown up with love and attention. It couldn't just be jealousy, could it? But he was still quite young, and there was always time to improve—or worsen. Aeryx grimaced.

"I want to give him one chance." Her serious expression then turned playful. "When you're not bleeding out everywhere, maybe then we can revisit you on your knees, beast."

Aeryx shook his head, shifting his weight as Tika's hoofbeats announced her approach. She halted, blowing fine snow dust from her nostrils at him, then took her nose and nudged him. "Hop on, it'll be easier than trudging through the snow." With his good arm, he gave Noel a boost, then hoisted himself behind her. Before he urged Tika on, Aeryx surveyed the area. Black dust swirled on top of the remaining snow—all that was left of the changelings. It was done, or close to it. The fight between the changelings and krampi had come to a close.

Aeryx sighed, nuzzling his nose into Noel's hair. This time, the press of her body against his reminded him of every curve beneath her clothing. Judging by the way her breath hitched, he wasn't the only one remembering their love making.

He nudged Tika's side, and she took off, up the hill toward his cottage. It wasn't a long ride, but given Aeryx's current state, he appreciated not trudging up the slope. Aeryx would've preferred lounging in the snow, staring up at the sky as he healed, but there were matters to attend to. Like changing out of his shredded uniform, and denying himself another taste of Noel in his bed.

The ride to his father's house proved quiet, enough so that Noel was able to take in her surroundings. This time, she didn't shiver violently in his arms.

"The trees are so tall!"

"You also have tall trees in your world." He cocked his head, squinting.

"Not this fucking tall. Is everything bigger here?" she teased.

He grinned against her ear. "You tell me."

Tika darted down a beaten path, quickening her stride as they grew closer to Aeryx's childhood home. The trees grew sparser, but evergreen bushes grew more prevalent, their gnarled limbs stretching out with thorns. Then the path gave way to a clearing, with a large cottage set back. Knee-high shrubs with red berries adorned the front winter garden. And a small porch led the way into the home.

His horse slowed her pace, snorting as she slid across the ground to a full halt. Aeryx hopped down first and peered up at Noel. She was staring at the house, her lips pursed.

"He's not going to hurt you." Although, he wasn't sure he could convince her otherwise. He *had* abducted her. Helping Noel down, he glanced toward the stable off to the side of the house. "I wonder if the tyrant is home..." Light smoke billowed from the chimney, hinting that Ryken was either inside using the hearth or he was nearby.

"Are you sure you want me to come with you? Because I may have a few choice words." Noel hopped down from Tika, then glanced up at him with an arched brow.

Oh, he was more than ready to interrogate Ryken. The rebel needed to learn a lesson. Aeryx huffed, rubbing Tika's neck before sliding from the saddle. "I don't know what he was thinking, but I swear he's not so cruel." It was the best word he could think of to describe his actions. Frowning, he motioned for Noel to follow as he traipsed up to the front stairs.

Without knocking, he opened the front door, and Ryken, who was lounging on the couch, jumped to his feet, muscles tensed and dark eyes wide. A piece of bread tumbled from his lips and onto the floor. He looked surprised to see Aeryx standing there and even more surprised to see Noel peering around his arm.

"What are you doing here? Why is *she* here?" Ryken sneered. "You're going to get in so much trouble when Major Enox finds out."

"Hello, brother, it's nice to see you too," Aeryx said dryly. "Why are you home?"

Ryken rolled his eyes. "Mama decided to scout a few more days and told me to come back."

Noel didn't bother disguising her laughter—it bubbled out even as she nudged Aeryx.

Ryken's face reddened. "Shut up, you mortal b—"

Before the words left his lips, Aeryx crossed the distance between them and grabbed Ryken by the collar of his shirt. "I would bite your tongue, little brother."

For a moment, something akin to fear flickered in Ryken's gaze. He lowered his eyes and narrowed them, suspicion replacing the fear. "You…" He looked to Noel, then back up at Aeryx. "You are even more foolish than I thought," he whispered.

"Sorry, kid, you'll be seeing more of me." Noel shut the door before she sauntered up to Aeryx's side.

Ryken's face twisted in rage—he looked as if he were about to spit in Noel's direction. Aeryx moved his hand and grabbed his brother's chin. "It is known to the king and queen, to father, that Noel and I are mated, so you can stop spewing your venom, Ryken."

Sometimes, Aeryx wondered why he'd asked Zira for a brother. Why he'd been so excited to hold the wriggling bundle when he was born. He hadn't always been a disagreeable prick, there had been times he'd glued himself to Aeryx's side. Slept in his bed, begged for Aeryx to train him or tell him stories from the barracks. Those days seemed so far away, like a faded dream.

Ryken's brows rose in surprise, then twisted as disgust swept across his face. "What the fuck? With a *human?*"

"Apparently it happens," was all Aeryx supplied, his tone sharp, warning his little brother to shut his mouth.

Ryken growled. "Fine, but I don't have to accept it."

That surprised Aeryx. His brows lifted, and he released his hold on Ryken. "It doesn't matter if you accept it or not. It is done. I expect you to be civil, do you understand?"

"And Ryken," Noel chimed in, an edge to her tone, "since we are getting to know each other, if you fuck with me like that again, or anyone for that matter, I'll use this new handy-dandy ability I gained." She grinned, her voice turning fairly playful. "It's called *frost fire*."

"What?" Ryken's nose wrinkled.

Aeryx patted him on the head, ruffling his blond wavy hair. "It's best not to poke the witch."

"Witch?" Ryken's voice went up an octave, his eyes sweeping over Noel in assessment. "She cannot be. Otherwise, she'd have…"

Unsurprisingly, Noel extended her hand, palm facing upward. Blue flames snaked along her skin, as if caressing her digits. When she rolled her hand over, they continued to lick her flesh. "I think I'm getting the hang of this witch thing, don't you?"

Aeryx couldn't help but grin. Pride swelled within his chest, that Noel—his *mate*—had power. With her, they could eradicate the vicious demons once and for all. There could be peace for Zira, himself, and his father. Knowing that those bastards would never portal back to Frosteria once banished to their realm.

"Give me a break," Ryken hissed. "You look like you're readying to rut her in front of me." He curled his lip in disgust. "I'm sorry I abducted you. Is that what you want to hear?" His arms crossed before him, lending him a sullen appearance.

"Probably as good as I'll get, right?" Noel glanced up at Aeryx, and he shrugged.

"You know, if it wasn't for her, I'd be dead. So would our

father." That was enough to silence Ryken's venomous mouth. "Oh, yes. She saved our asses."

Ryken rubbed the back of his neck, scowling at the floor. "I'm sorry," his tone was less acidic and more genuine.

Noel rolled her eyes. "Yeah, apology accepted, kid."

"As much as I'd love to stay and have a one-on-one chat with you, Ryken, I need to head to the fortress. Be careful." He gently smacked his brother on the back of the head, ruffled his hair again, and when he squirmed to get away, Aeryx pulled him in for a hug. "Stop being such a prick." He squeezed, then released him, grinning.

Ryken swiped at his head, attempting to smooth out the tousled waves. "Better be on your way."

Turning away from Ryken, he strode toward the door and opened it. The familiar cool breeze washed over him, rustling his hair against his face. Noel dipped beneath his arm and pressed into his side, a small action, but one that made his heart gallop. He bent his head and brushed a kiss to her temple.

"Ready to show off more of your skills?" He murmured against her ear.

"I think I much prefer to be back at your cottage." She smiled, but he could hear the hint of nervousness in her tone.

"I won't let anyone near you, understand? And if they try, I'll cut them down, and you can use your frost fire to reduce them to ashes." He winked. "I promise, princess."

She sighed. "All right. If I have to…"

"Unfortunately," he grumbled.

Stepping outside, he called Tika, and she galloped through the frost-covered trees, letting loose a high-pitched whinny. When she came to a sliding halt in front of them, chunks of snow spewed onto Aeryx's thighs and chest. He grunted and flicked his hand down his uniform.

"Someone has an attitude." Noel nodded to the horse and laughed. "I like it."

Tika tossed her head, her mane chiming against her smooth neck. The sound was similar to that of laughter, which Aeryx didn't appreciate.

"Enough sass out of you," he said to Tika, but peered over at Noel, who sidled up to him and waited for a boost. She'd seemingly gotten used to mounting Tika already. She was a fast learner, and if she wanted to remain in Frosteria, she'd have to be.

Once Noel settled, Aeryx pulled himself up behind her. She leaned against him, molding into him perfectly. Despite being against the bond, refusing to believe there was a perfect match out there for him, he understood now, that the magic that bound them together knew what the hell it was doing. Leaning forward, he brushed a heated kiss along the exposed edges of her mark.

Noel inhaled sharply. "I thought we were supposed to be going to the fortress?"

Aeryx's nostrils flared as he scented her mounting arousal. His cock twitched, pressing against the curve of her ass. Through the bond, he felt the burning need growing between them. "Unfortunately, we have to." His voice came out roughly as he dragged his hands along her thighs. "After, you are mine."

Noel laughed, and it sounded huskier than usual. "You think so? Maybe it'll be *me* showing you who belongs to who."

"We'll see about that, princess." He nibbled the tip of her

ear, then pulled away as he urged Tika forward. She leaped into a steady gallop through the snow and darted around the tall pine trees as though it were only a game.

The fortress wasn't far from his father's home, which was precisely what he'd wanted when it was built. Aeryx recalled the day he'd announced they'd be moving out of the captain's quarters in the barracks and into a home with Zira because they'd outgrown the small space. He hadn't known it then, but Zira had been with child.

It was too soon to even consider such a thing with Noel, yet Aeryx couldn't deny the thrum in his veins, the stirring of desire to one day have that for himself too.

Tika's hooves pounded on the frozen snow, kicking up dust in their wake. She lifted her head, whinnied, and it echoed off the trees, rolled around across the grounds, announcing they were arriving at the fortress.

A familiar acrid scent tickled his nose, and Aeryx knew it was the furnace. Through the treetops, black smoke billowed into the sky.

"What is that?" Noel murmured.

"That… is our equivalent of a fire in the woods. If you think the horde you witnessed was anything…" It wasn't. Villages saw far more swarms than those mere forty changelings. "At least now, when they're banished back to the afterlife realm, they're gone." His arms tightened around her and he leaned his weight forward. "Thanks to you."

As Tika emerged from the woods, the fortress came into view. The tall spires stabbed toward the sky, and in the court-yard, trainees lined up, readying to follow the lead of their commanding krampi. But Aeryx didn't see his father, nor did he hear any orders being barked.

His gaze shifted toward the whipping poles, and as if it were happening before him, he recalled Noel's small frame as Zira whipped the wretched fuck who'd possessed her. She hadn't been the first body he'd seen whipped, but still, it never left a warm fuzzy feeling inside him. Not even as he aged and it became his mission. It never got easier.

Never again would changelings terrorize mortals.

Tika stopped in front of the fortress and pawed at the ground. Aeryx was hesitant to dismount, knowing how reluctant Noel was to head inside. He frowned and took in the building, trying to see it from her perspective.

The structure was ivory, just like the furnace and barracks —he supposed it was meant to blend in with the snowy terrain. There were few windows that the sun could glint off of, and again, he assumed it was a form of camouflage. On the top, where the spires twisted like gnarled tree branches, there was a balcony where scouts could survey the horizon for any impending threat.

"I suppose we should get this meeting over with…" Aeryx grumbled, tension rising within him. Not that the major could deny them when they'd received his father's permission, and in so many words, the king's too.

Noel turned to face him, her colorful hair tumbling into her eyes. "Hey."

He lifted his hand, brushing the strands from her face. "Yes?" His lips twitched into a small smile.

"We already got the big 'okay', so, we can always tell him to fuck off, right?" She lifted her hand, wiggling her fingers as if on the verge of conjuring her flames.

Aeryx couldn't help but erupt in laughter, then he took her wrist and brought her hand to his lips. "Please don't tell the army's major to fuck off, or blast him with your magic. I don't think either bodes well for me or my place among the other warriors."

Noel flexed her fingers, then tapped his nose. "You're no fun."

Aeryx rolled his eyes and escorted her inside the fortress. Little by little, the tension crept back in, and by the time he reached the major, who stood with his hands clasped behind his back, Aeryx had fallen into the warrior he was born to be.

"Major," Aeryx grunted, pounding his fist to his chest as he bowed.

Long, ebony braids tumbled down the major's shoulders, dangling at his chest. "At ease," Enox said, his gaze flicking from Aeryx to Noel. "Word has traveled fast, but let's find somewhere a little more private." He motioned toward the hall and walked away.

Aeryx didn't so much as glance at Noel, but his hand sought hers out, and when he found it, he gave it a squeeze, hopefully reassuring her.

It was far too quiet in the fortress—they didn't pass a single krampi. Likely because they were out rounding up the last of the changelings, banishing them once and for all.

Noel stumbled as she stared down the long hallway. Despite not having many windows, the white walls reflected light, but it also was dull to look at, now that Aeryx considered it. Especially after he'd stayed in the colorful house belonging to Ivy's aunt.

Enox led them to a meeting room. Inside, the walls were a deep green, the color of pine needles. One floor-to-ceiling window rested on the far side of the room, giving them all the light they needed.

"You can close the door," Enox offered, jerking his chin. His expression remained neutral, and gave nothing away.

Noel closed it, then sidled up to Aeryx's side, her hands shaking slightly.

"I hear congratulations are in order." The major's eyes slid to Noel, and although he wasn't a foe, Aeryx stepped forward. "Easy. She is your mate, and I won't dispute that. I'll accept it as I would any other. But, I need to hear you say it won't affect your abilities in our army. That you won't spend your days rutting like a spring buck."

Aeryx squinted, unsure of the reason he was even there. If it wasn't to debate on whether or not Noel could truly be his mate, then why was he required to speak with Enox? "Major I—"

"Vow it."

He thought about it a moment, tamping down the reflex to chuckle. Although he could spend his free time finding new ways to fuck Noel, he had other duties, too. "I vow to not let my mate interfere with my tasks in the army."

Enox nodded, clapping his hands. "Good, because before you left for the mortal realm, your father and I had a chat..." When he dropped his hands, Enox glanced over Noel, assessing her. "And another witch in Frosteria. I hear we have you to thank, so on that note, I hope you'll always have Frosteria's best interest in mind."

"What?" Noel squeaked.

"Don't worry. We won't require you to do anything, but should the king need you, I have a feeling he'll come knocking on your door." Enox chuckled.

It took a moment for Aeryx to register what had been said.

He pinched the bridge of his nose and squinted. "I don't understand."

"I'm abdicating my position to your father, and in turn—" A rapping on the door shattered the moment, and when the door opened it was his father, who winked as he strode in. "Captain." Enox inclined his head, his ebony horns jutting toward the white ceiling.

Korreth rubbed the back of his neck. "Apologies, a few stragglers needed to be brought to the furnace."

Enox lifted his brows, as if waiting for Korreth to say something. "I told him I abdicated…" He motioned with his hand to continue on.

Korreth's lips twitched into a broader smile that reached his eyes. "Ah, so," he closed the distance between them, and he had to glance up to look Aeryx in the eye. "If you'd take the position, I'd like to name you captain of the army."

Aeryx's mouth gaped. His heart thundered in his ears, and for a moment, he believed it was a dream. That he couldn't be here, in this room, with his mate, his father, and the major.

"What do you say, son?" Korreth prompted.

"Umm, fuck yes?" Noel whispered none too quietly, her nerves seeming to have dissipated. Her outburst drew the attention of Enox and Korreth, who stared in surprise.

Aeryx slanted Noel a look and shook his head. From the time he was a child, it'd been his dream to be in the army and to one day lead it. Now, the opportunity was being offered to him…

"I accept," the words tumbled from his lips, but it didn't sound like his voice.

"Very good," Enox declared. "Major Korreth and Captain

Aeryx… it has a nice ring to it." He glanced around the room, nodding to himself as he strode toward the door.

"But, why?" Aeryx's voice rose an octave.

"By next week, I'll have transitioned out of the fortress. As for why, I am tired, and my mate deserves time with me." He paused, sighing wistfully. "I have no doubt you'll both go above and beyond for the army, as you already do." With one last look around the room, Enox slid out the door, leaving them.

"You knew?" Aeryx turned to look at his father.

"Suppose I did." He grinned.

The by-the-book krampi warrior had kept such a grand secret from his son? Aeryx narrowed his eyes, then his features relaxed as he chuckled.

Aeryx closed the distance between Noel, dipped his head down, and captured her lips. His tongue slid over hers, and the taste of her burst in his mouth. When he withdrew, she was smiling up at him, and his father cleared his throat.

Now he had everything he could possibly want.

CHAPTER 25

NOEL

"WHAT THE HELL DO YOU MEAN YOU'RE MOVING?" WINTER wrinkled her nose.

"Seriously?" Holly shrilled, slapping her thighs. "You just met some random guy and got married?"

"I mean, he's like, my soulmate…" Noel shrugged with a love-struck sigh as they stood in the middle of the sorority house living room. She knew it sounded stupid, but she couldn't tell them the complete truth. Not with how seeing Aeryx had affected Winter. Noel couldn't put into words everything she felt, that she was now a witch, and how even if the mate bond wasn't beating like a heart inside her, she still would've chosen to try things out in Frosteria.

"He didn't pay you to marry him, did he?" Winter pursed her lips, her hands on her hips.

"You can tell us if you're one of those mail-order brides," Holly added. "We promise not to judge. Hell, for the right price, I'd become one myself."

Noel pinched the bridge of her nose, her body shaking with laughter.

"What?" Winter's voice rose an octave. "It happens!"

"I'm definitely not a mail-order bride." Noel rolled her eyes, then held out her arms, surprising herself by initiating a hug first. "Now, come here." She drew Winter and Holly to her, and they tightened their holds. "I'm going to miss you guys so much, and you can take whatever you want from my side of the room since I can't take everything."

"That doesn't help at all," Holly whispered, her voice breaking into a sob. "But I may steal your bed. Mine's hard as hell."

"It's yours." Noel smiled, tears pricking her eyes.

They pulled apart and drank the rest of their coffee while chatting for a little longer about Winter and Holly's newest videos.

"You better not act like those cunts who get married and never talk to their friends again," Winter called toward Noel as she shut the door. Even if she had to take a portal weekly or less to Vermont, she would make sure to text her.

Noel pressed a hand to her mate mark—that was hidden beneath a turtleneck shirt—as she peered up at the sorority house, its red brick, and its trimmed bushes. The house had been her first real home since her mom had passed. It wasn't as if she couldn't come and visit every so often, but it still felt like this was a goodbye.

Ivy was still in class, and Noel sent her a text asking her to meet at the same place in the woods where they'd been last.

Ivy: You're back! You will tell me EVERYTHING!

Noel smiled and tucked her phone into her backpack. Earlier, she'd sent her dad a text, telling him she was moving to Europe with her new husband. Most parents would've flipped their shit, but not her dad. He hadn't been her dad in a long time, though. There wasn't even a scathing call with him begging her to come home, just a simple text with the words, *I wouldn't expect anything less from you.* Even though it hurt like hell, she shrugged it off because sometimes blood families weren't like the ones that were made.

If her mom were still alive, though, she would've been with her every step of the way. She glanced up at the sky, not knowing where her mom was now, but she believed she was looking down at her. "I'm still not perfect, but you never needed me to be," Noel said, hoping her mom could hear her before she gripped the handle of her luggage and dragged it in the direction of her destination.

Birds chirping and insects buzzing filled the woods when she entered, and she plopped down against a pine tree to wait for Ivy. Aeryx had dropped her off at the portal and would be picking her up in a little while. Since it was her first time traveling, she hadn't wanted to go by herself just yet, but next time she would attempt to take a stag. And hopefully not fall and die.

She still couldn't wrap her head around the fact that she and Aeryx were fated mates—it was something she'd only read about in stories. But fuck, it was real. He was now the captain of the Immortal Army, and what had her dumbass decided to do? Become a warrior. *Her.* She smiled to herself.

The snapping of twigs echoed, and Noel jerked her head up to find Ivy breaking through the trees, her red hair pulled up into a messy bun.

"All right, why did you have me meet you in the woods

instead of back at the house?" Ivy cocked her head. "Something's up." She knew Noel so well.

Noel stood, brushing the dead leaves from her jeans. "I'm not coming home."

Ivy's face fell. "What do you mean? I thought you were going to tell Aeryx your feelings, then come home."

"Things veered from my original plan. Oh, and you're going to *love* this story. Trust me." Noel then went into detail about everything that had happened in Frosteria, the kidnapping, the mate bond, its effects, the changelings she faced, being a witch, and then about the fucking hot king and his badass shifter queen who ruled there. "This is the real kicker… in Frosteria, Aeryx doesn't look like a beast. He looks like us, only sexier and with horns."

Ivy blinked, seeming to take everything in before a huge grin spread across her cheeks. "Like Tim Curry in *Legend*?"

"What? No! He's not *red* and you've seen his horns—they're big but not *that* big." Noel laughed, trying to swipe the image away of how big his dick would be if his horns were that size.

"Too bad." Ivy chuckled. Her grin then fell from her lips as she ran to Noel and circled her arms around her, yanking her into a tight hug. "But now I'm not going to see you every day. Who am I going to laugh with when Holly and Winter do something stupid? You're the only one who can relate to the movies I watch."

"I can come back and forth." Noel sniffed, hot tears spilling down her face. She would miss things here—but nothing and no one more than Ivy.

"I knew one day we wouldn't live together anymore, but I didn't think it would be this soon." Ivy lifted her head and her grin was back. "So this means you got the prince and the beast all rolled into one. Epic ending."

Noel bit her lip, a thought crossing her mind. "Meet me here in a week. I'm going to have a damn good surprise for you."

As Noel stepped through the barrier, leaving Ivy behind, a deep red sled was already waiting in the snow for her. In the front seat, both wearing their dark warrior tunics, sat Aeryx with a bright smile and Ryken glowering beside him like he wanted to be any place but there. Even though Noel didn't go around kidnapping when she was his age, she had stolen, and her attitude toward people back then was completely snotty. She understood a bit better where he was coming from, and if teen years sucked for humans, then she was pretty sure they could be just as shitty for krampi.

"You're right on time." She smiled, the bond inside her pounding, the energy drumming.

"We've been here for a while and just finished training," Aeryx said with a wink.

Noel tossed her luggage in the back of the sled and her pack in the front. She slid beside Ryken, a grunt slipping from him when her arm rested against his.

"Hello to you too," she said to the younger brother, then glanced at Aeryx. "I wish Ivy could've come." At least for a visit. Even though Noel could stay in Frosteria, other mortals still weren't allowed. But Noel wasn't always good with rules, and that was one she might have to bend.

"You can always visit her whenever you want." Aeryx jostled the reins, the elk jolting forward.

The wind thrashed her hair, and Ryken moved his hand when a lock brushed his skin. She arched a brow at him. Aeryx had decided to have Ryken train alongside him so he could spend more time with his brother. He was doing what her father hadn't. Even when she was being distant, even when hateful, she'd still needed him. And Noel wanted to help Ryken too.

Noel leaned forward and unzipped her bag, fishing out the black object. She nudged Ryken with her elbow. "I brought something for you, kid."

The frown fell away from his face, replaced by a curious expression. He took the object from her and rolled it around in his hand. "What is it?"

She'd remembered the story Aeryx had told her about how Zira had given him the music box when they'd become a family. Zira had been open, loving, and wanted them to grow closer. Noel needed to do the same thing, a fresh start between them, even though she was sure as hell his attitude wouldn't vanish overnight.

"A Magic 8 Ball." She shrugged, turning it around in his hands so the part needing to be read for someone's fortune was visible.

"Magic?" He eyed her skeptically.

"Well," she drawled. "You shake it and it predicts an answer to your question. Ask it something that will have a yes or no outcome."

Ryken squinted, seeming to concentrate as he stared at the ball. "Will Noel ever go home?" He shook it with force, a small clink sounding. "No."

Noel grinned and reclined against the back of the seat. "Looks like I'm here to stay, little krampi."

Ryken rolled his eyes, but the edges of his lips tilted upward, a barely-there smile showing. Surprising her, he brought the ball close, not giving it back to her as she'd expected. It was good enough.

"One more thing." She then took out a jar of peanut butter and placed it on his lap. "You can also have one of your brother's gifts, but don't tell him."

"I heard that," Aeryx sang.

"Don't worry." She laughed. "I have more for you."

"What is it?" Ryken blinked at the jar.

"Something that will rival your favorite stew, brother." Aeryx chuckled.

As they headed toward Ryken's home to drop him off, Noel looked out at the landscape, taking it all in. A winter wonderland that lasted forever, and lucky for her, she preferred the snow.

Pale blue hawks soared above them, and a white bear traveled across the hilly landscape. Although she might miss technology, nothing compared to this nature.

Ryken's cottage slipped into view, and holly bushes dotted with bright red berries lined the garden. A blonde woman stood outside, brushing Dral's fur. When she glanced over her shoulder at them, Noel saw she was a krampi, her black curled horns glistening beneath the sun.

As realization struck her, Noel's eyes widened in surprise. "Is that Zira?"

"That's right." Aeryx smirked. "You haven't seen her in this form."

She was maybe one of the most beautiful women Noel

had ever seen. Ethereal. Zira's brown eyes met hers when Aeryx came to a stop. Noel took a deep swallow—Zira would've heard everything by now. About her stealing the stone…

"Hello, Mama," Ryken said, leaping out from the sleigh, his boots crunching against the snow.

Zira ran her fingers through his blond locks and patted his back before he headed inside. Noel had asked Aeryx not to tell his parents what Ryken had done to her because she really did want to give him that chance.

Zira turned once again to Noel, her movements relaxed as she walked to them. "Welcome home, Noel."

"I'm sorry," Noel rushed out, guilt churning in her stomach. "I was going to give the stone back, but when I returned, you were already gone."

"Ryken gave it back to me." Zira batted her hand in the air. "You did what I would have done. And in this instance, it worked out for the best. So thank you for helping our world, daughter."

Noel's eyes widened. Zira called her *daughter*. She'd only met the krampi a couple of times in her life, and she was already treating her like family. Ivy and the sorority girls had done the same.

"I think you two need to take the rest of the day off because tomorrow"—she glanced at Aeryx, her eyes sparkling —"you'll have *captain* duties to take care of."

"Supper tomorrow evening?" Aeryx asked.

"As always. We'll have lots of new things to discuss. Now, go before Korreth comes home and tells you to get to work." She laughed, shooing them away with her hands.

They said goodbye and Aeryx snapped the reins, the elk barreling forward.

"What you did for Ryken was nice," Aeryx said.

Noel scooted closer, so there wasn't any space between the two of them. "I think I scared him enough already."

"He deserved it after the shit he pulled."

Noel didn't disagree with that in the slightest. "So, are we going home now?" They passed a village of cottages, some stone, others wood. Nothing like the modern houses that cluttered the town near the cottage.

"Is that where you want to go, princess?" He traced his lower lip with his thumb, and heat spread through her at seeing the small gesture.

The world was too beautiful, too new, to be cooped up inside. "No, take me somewhere relaxing."

Aeryx wrapped an arm around her, his nose brushing her temple. "I know just the place."

It didn't take more than fifteen minutes before they ventured through a forest, filled with skyscraping trees covered in snow, to a glistening river.

Aeryx untacked the elk from the sleigh, letting them roam free near the river, where they drank beside a white fox that seemed to study Noel. A low humming flowed within her as she looked at the small animal, as if they were connected on some level. And then it darted into the forest, the humming quieting.

"That was odd," she said. "I think I felt some sort of magical connection with the fox for a second."

"You may have just met your familiar." Aeryx grinned. "He'll return when he's ready." He then grabbed Noel's hand

and took her farther down a narrow path. Taking the blanket from under his arm, he unrolled it for them to sit on.

"When we get back to the cottage, you can add whatever you want to make it feel like home. It's not only mine, it's *ours*."

"Aeryx, are you sure about that?" Noel shot him a devious grin.

"You can flip it upside down for all I care." He draped his arm around her, and she leaned her head against him while they listened to the river's gentle sounds. It was strange seeing the cold, but not feeling like she needed a jacket, or clothes…

"Give me a second," he said softly. She watched with a raised eyebrow as he went to the stream, shaping the water into something. The liquid weaved together, creating sharp edges and rounded layers until a crystal-clear crown rested in his hand.

"I thought you may need this, princess." He chuckled, sauntering back to her, his muscles flexing beneath his tight pants.

Her heart warmed at the sight of his gift, and she smiled while taking it from him. "So cheesy, yet so romantic. I've never received a crown made from ice before."

"Damn, so you've had crowns?" He lifted a brow at her.

"Plastic ones with fake jewels." She pushed a tendril of hair behind his ear. "Nothing like this though."

Noel's gaze locked on his deep brown irises until the feelings within her took on a new shape, tightening, stretching, a craving taking root. Her breaths grew ragged as she inhaled his comfortable scent, her heart increasing. She trailed her fingers along his neck and interlaced them in his hair. His arm fell to her waist, drawing her closer.

She leaned in, her nose brushing his. "I've never been fucked in the snow before."

"Do you want me to make that happen?" He smirked.

"Hell yes." She laughed, her lips finding his. Only now, their kiss wasn't animalistic like when they'd first had sex— this was something different but just as good. Noel didn't want to rush this time—she wanted to take in every inch of him, explore every part of him. She was claiming Aeryx as hers, and hers only. And the territorial side of her never wanted to let him go. An immortal life was something she never expected, but if this was what she would feel for an eternity, then let the flame stay ignited, burning brightly. Not only that, but to train with Aeryx and the krampi army, to help protect another world, along with her old one at the same time, was worth every breath.

Noel helped him remove his tunic, then trailed her fingers to his pants, unlacing the ties. He slid them off and took her in his arms, laying her in the snow. It was slightly cool against her, but the spark in Noel worked its magic, her frost fire warming her skin and his.

Aeryx's lips slanted across hers, his teeth softly biting her lower lip, his tongue flicking the seam before he kissed her again. More and more. She grasped his throbbing cock and he growled, tossing his head back as she stroked him, her thumb circling his tip. His hips rolled forward, meeting each of her strokes.

"I need to be inside you," he rasped.

His mouth pressed to hers, and he drew down her pants, along with her panties, until she was completely naked and needing him too.

He bit his lip as he took her in, and the aching feeling

inside her grew. "I love you, beast," she finally said, her heart slamming against her rib cage at what she was admitting.

"I love you, princess." And then his lips found hers again, as if he couldn't get enough of her mouth, just as she couldn't his.

Aeryx's hand cupped her mound, and she moaned while his skilled fingers rubbed her clit, dipped inside her. And then his cock was lined up at her soaked entrance. With one motion, he buried himself inside her, making her moan even louder. He trailed kisses down her neck as he thrust, each movement driving her over the edge. Then he rolled them to a sitting position with her in his lap, for her to continue claiming him.

Noel rocked against Aeryx, his fingers in her hair, his other grasping her breast, kneading it with sensuous movements. Sex had never been like this, and it wasn't because he was otherworldly either, it was because no matter how slow or fast their bodies worked, love echoed around them. True fucking love. It had been there, ever since they'd met as kids —she just hadn't known it. But the memory had always stayed lit within her heart until it blazed when she'd met him again.

Her hips picked up their pace, circling and moving harder, the magic stirring inside her, his magic caressing hers. And then together they came, the orgasm barreling through them, her shouting, him roaring.

Aeryx took them both to the ground, tucking her into the crook of his shoulder. Their chests heaved, and he whispered while kissing the top of her head, "I quite like this bond."

"I quite fucking like you, and I'm always going to claim

you." Noel grinned. "I guess you can have your jar of peanut butter now."

"And after that," he said, his voice deep. "I'll show you precisely how *I* claim."

"Challenge accepted."

EPILOGUE

AERYX

A LITTLE OVER A WEEK HAD PASSED SINCE AERYX'S LIFE HAD been altered. For the better. He'd been named captain of the Immortal Army and Noel had claimed him as her own. Sometimes, when he woke, he'd wondered if it had all been a dream, only to find her warm flesh nestled against his naked chest.

However, today, he was on the hillside next to a portal, standing beside his cousin, Efraun, because he'd hunted Noel down for him. She'd been missing, and while Aeryx was confident that she could largely handle herself, she was still new to his world. When he couldn't find her, only to discover a stag was missing from the stable, he enlisted his cousin's help.

Snow drifted on a light breeze, casting flakes against Aeryx's cheeks. They melted on contact, creating streams down his face.

Efraun's chestnut braids rustled as the wind picked up.

"Why would she return to the mortal realm?" He quirked a brow while scratching his chin.

Aeryx stared at the portal, the blue flecks spitting outward as it circled. "I don't know." He ground out the words, glowering off to the side. Still, he'd offered for her to go and visit any time she wished, but to at least let him know because of the lurking danger still there. The changelings' population was on the decline, and their threat was minimal, but a part of him was afraid. Perhaps not that she'd find herself in the clutches of a demon wanting to tear her to shreds, rather, what if she got trapped in the mortal realm?

It was a foolish worry, but still, the invisible tether that bound them together tugged at him, grating on his nerves.

Efraun stepped closer—his long fur coat billowing behind him did nothing to cover his bare chest. "I see." Sidling up next to Aeryx, he peered at the swirling blue ring before them. "I also hear that congratulations are in order, Captain."

Aeryx's teeth grazed his bottom lip. His cousin's words sounded distant, and it took a moment for them to register. "Hm? Oh. Yes." Squinting, he turned to glance at Efraun, his hazel eyes trained on him.

"And, as it were, Captain, I have some news regarding that darling *little cat* in the mountain." Efraun tugged at invisible whiskers on his face, chuckling. His expression grew serious as he continued, "A friend's village was attacked by Schnookums."

Aeryx snorted. "Schnookums? Is that what you're calling it now?"

Now that had Aeryx's attention. The Jólakötturinn was commonly known as the Yule Cat, but there was nothing cuddly or affectionate about the wretched monster. Since the changelings had dwindled in Frosteria, the cat had crept from the mountain and started ravaging a nearby krampi village.

His father had relayed the tragic events. Unlike the changelings, who left a heart behind as a token, the Jólaköttturinn hunted its prey and played with it even. Clawed it, stripped them of clothing, then ate them whole. The only proof the monster had been there, was the blood bathing the ground, and the tracks it left behind.

Efraun clapped his hands together, rubbing them. "Yes, or maybe Mittens."

He blinked at the nickname, wondering why the hell it even needed one. "Why?"

Efraun's lips tugged into a broad grin. "I imagine his toes are white."

Aeryx gaped at his cousin and wondered what went through his head. It was also no wonder he never joined the army—it would've dulled his odd sense of humor. The wilderness suited him, where he could convene with the realm. In Aeryx's younger years, he often took walks with Efraun in the woods, and soon they'd be surrounded by animals. Stags, birds, foxes, and wolves. They flocked to him, and when Aeryx asked why, Efraun only shrugged and said it had something to do with being still enough in his mind and spirit. Someone like that wouldn't last in the army.

"Is the bastard gone already?" Aeryx's muscles tensed as if he were readying to call Tika and leap onto her back.

"Unfortunately." Efraun turned away, the wind whipping his braids across his face. "But the cat left destruction in its wake." He sighed, then faced Aeryx again, stepping a little too close. "Something viler always seems to rise here."

Lifting his hand, Efraun poked Aeryx's nose, causing him to swipe at it.

Aeryx wrinkled his nose. "Enough of that."

"You looked a little too much like your father just then." He shrugged, unapologetic.

Aeryx squinted at him, wondering if he didn't grasp the situation. "Because it's a *serious* matter, Efraun."

His cousin nodded gravely, his shoulders still relaxed though. "It is. And I'm sure Frosteria's finest warriors will handle it."

And yet, he was still joined in the battle with the changelings, had even slaughtered his fair share of the bastards, too.

Aeryx frowned. "Why don't you join us? We need you."

Efraun lifted his hands, shaking his head. His braids, decorated with tiny green glass beads at the ends, jangled. "No. I'm no warrior." He placed a hand to his chest. "I'm better off in the woods alone."

As the words tumbled from Efraun's lips, laughter spilled from the portal. Aeryx recognized the beautiful sound of *her* laugh. He turned just in time to see Noel's perfect body slip into view. She was breathless and smiling, but when her gaze caught his, she froze.

Noel's eyes widened. "Um..." She stumbled forward as another body collided with hers. A female with red hair crashed into Noel's back. This one, Aeryx knew, and he frowned. "I thought you were going to be at the barracks?"

"Noel," he said firmly, sounding more like his father than anything. "What the hell are you doing?" Confusion rumpled his brow as he looked between Noel and Ivy.

Ivy's red hair tumbled from her shoulders. She curled in

on herself as the bite of their world sunk into her. "Aeryx?" Ivy whispered, staring at him.

"I told you." Noel sauntered up to him, all confidence and swagger that he couldn't help but smirk at.

"Hello, Ivy. I wasn't expecting a visit from you, otherwise, I'd have brought a coat." Aeryx turned to look at Efraun, who'd ceased smiling altogether and was gazing intently at Ivy. It was odd seeing his cousin so serious and focused on someone else. The only time he recalled seeing him in such a state was when his mother had died. "This is my cousin Efraun."

Ivy's eyes locked onto the other male and she sucked in a breath, then took a step back.

Noel's brows furrowed as she exchanged a glance between the two of them. "All right, guess you've seen what I mean about krampi. They're not big sexy beasts here, just big sexy men with horns."

Efraun's typical, jovial expression still hadn't returned, not as his gaze remained latched on Ivy, his lips parted, his chest heaving.

Noel, having picked up on the growing tension, turned toward her friend. "Now that you know, let's get you back home and warmed up." But as they turned back to the open portal, Noel's arm pushed through to go into the mortal world while Ivy's didn't.

"Aeryx?" Noel turned to look at him, blinking rapidly.

He'd never seen anything like this before. A sinking feeling washed over him and he glanced toward his cousin.

Efraun, who's eyes remained focused on Ivy, finally spoke. "You're my mate."

TRAVEL BACK TO FROSTERIA . . .

Even a fated mate can face rejection, no matter the temptation.

Efraun is a tracker, not a warrior, and spends his free time alone in the woods. Yet when he finds himself fated to a mortal who refuses to give him the time of day, he has no other blasted choice but to prove himself, not only with his heart but his adept touch.

Ivy had always dreamed about college because that was what society dictated. Her choices have never been her own, even when she finds herself trapped in a frost demon world, destined to a male who looks as though he could pleasure any woman. She won't give in though, no matter how enticing he proves to be.

But when trouble knocks, Ivy and Efraun are forced to work together on a perilous mission. All bets are off as the mate bond tugs at them, drawing them closer.

Perfect for fans of Laura Thalassa, K.F. Breene, Raven Kennedy, and Elizabeth Briggs. Frost Touch is book two in this highly-addictive fantasy romance series with fated mates, plenty of spice and banter, and a frosty world you would want to get lost in.

FROST TOUCH

Book 2 in the Demons of Frosteria Series

COMING SOON

ACKNOWLEDGMENTS

Are you craving peanut butter now? We hoped you loved reading Aeryx and Noel's fated mates story! We really wanted to put a bit of beauty in the beast and show how it is definitely what's inside that counts.

Our first big thanks is to our families, who inspire us each day. The story wouldn't have happened without Amber H., Jerica, Lou, Hayley, Vic and Ann. You helped pull this story together and thank you from the bottom of our hearts. To Jackie, who did a fantastic job with editing!

And one more shoutout to our readers! We love you and hope you now want to learn more about Krampus! We are so excited for you to read about Ivy and Efraun's dark, romantic, and fun journey next!

THE OFFICIAL PLAYLIST

Want to listen along while you read and immerse yourself into the world? Listen to the playlist below!

1. Black Leather by KEiiNo
2. Monsters by All Time Low
3. Electric Feel by MGMT
4. The Evil Folk by KAAZE
5. I Love U by Chainsmokers
6. Scary Monsters and Nice Sprites by Skrillex
7. Shut Up and Dance by Walk the Moon
8. Would You Love A Monster Man? By Lordi
9. Monster by LUM!X, Gabry Ponte
10. Aurora by K-391, Røry

ABOUT ELLE BEAUMONT

 Elle Beaumont loves creating vivid and fantastical worlds. She lives in southeastern, Massachusetts with her husband and two children. When not writing or chasing around her children, she enjoys making candles. More than once she has proclaimed that coffee is her lifeblood and it's how she refrains from becoming a zombie.

Stay up to date and receive some free books by signing up for her newsletter! ellebeaumontbooks.com/newsletter

Join Elle's Facebook group and hang out with her
facebook.com/groups/ElleBeaumontStreetTeam

For more information visit
www.ellebeaumontbooks.com
Follow Elle on social media!

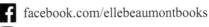 facebook.com/ellebeaumontbooks
 instagram.com/ellebeaumontbooks

MORE FROM ELLE

Standalones

The Dragon's Bride

The Castle of Thorns

Beneath the Willow

Demons of Frosteria

Frost Mate

Frost Claim

Frost Touch (Coming Soon)

Immortal Realms Trilogy

Seeds of Sorrow

Tides of Torment (June '23)

Wages of War (Feb '24)

The Hunter Series

Hunter's Truce

Royal's Vow

Assassin's Gambit

Queen's Edge

Secrets of Galathea

Brotherhood of the Sea

Bindings of the Sea

Voice of the Sea

King of the Sea

ABOUT CANDACE ROBINSON

 Candace Robinson spends her days consumed by words and hoping to one day find her own DeLorean time machine. Her life consists of avoiding migraines, admiring Bonsai trees, watching classic movies, and living with her husband and daughter in Texas—where it can be forty degrees one day and eighty the next.

Stay up to date by signing up for Candace's newsletter! http://eepurl.com/dhV0yv

Join Candace's Facebook group and hang out with her facebook.com/groups/candacesprettymonsters

Follow Candace on social media!

facebook.com/literarydust

instagram.com/candacerobinsonbooks

MORE FROM CANDACE

Wicked Souls Duology

Vault of Glass

Bride of Glass

Marked by Magic Duology

The Bone Valley

Merciless Stars

Cruel Curses Trilogy

Clouded By Envy

Veiled By Desire

Shadowed By Despair

Cursed Hearts Duology

Lyrics & Curses

Music & Curses

Letters Duology

Dearest Clementine: Dark and Romantic Monstrous Tales

Monstrous Tales

Dearest Dorin: A Romantic Ghostly Tale

Campfire Fantasy Tales

Lullaby of Flames

A Layer Hidden

The Celebration Game

Mirror, Mirror

Faeries of Oz Series

Lion

Tin

Crow

Ozma

Tik-Tok

Demons of Frosteria

Frost Mate

Frost Claim

Frost Touch (Coming Soon)

Vampires in Wonderland

Rav

Maddie

Chess

Knave

Standalones

Between the Quiet

Hearts Are Like Balloons

Bacon Pie

Avocado Bliss

These Vicious Thorns: Tales of the Lovely Grim

MORE BOOKS YOU'LL LOVE

If you enjoyed this story, please consider leaving a review!
Then check out more books from Midnight Tide Publishing!

Come True by Brindi Quinn

★A jaded girl. A persistent genie. A contest of souls.★

Recent college graduate Dolly Jones has spent the last year stubbornly trying to atone for a mistake that cost her everything. She doesn't go out, she doesn't make new friends and she sure as hell doesn't treat herself to things she hasn't earned, but when her most recent thrift store purchase proves home to a hot, magical genie determined to draw out her darkest desires in exchange for a taste of her soul, Dolly's restraint, and patience, will be put to the test.

Newbie genie Velis Reilhander will do anything to beat his older half-brothers in a soul-collecting contest that will determine the next heir to their family estate, even if it means coaxing desire out of the least palatable human he's ever contracted. As a djinn from a 'polluted' bloodline, Velis knows what it's like to work twice as hard as everyone else, and he won't let anyone—not even Dolly f*cking Jones— stand in the way of his birthright. He just needs to figure out her heart's greatest desire before his asshole brothers can get to her first.

COME TRUE: A BOMB-ASS GENIE ROMANCE is the romantic, fantastic second-coming-of-age story of two flawed twenty-somethings from different realms battling their inner demons, and each other, one wish at a time.

Available Now